UNFORGETTABLE NOVELS
OF THE WEST
BS . . .

Cole Mas⸺erritory
looking for⸺ and found a bloody
range war instead . . .

DURANGO GUNFIGHT
Quint Cantrell wants to bury his past. But the
Hardester clan wants to bury *him* . . .

MAVERICK GUNS
Clay Mason's brother has been marked for
death by a sly killer—but when you take on
one of the Mason clan, you take on *all* of the
Mason clan . . .

MONTANA BREED
Young Rafe Gunn wanted to look into his family's past. But first he had to look death
square in the face . . .

APACHE BLANCO
Trace Gundy has a chance to make a small
fortune and a fresh start. But in helping a
rich man's son escape from prison, he could
get himself locked up—or worse . . .

GUN BOSS
Raised by an Apache tribe, Trace Gundy never
forgot his lessons in survival. Now, to avenge
the loss of his beloved wife, he will call upon
the fighting spirit he learned as a boy . . .

2.25

POWDER RIVER

JACK BALLAS

JOVE BOOKS, NEW YORK

POWDER RIVER

A Jove Book / published by arrangement with
the author

PRINTING HISTORY
Jove edition / October 1995

ISBN: 0-515-11727-7

A JOVE BOOK®
Jove Books are published by The Berkley Publishing Group,
200 Madison Avenue, New York, New York 10016.
JOVE and the "J" designs are trademarks
belonging to Jove Publications, Inc.

PRINTED IN THE UNITED STATES OF AMERICA

10 9 8 7 6 5 4 3 2 1

To my sons, Byron and Kirby, and to one of
my best fans, my only grandson, Zachary.
Thanks, boys, for being you.

CHAPTER ONE

★ ★ ★

Here on the Powder River, between Milestown and Ismay, Montana, cold gripped the land like an icy fist. Case Gentry, his wife, Anne, and two children—Mark, ten, and Brandy, eight years old—huddled out of the wind and snow in their ranch cabin.

Mark and Brandy washed and dried the dishes. Anne sat next to Case in front of the fire, her fingers busy darning a pair of socks. They talked of Case's upcoming trip into Miles.

Shod hooves sounded against the frozen ground.

Gentry motioned them for quiet, stood, wrapped his gun-belt around his waist and cinched it tight. "Get away from in front of the door." Without a word they did as told.

The horse stopped and leather squeaked when the rider shifted his weight to dismount. Gentry moved to stand at the side of the door.

"Hello the house," called a voice from outside.

"We're here." Gentry cracked the door enough to see a man, slim, of medium height, unshaven, and dirty, standing outside. He wore two guns, each with a silver star inlaid in its grip. He wore his holsters low, tied to his thighs. Gentry had heard of those guns before. Being dirty in this weather didn't bother Gentry, but the tied-down holsters, worn low, did.

"Don't want to seem unfriendly, stranger, but shuck your hardware and hang it on your saddle horn," Gentry said.

1

"Don't mean you no harm, friend. Just want to get in out of the cold."

Through the crack, Gentry studied the man, didn't like what he saw—but couldn't turn anyone away in this weather. "Shuck your guns and come in."

The stranger did as he was told. "Now hang that big Bowie knife alongside of it," Gentry said.

While pulling his knife case from his belt, the man looked over his shoulder. "You ain't a very trusting man, are you, friend?"

"That's the second time you called me friend. Now, come in an' we'll see if it's true."

The stranger came in, bringing with him a gust of cold air. He walked directly to the fire.

"Name's Bent Bowdry, from down Texas way. Howdy."

Gentry's gut tightened at the name. Bent Bowdry was a cheap, two-bit Texas gunhand. He hired out, seemingly always on the wrong side during range wars. This day and time, even as sparsely settled as was the West, a man couldn't get away from his reputation.

Gentry looked him in the eyes a moment, then said, "Heard 'bout you, Bowdry, none of it good." Not offering his hand, he continued, "I'm Case Gentry." At this, Bowdry's head snapped up. He knew the name.

Gentry had been a Texas Ranger for two years before heading north with a trail drive. He never figured himself a fast gun, but was feared because he never gave up on finding the man he was looking for, and many said his first shot, handgun or rifle, never missed.

"Warm yourself, an' I'll give you a cup of watered-down coffee. Then you're gone. Or you can sleep one night in the stable. One night, that's all."

"Don't seem like you want to earn the name 'friend' I tagged you with."

"Bowdry, I ain't never been friends with the likes of you. Warm up an' get." Gentry kept his hand close to his Colt.

Bowdry's eyes, an oily sheen to them, kept seeking

Anne's perfectly proportioned figure as she moved about the room. Gentry would not head for Milestown unless Bowdry rode ahead of him, every step of the way.

"I'll sleep in your stable. It's a long way to Milestown."

Bowdry took his time sipping the weak coffee Anne handed him. He finished and handed her the cup. "Yore man didn't see fit to tell me what name you go by."

Gentry said, "She ain't gonna tell you it neither. Head for the barn."

As soon as the door shut behind him, Anne said to her husband, "Case, I've never known you to be so rude. Why? Besides being dirty, he seemed all right."

Gentry pulled his belt from the buckle, changed his mind, and rebuckled it. As long as Bowdry was around he'd wear his gun. Finally his gaze 'ocked with Anne's. "Little girl, that man is more dirty insic? than he is outside. Never met him before, but heard about him when I was a Ranger." He chuckled. "Reckon you could say he's heard 'bout me too."

The children finished the dishes. Gentry knocked the dottle from his pipe, and the day was so far gone Anne had trouble seeing to continue her darning. It was time to light the lantern; instead they got ready for bed. No need in wasting coal oil.

Mark and Brandy slept in the loft. Heat from the fireplace rose into it and kept it warm. Gentry and Anne climbed the ladder, tucked them in, and kissed them good night.

"Tell me a story?" Brandy asked, her eyes wide and hopeful.

Anne shook her head. "Not tonight, dear. I want to talk with your papa a little."

For a while after putting the children to bed, Gentry and his wife sat in front of the fire, watching it die to glowing embers, not talking, but comfortable in the silence that surrounded them. Then, as though reading each other's minds, they stood and went to their bed, separated from the rest of the room by a blanket hung from the ceiling. It was built against the back wall. Gentry build it there for the additional strength the cabin uprights gave it.

Long after they went to bed, Gentry held Anne close to him. "You're thinking of something, Case. What is it?"

"Just thinkin' maybe I'll lay out the chores for the children in the mornin' and make my trip to Miles. No point in waitin'."

Anne chuckled. "You're going to make sure Bowdry goes too, aren't you? You didn't like him looking at me. Can't say I liked it much either. It made me feel . . . dirty."

Gentry said, "Think you're smart, don't you? You read me all the while. Yeah, that's what I had in mind." They went to sleep like that, lying close. He never felt like a whole man unless Anne was within reach.

The next morning Gentry told the children the chores they were to do while he was gone. Before going out the door to saddle his horse, he squatted in front of Mark. "Son, whenever I ain't here you're the man of the family. That means you gotta take care of your ma and your sister— keep 'em safe. What I want you to do is, load the twelve-gauge, keep it with you when you're doin' chores, an' in the evenin's lock the door an' don't let no one in. Got it?"

Mark stood a little straighter. "Yes, sir, Papa. You do what you gotta, an' don't worry. We'll be all right."

Pride in this little boy of his swelled Gentry's chest. He pulled Mark into his arms and hugged him, then Brandy, and last a hug for Anne that lasted twice as long. When he released her, he shifted his handgun to the pocket of his buffalo robe, pulled the robe tight about him, tied the leather thongs to hold the robe together, and left.

Bowdry's horse was in the barn, but Gentry didn't see the slim gunman. "Bowdry, time to hit the trail, gonna be a cold ride."

From the hayloft, Bowdry said, "You riding too?"

"Yep."

"Which way you goin'?"

"Milestown. We'll ride together."

The night before Bowdry had said Miles was his destination, now he hedged. "Reckon I changed my mind. Figure to ride over to that little settlement on O'Fallon Creek, believe they're beginnin' to call it Ismay."

Gentry threw the hull over his horse's back and pulled the cinch straps tight. He rode a Texas rig, and it, unlike others, was cinched front and back. While tightening them, he stood with his horse between him and the ladder to the loft. "Come on down, Bowdry. You gonna be gone soon's I am. Ain't leavin' you here with my missus and kids."

"Go ahead, Gentry. I ain't gonna hurt your family." A scrape and two sharp thuds on the floor above told Gentry that Bowdry stomped into his boots.

The way Bowdry looked at Anne the night before and now his decision to go to Ismay told the whole story. He didn't intend going anywhere. Gentry drew his Colt from his buffalo robe.

He stood behind his horse until Bowdry had both feet on the ground. "You ain't goin' to Ismay. Saddle up an' be damned quick about it. You an' me, we're goin' to Milestown. We ain't ridin' together either. You're ridin' bout ten feet ahead of me all the way, an' if you got any other ideas, I got this .44 pointed straight at your gut. It says we gonna do it my way."

Bowdry only looked at him, but Gentry read pure poison in his eyes. Gentry told him to drop his gunbelt and knife and to stand about three feet from the wall, lean into it, and spread his legs.

He felt for a hideout and found a .32-caliber derringer in the top of Bowdry's boot. Satisfied he had his man disarmed, he shoved his own pistol into his coat pocket, hung Bowdry's weapons from his saddle horn, and they rode out. Icy wind cut into Gentry's lungs.

The only caution he need use now was to keep distance between them.

Bowdry wasn't his only worry; renegade Sioux refused

to stay on the reservation. Gentry didn't blame them. The government seemed set on starving them. Many of the young ones simply pulled stakes and left. Even in the heart of winter he reckoned they would fare better than being herded like a bunch of sheep. If he'd been a Sioux, he'd leave too.

Empathizing with them didn't make them any less dangerous. His gaze constantly searched ridges, tree lines, the lips of ravines, and large boulders for movement that might signal an enemy, although in this weather they'd probably hole up. A glance at Bowdry every time his eyes swept the countryside kept him aware of *that* danger.

The gunslinger kept letting his horse slow. Every time he did, Gentry told him to move ahead again. Every few feet Bowdry swung his head to the side. He knew Bowdry tried to gauge the distance between them in order to jump him.

About halfway to Miles snow started again, and the wind hadn't let up. Bowdry dropped back a few feet. "Let's find a place an' make camp, Gentry. Way this weather's goin', we ain't gonna make it by dark."

"Move that horse ahead an' keep goin'. Anybody don't make it, it's gonna be you."

Bowdry jerked the reins and moved ahead. "Put that side gun in your holster and gimme a chance, you'll be the one what won't make it."

Gentry grinned. "I oughta do that, but I got you where I want you anyhow."

The slate gray sky darkened. Cold and blowing snow washed smells from the air. Wind whined incessantly, killing all other sound. Gentry wondered whether he could pull the trigger of his handgun if he had to. His hands felt like cardboard. "Drop back until I tell you to stop." Bowdry did as Gentry ordered. "Don't get any ideas. You'd be dead 'fore you left your horse."

Gentry cast a worried eye at the horses struggling in snow over a foot deep on level ground. And night had settled in. He saw Bowdry as only a shadow and decided to tie him.

"Hold up. Climb down and put your hands behind you."

Bowdry did as told, but when Gentry came close, he took a roundhouse swing at him. His fist caught Gentry on the cheekbone. Gentry threw his arm up to ward off a left coming at his chin and hooked a right to Bowdry's gut. The punch didn't phase the slim gunman. His heavy coat padded the blow.

Have to work on his face, Gentry thought, and swung a hard right to Bowdry's nose. Blood spurted. Gentry followed with a left hook that landed flush on the gunslinger's chin. Bowdry threw a right cross that caught Gentry alongside his head.

Looked like Bowdry figured the coats as protection also. Gentry shook his head. Slim as he was, the gunslinger could hit.

They threw punches that missed, and backed off to catch their breath. Cold air cut like a hot knife into Gentry's lungs. Neither of them could stand much of this. He stepped into Bowdry and punched straight out with his left and followed with a right uppercut.

Bowdry went down, rolled, and came to his feet, his hands full of snow. Gentry moved in for another swing and Bowdry tossed the snow in his face, blinding him for a moment. Gentry took another right to the chin. He went down and rolled. Bowdry ran for Gentry's horse—and his weapons.

Gentry's hand dipped into his pocket for his pistol. "Don't do it, Bowdry. Don't want to kill you."

Bowdry's hands stopped short of grasping the grip of his handgun.

"Now lie down, flat on your stomach, hands behind you."

This time Bowdry didn't try anything, probably too tired, Gentry figured. He trussed Bowdry's hands, dragged him to his horse, jerked him to his feet, had him mount, and tied his feet under his horse's belly.

When he climbed back on his horse, Gentry knew they were in trouble. The fight had caused them to sweat. With temperatures about forty below, if sweat froze to their bodies, they were dead. Milestown better be close.

The horses plodded on, heads hanging. Gentry felt warmer. He shook his head to clear his vision and looked at Bowdry slumped in the saddle. "Bowdry? Bowdry, you all right?" He got no answer. The weather hadn't warmed—they were freezing to death.

He tried to figure something he could do—make camp—something. He couldn't think clearly. He faded in and out of consciousness. While lucid, he feared falling from his horse. That *would* be his end. He tied his hands to the saddle horn.

After hours, maybe only minutes, it could have been a week for all he knew, he topped a hill and thought he saw lights. He again shook his head to bring his eyes into focus. There were lights down there. He kicked the gelding to a faster pace. The lights shimmered with a sort of halo about them. Gentry squeezed his eyes shut and looked again. This time he wasn't certain he'd seen lights or anything else. Snow swirled, throwing up a curtain between him and where he thought he'd seen hope.

CHAPTER TWO

★ ★ ★

Anne, a lump in her throat so large she couldn't swallow, watched Case ride out behind Bowdry. To the children she tried to show a cheery face, but her hands, held in front of her, gripped each other so her knuckles showed white.

"Father," she prayed, "please keep him safe. He's making this trip, not to buy supplies as he wanted me to think, but to buy us a few small things for Christmas, to bring us a little happiness. The only happiness we want is having him here." She watched until the two riders disappeared around a bend in the trail.

A look at the children showed them watching their father just as she did. "Come, we have work to do. Mark, bring in a load of stove wood. Brandy, run down to the cellar and bring up three medium-sized potatoes." She thought if they stayed busy they wouldn't worry or miss their father so much. She didn't fool Mark for a minute.

"Mama, now you stop worryin'. Papa's gonna be all right. I'll take care of you 'til he gets back."

Anne squatted by the step to the front porch. Case started the porch before the weather turned bad—said he'd have it finished in time to sit on when the summer came again. She pulled both her children into her arms and held them close.

"Bless you, little ones, we love him so much, don't we." She held them tightly a moment, then turned them loose. "Shoo, now. We have work to do. Don't want your father

9

coming home and finding nothing done. He'll think we're lazy."

That afternoon she noticed Mark didn't get far from the shotgun while he was doing his chores. She wouldn't be surprised to see him lay it on the floor at the side of the bed. Case had entrusted him with their safety, and the little ten-year-old boy showed he would stand between them and harm. *He* was her *little* man.

When she took Brandy to the barn to give her another lesson in milking, Mark stood in the doorway, the .12-gauge cradled in the crook of his arm.

Anne brought a small amount of warm water to wash the cow's udder, and to make it more comfortable rather than grip her teats with cold hands. "Watch this, Brandy. You close your fist, but not tight, close to her bag first, then close each finger in sequence until you get to your little finger, pulling gently on her teats as you close your fist. This pushes the milk out and into the bucket." She did it a few times, slowly, to let Brandy see how it worked, then let Brandy try.

"Good, good. See what a nice stream you had." Anne smiled to herself—of course the stream of milk should have gone in the bucket instead of all over her and Brandy. "You'll learn to guide the stream so it'll hit the bucket every time. Now let me finish up. We'll try it a little more every day until you are as good as me."

"Oh, Mama, you reckon I'll ever be *that* good?"

Anne smiled. "Yes, dear, you will." She couldn't help thinking there would be many times in weather like this when Brandy would wish she'd never heard of milking.

"Mama," Mark cut into her thoughts, "rider comin', ridin' slowlike. Y'all stay here in the barn 'til I see if it's all right."

He crept out and slithered behind Brandy's mounting stump. A rider rode into view slumped over his horse's neck, holding to the mane. Dressed in buckskins, with a buffalo robe covering most of his body and with a hat made of the same, Mark couldn't tell much about him.

The pony stopped by the front stoop. Sagging, the bundle of fur leaned to the side, the mane slipped from his fingers—and he fell to the ground.

"Mama, looks like we got a hurt man out yonder by the porch." Mark kept his eyes on the rider, holding the shotgun, ready to shoot if he saw any sign of danger. "I'm gonna walk out yonder and see if we know him. Come out when I call."

He stood from behind the stump, kept the man in full view, and slowly walked toward him. He couldn't see the rider's face. He needed to take off the hat wrapped around his face in order to see, and he couldn't do that and handle the shotgun too.

"Mama, you an' Brandy come on out here. This here man's hurt, need some help seein' who he is."

Walking toward him, Mark caught the smell of wood smoke and bear grease. The man smelled like an Indian. Without taking his eyes from the rider, Mark held the .12-gauge out for Anne. When he felt its weight taken from his hands, he moved to the other side so as not to block his mother's view. Carefully, he reached for the hat the man wore and removed it. The man didn't stir, he was out cold—and he was a Sioux warrior.

A jagged gash, still bleeding, cut through the Indian's scalp to white skull underneath. Still squatting by the warrior's side, Mark looked up at his mother. "What we gonna do, Mama? Cain't let him just lie here. He'll freeze to death."

Anne studied the Sioux. It would be foolish to take him in the house, but if Mark held the shotgun on him maybe it wouldn't be so dangerous.

No. She couldn't jeopardize her children like that. She wouldn't do it. Oh, how she wished Case were here. Anger built in her throat. Indian or not, she couldn't leave a human being out here in the cold.

Maybe she and Mark could each take an arm and drag him into the house. She could hold the shotgun in her other hand. She looked at the warrior closely. He was young, not over twenty-five years old. Handsome, she thought, then studied on it another few minutes. As Mark said, she couldn't leave him out here, hurt as badly as he seemed.

"Mark, stable his horse, then come here and take one arm, I'll take this one and handle the shotgun. Brandy, open the door while your brother puts the horse away."

Slowly, careful not to bump his head on the porch, they dragged the Indian inside. A kettle of water already boiled on the stove. "Here, son, take the gun and keep it pointed at him."

Anne gathered a handful of quilt swatches, knelt at the warrior's side, and placed the kettle of hot water on the floor next to her. "Gracious, there's dirt and small pieces of rock buried in this cut."

"Yes'm, I seen some scrapes on the side of his horse with some of the same stuff in 'em. Horse must have fell with 'im."

Anne spent over fifteen minutes cleaning the Sioux's wound, then looked at Brandy. "Get me my sewing box, please." She spent another fifteen minutes or so stitching the man's scalp. He never stirred or moaned, although she became aware, when about half through, the Sioux stared at her with black, emotionless eyes.

"Brandy, warm that broth I was going to use for soup and bring me a bowl."

Anne put the bowl of broth on the floor alongside the kettle and spooned a little at a time into the warrior's mouth. Before she finished he lapsed into unconsciousness again.

She and Mark took turns during the long night sitting with the man, holding the shotgun on him when it was their turn. He was restless and tossed and turned several times in his sleep. He moaned a few times, and Anne had to smile.

A Sioux warrior would never moan if awake—it wouldn't be manly.

Dawn seeped into the room, gradually pushing darkness from the corners. Anne's turn to watch, she put another log on the fire, glanced at the Indian, and settled back into her rocker. The extra log warmed the room; Anne's eyes drooped, she forced them open, then they closed.

Her eyes snapped open. She'd dozed off and it was full daylight. She looked at the Sioux. The same black eyes stared at her, only now there was a bit of sparkle in them, and Anne would have bet a slight smile crinkled the corners of his mouth. He rolled over, tried to stand, tried again, and made it on his third try. She lifted the barrel of the .12-gauge to point at him.

Still looking at her, he touched the bandage on his head, hesitated a moment, then walked unsteadily to the door and left. Anne had the distinct feeling he wanted to say something, maybe thank her, but didn't know how. She stood at the window and watched him ride from the stable.

For the next couple of days after the Sioux left, Anne kept the children busy so they wouldn't miss Case so much. She stayed busy too, but couldn't keep him from her mind. He'd ridden to her father's ranch in weather much like they were now having. Said he was looking for shelter and could he stay until it thawed a little.

He was up from Texas, came up with a trail drive. Her father hired Case, not knowing that a year later Case would ride from the ranch with his daughter as his new bride.

She didn't start looking for Case to return from Miles until the third day. By nightfall she gave up. The weather turned colder, snow again started, and the wind blew up a blizzard. Her chest tightened with fear. She hoped Case hadn't started out in this weather. Every few moments a glance at the window showed snow building against it. Her nerves turned raw with fear.

She cooked supper early so they could eat and get in bed before nightfall. They wouldn't have to use their small amount of coal oil: the fireplace shed enough light to un-dress by.

Anne lay awake long into the night, wondering where her husband slept and if he was safe.

When she went outside the next morning, although she'd heard nothing unusual during the night, a six-point buck lay in drifted snow on the unfinished porch outside the door. The young warrior had thanked her.

Chancing he had seen lights at the bottom of the hill, Gentry headed that way. the ride down seemed forever, and Gentry thanked his god, the Indians' god, and every other deity he could think of on the way into town.

When he reached the end of Main Street, he stopped and searched its length for signs of life. Not a person stirred. He nudged the gelding ahead, looking from side to side, hop-ing to see someone in or around the buildings. The smell of wood smoke told him fires were inside those buildings—fires and warmth. None of the stores or offices were open.

The weather had driven everyone to bed early. He couldn't estimate the time, but hoped the saloons were still open.

Down the street a ways, a tin-panny piano tinkled. Gen-try homed in on the sound. He wanted to shout, but could-n't. He'd been clinching his jaws until they felt frozen in place

In front of Tate's Range Rider Saloon, he drew rein and tried to climb from his horse. His mind ordered his legs to swing over his horse's rump, his hands to hold on to the pommel. Neither would do as ordered. Too, his brain wouldn't hold a thought long enough to make any part of him work.

No one was outside, but the piano jangling inside said people were there. He muddled that thought around awhile, then figured if he rode his horse onto the boardwalk he might get attention.

Holding the reins of Bowdry's horse, Gentry prodded his gelding to the rough wooden planks. The bay stepped dain-

tily to the walkway, single-footing as though afraid he'd
fall through. Gentry feared the same thing.

The hollow sound of hooves on the walk didn't bring
anyone. Gentry sidled the gelding next to the door and
kicked on the solid wooden panels. He kicked, and waited,
seemingly hours. He kicked again, same results. He thought
to try again to break the door down with his horse's shoulder. He kicked one more time. The latch scraped against the
wood and the door opened.

Men swarmed around. Gentry opened his mouth to tell
them he was frozen. Words formed in his mind, but his
mouth wouldn't push them out.

Hands cut the thongs that held his wrists tied to the saddle horn. They lifted him from the saddle and carried him
into the saloon, placing him and Bowdry on a pool tale side
by side. Gentry stared up at the circle faces, still unable to
speak.

A man, large on anybody's scale, looked at those surrounding the table. "Anybody know these men?"

Gentry figured the man was Tate, the owner. He wanted
to yell at him, "Hell yes, they's at least four men here who
know me." The words froze in his throat.

Someone at the foot of the table, Gentry couldn't tell
who, said, "Yeah, the bigun there, with the shoulders a mile
wide, that's Case Gentry. He ranches over yonder on the
Powder, east of here. Used to be a Ranger down Texas
way. The one with his hands tied? Don't know 'im. Better
let the marshal keep 'im 'til we get somethin' outta Gentry.
He must of had a reason for bringin' 'im in tied hand an'
foot."

Gentry tried again to say something, and only managed a
grunt. Someone brought a pile of blankets and covered
them. Someone else said, "Get the doc. We'll try to get
their blood flowing while you're gone. You, Slim, get a jig-
ger of whiskey. We'll trickle a little into each of them."

Things faded in and out after that. Gentry tried to keep

his attention on what those around him said, but he finally gave up and closed his eyes. He'd never been so tired.

After what seemed only minutes, he opened his eyes a crack. Bright sunlight streamed through a window with a flimsy curtain. Where was he? What was he doing here? Where did the sun come from? The last thing he remembered was cold and snow.

He moved his eyes from side to side. He lay in a room skimpily furnished, only a washstand, a chair, and the bed he lay upon broke its drabness. He was shivering, cold—but he sweated. Something wasn't right. Trying to turn over, he couldn't. A mountain of quilts and blankets covered him.

He positioned his hands under the covers to push them off when he saw he wasn't alone. A right pretty, but tired and faded looking woman sat by the bed.

"Sorry, ma'am, didn't notice you sittin' there, was about to get up."

"Mr. Gentry, you ain't gettin' up. You was nigh froze to death when they brought you to my room. The doctor was in again this mornin' to look at you. Says you got pneumonia. You gotta stay in bed, or you gonna die. You got a terrible fever right now."

Another chill took him. He couldn't stop shaking, and sweat flowed from him. He pulled the covers tighter around his body. "Gotta get up. Gotta get word to my wife an' children. They gonna be worried sick 'bout me."

"Mr. Gentry, I'll try to find someone to go tell 'em. Ain't much chance o' that though. Hear tell the temperature's done dropped to fifty below. Nobody's goin' out in that weather."

Gentry ran his hands down his sweat-soaked body and felt nothing but skin. The fever was nothing to the warmth that flooded him from his toes to his head. "Who undressed me? Where's my clothes? Where am I?"

"You're in my room at Deadwood Joan's House of Pleasures, an' you got nothin' I ain't seen before. When they

brought you in, this was the only place in town you mighta
stayed. Every room in town was full. I undressed you, an'
put you to bed.

"I give up my bed for you. Well, I didn't give it up com-
pletely. You an' me, we done shared that bed for three
nights. Looks like 'til you get well we gonna spend a few
more nights together under them covers."

Blood surged to Gentry's face again. "Ma'am, I 'preciate
your kindness, but I'm a married man. I gotta get outta
here."

She laughed, maybe one of the few real laughs she'd had
in a long time. "Stop callin' me ma'am, my name's Sara.
And don't worry, cowboy, you're safe with me. Although
not many men handsome as you, married or single, are in a
hurry to get outta my bed. Now lie down. We gotta get you
well."

Another chill took hold of him. He didn't care where he
was, all he wanted to do was stop shaking, get well, and get
out of here. Sara left the room and less than an hour later
was back. She had a glass of hot water with her.

Handing the glass to Gentry, she said, "Went down by
the Tongue, they's a bunch of willow trees growin' along
the bank. I scraped the inside bark and made this concoction; it'll stop your fever." He didn't argue. He'd known
about this a long time. The Comanches and other tribes
he'd known used it. His mother had picked up its use from
the Caddo Indians in East Texas. He took the glass in a
shaking hand and drank every drop the glass held. It wasn't
long before he fell asleep.

When he woke, Sara sat by his side again. For all he
knew she'd been there all the while.

She smiled. "Feelin' better, Mr. Gentry?"

He nodded. "Yes, ma'am. Seems the fever's gone."

"It is. I been checkin' you every few minutes." She
leaned close to the bed and whispered, as though afraid
someone would hear, "Mr. Gentry, we gotta get you well.
That man you brought in, Bent Bowdry? Well, the marshal

finally let him go when he couldn't find no wanted notices on him, an' now he's done took up with another no-good.

"They say they gonna kill you when you come outta here. Marshal says he cain't do nothin' about it until they shoot you." Sara frowned. "Seems sorta dumb. Reckon I ain't never gonna understand the law." She again leaned close. "We'll slip you out the back door when you're well enough an' you can head for home."

Gentry stared at her a moment. "Bless you, Sara. Know you mean well, but I can't run. Every man from here to El Paso would figure me a coward. I'll stay, but I'm gonna get real well first."

He slept well that night, and the next day the "nice" ladies of the town sent their menfolk into the house of fallen angels to take Gentry from its influence. Sara had heard what they would try to do. She was ready.

A knock sounded on Gentry's door. Sara stood, reached into her handbag, and pulled out a .32-caliber pocket pistol. "Come in, it's unlocked."

Four men tried to enter the room at the same time, finally backed off and came in one at a time. "What was it you gentlemen wanted, Mr. Dean?"

"Well, now, Sary, our wives think we ought to take Mr. Gentry to one of our houses to get well. This—well—this . . . "

"This place ain't good enough for him?" Sara cut in. "Well now, I'll tell you, it was good enough when he needed doctorin' day an' night. I didn't see none of you come around to help then, and you damn sure ain't takin' him out in that weather now. You'll have 'im right back where he was. I'm keepin' 'im."

"Now, Sary, listen to reason. We got room for 'im. We can move 'im an' you can go back to work. Besides, our wives gonna raise teetotal hell if we don't bring 'im out."

Sara waved her small pistol. "Sir, you ain't never seen no teetotal hell raised nowhere, less'n you try takin' Mr. Gentry outta here. Then I'm gonna show you some real hell raisin'. Y'all git."

They left, closing the door softly behind them. Gentry looked at Sara a long minute. "Ma'am, reckon I been too sick to think. You ain't been able to earn a livin' since you taken me in. Don't know how I'll make it up to you. Ain't got but a few dollars I was gonna get my wife an' chilun some Christmas with, but I'm gonna give it to you. Know it ain't gonna be enough, but you're sure enough gonna take it."

"Mr. Gentry, I ain't takin' one nickel of your money. All the girls, includin' Deadwood Joan, been splittin' their earnin's with me ever since you been here." She grinned. "Ain't tellin' them, but I been makin' more while takin' care of you than I ever made doin'—uh, doin' . . . "

"Don't say no more, Sara. You'll never know how much I thank you." He chuckled. "And, wait'll I tell Anne where I been spendin' my time since I left home. Lordy day. I'll bet she'll never forget it."

"Aw, Mr. Gentry, you don't need to tell her. I'll . . . "

"Oh, no you don't. I'm gonna tell her. Wouldn't miss the look on her face for nothin'."

Two more days and Gentry was taking coffee with "the ladies" in the kitchen. Three days after that he told them he better leave. He had Christmas shopping to do. Too, he had a gun date with Bowdry and his new found sidekick.

He wondered who Bowdry had picked up with, although it wouldn't be hard to find hard cases in any western town. Would he have to fight both of them or would Bowdry try him alone. If he had the slim gunman figured right, he'd do it the safest way he could. Gentry shrugged. He'd have to fight them both.

CHAPTER THREE

★ ★ ★

Gentry hated to leave the warmth of Deadwood Joan's kitchen, but he was long overdue at the ranch, and he still had things to do here. "I'll stop in an' say 'bye 'fore I leave, Sara. Know money won't pay for what you did for me, ain't got much of that anyway, but I'll make it up to you somehow."

"Don't worry about it, cowboy." That gleam came to her eyes again. "I sort of enjoyed it." Gentry felt his face turn red as his long handles. He left before he caught fire and melted.

Outside, the weather still had a bite to it, but the wind had stopped, making it seem warmer. He glanced around to get his bearings. Deadwood Joan's house sat close to the banks of the Tongue River. Only a vacant lot separated it from Milestown's business district bordering, on both sides, a rough, windblown, frozen roadway. He headed for the center of town.

At the marshal's office, Gentry told him why he'd brought Bowdry in, along with a little of the background on the man as he knew it. "Ain't done nothin' outside the law I know of."

Marshal Bruns slanted a sour look at him. "You hear he's set himself up to kill you?"

Gentry nodded. "Yeah, heard 'bout that. I can take care of *him*. He never was as good with a handgun as he figured."

20

Bruns tamped his pipe and put fire to it. Through a cloud of smoke, he said, "He's picked up a partner from somewhere. Seen 'im around a few times. He looks saltier than Bowdry."

Gentry shrugged, trying to appear confident even though his stomach felt like it had worms crawling in it. "Marshal, reckon I gotta take what comes. Used to, I wouldn't be worried 'bout it, but I got a wife an' kids now so I better not miss."

"You very fast with that .44?"

"Don't know. I'm still here, an' I been in a few scrapes. Fair to middlin', I reckon."

Bruns stood. "Gentry, I'm not supposed to do this, but if you can set it up outside of town, outside of my bailiwick, I'll side you."

Gentry was shaking his head before Bruns finished his sentence. "You know I cain't do that. I'd have to leave the territory. 'Preciate the offer, but I saddle my own broncs."

"Figured you'd say that." Bruns stuck out his hand. "Good luck. If you win, you got no trouble with me. If you lose, Bowdry and the other one's got plenty of trouble."

Gentry chuckled and shook Bruns's hand, then his face stiffened and he felt his eyes turn hard and cold. "Bruns, they don't have to lose to have plenty of trouble. They already got it. Then, I gotta be gettin' home. My missus will be frantic if I don't get home right soon, probably is right now."

"You're not thinkin' to try that ride again? Hell, man, it ain't warmed an ounce since you rode in, fact is it's colder—wind just stopped blowin'."

"Yep. 'Fraid I better. My wife an' kids are out yonder alone. Feel better if I'm with 'em."

Bruns nodded. "Know how that is, but play it safe as you can." Gentry threw his hand up in a casual good-bye and left. He angled across the street to Leighton's general store.

When he closed the door behind him, he headed straight for the potbellied stove in the middle of the floor. It glowed a cherry-red, and the aroma of coffee beans, tanned leather, tobacco, and peppers mixed with scents from clothing and goodness knows what else filled him with a sense of well-being.

"Howdy, Gentry. Hear you been mighty sick—pneumonia. How you feeling?"

Gentry nodded. "Feelin' good. Got a few things to buy. Got eighteen dollars an' a dime. Don't let me go over that."

"Gentry, I'll carry you for long as it takes to make your outfit pay. Hell, get what you need."

Gentry pulled his hands away from the stove's heat. "'Preciate it, Leighton, but I'll make it as long's I can. Ain't to that point yet."

Leighton shook his head and muttered, "Stubborn as an old mule, and so prideful won't take help even when it's offered."

Gentry walked around the store, sighting the things stocked there. He mostly wanted to get some idea what he might be able to afford as gifts. A doll took his eye. Brandy had never had anything but a gnarled wooden carving he'd made as soon as she could walk. Sure didn't seem like eight years since she was a chubby, cuddly baby. He set the doll aside. If he could afford it, she wouldn't have to play at dressing that old carving anymore.

In a case alongside the pistols, a hand mirror, a comb, and brush rested in a small wooden box. Gentry hovered over the case several minutes, wanting it for Anne so bad it hurt. He imagined her sitting on the edge of their bed, brushing her glorious mane of auburn hair. Then she'd pick up the mirror and her green eyes would sparkle when she saw herself.

Now, she had only a shard broken from a mirror in some distant past. He remembered finding the mirror, all of it broken except the small piece he'd brought home. He'd found it in the burned-out skeleton of a wagon.

He searched through the store three or four times, and always ended up back at the case, looking at the mirror set. He put it aside with the doll.

His son, Mark, had known nothing but work. Most of the time he shouldered a man's load, helping his dad set fence posts, brand cattle, ride fence, and all the odd jobs Gentry saddled him with. A lump swelled in Gentry's throat, and his chest tightened. Thinking of his son always did this to him.

He had watched Mark play with a board he'd carved into the likeness of a rifle. The boy needed a real one, unless they cost too much.

Gentry walked directly to the rifles hung from pegs on the wall behind the counter. He knew, right off, he couldn't buy a new one; some new ones ran as much as sixty dollars. He moved on down the wall to look at those Leighton had taken in on trade, some of them pretty badly used.

A Henry .22 hung on a wooden peg. It had a price tag of three dollars and a quarter.

Gentry lifted it off the peg, checked its action, sighted down its barrel, and put it back. It was in good condition. The stock was a little roughed up, but he could smooth it.

He had to remember the staples Anne had told him she needed. A roll of brown wrapping paper took his eye. He tore off a strip and wrote down the things he needed first, he then added the mirror set, the doll, and the rifle. Looking at the list, he shook his head, knowing he hadn't enough money to cover it.

With enough left over, he had thought to buy a couple pounds of tobacco. He'd been packing his pipe with kinnikinnick longer than he could remember. A pipeful of real tobacco would be a treat. He left the tobacco off the list.

"Leighton, how 'bout seeing what this comes to. Include that Henry .22 you got there on that end peg. Make that flour a hundred-pound sack, fifty pounds of coffee, and the same with sugar." He handed Leighton the list, tamped, and lighted his pipe.

Leighton wrinkled his nose. "What the devil you smokin' in that old corncob?"

Gentry tensed. Having people know how broke he was didn't set right, even though he'd told Leighton only a few minutes ago. His face stiffened, and his jaw set. "Kinnikinnick. I like it."

A slight smile creased the corners of Leighton's mouth. "Uh-huh."

Leighton put figures by each item Gentry had written down, erased some, and tallied the amount again. Finally, after doing it three times, he pushed the list toward Gentry. "Comes to nineteen dollars an' twenty-three cents."

"Reckon we can cut back on the coffee. How much coffee can I buy with the money I told you I had?"

Leighton pulled the paper toward him, then pushed it back. "Tell you what, you help me move an' stack some goods I got in the back room, we'll call it even."

Gentry stared at him a moment, turned his head to blink back moisture he felt shame over, then again turned his look on his friend. "Leighton, know you shaved prices on everything, probably even lost money on this deal, but I ain't got the guts to put my pride ahead of it. C'mon. Let's move them goods so you can move 'em back after I leave."

Leighton chuckled. "I really do have some stuff needs movin'. An' besides, if I didn't charge you quite enough this time, believe me, I'll get it back next time you're in."

They spent a couple of hours rearranging stock, and while Gentry finished the job, Leighton went up front and packaged his goods, putting them all in a couple of gunny sacks Gentry could sling across his horse's rump.

Everything packed, Leighton glanced at the tins of tobacco and pulled a four-pound can from the shelf. He pushed it deep into the gunny sack and pulled a corner of the coffee bag over it, muttering all the while. "Likes kinnikinnick, does he? Danged hard-headed, stiff-necked sonofagun. If he had a wagon with him, I'd bust his pride wide open. He'd take help from a friend, or I'd bust him one in the chops." He chuckled. "Naw. Don't think I'd want to try busting him one—too big."

When Gentry came back to the front, Leighton asked, "When you leavin' for home?"

Gentry looked at the old Regulator clock on the wall. Half past ten. "Reckon if I leave now, I can make it soon after dark." Then he said to himself, "Got no place to sleep noway."

"Don't be a fool, Gentry. It's forty, maybe fifty below out there, and the wind's pickin' up again. Stay 'til mornin'."

"Don't look like it's gonna get any better. I'll think on it though." He slung the gunny sacks across his shoulders. "Thanks again for what you done for me today. Ain't gonna forget it."

"You better forget it. I already have. Besides that, you better get somethin' to eat before you leave, gonna be a long, cold ride." He dropped a quarter in Gentry's shirt pocket. "Buy yourself some dinner."

Gentry knew to protest would be useless. He shouldered his supplies and went down the street to the cafe. The only thing he'd had in his stomach since early the day before was the coffee he'd had in Deadwood Joan's kitchen. Now that he had money to eat on, he let his stomach tell him how hungry he was.

The cafe, a gray, unpainted clapboard shack, looked a lot better inside. Red checkered oilcloth covered the tables. The windows were curtained, and the food caused Gentry's stomach to growl. The quarter Leighton put in his pocket covered a big bowl of stew, corn bread, and all the coffee he could drink. When he finished, he felt he could ride home and back again.

Despite Leighton's warning to stay overnight, Gentry went from the cafe to the livery stable, put his supplies in the stall with his horse, and headed for Tate's. He wanted to thank him for thawing him out the night he rode in.

Then he thought of Bowdry. He shrugged. Bowdry and his sidekick would have to wait, he wanted to get home.

When he walked from the warmth of the livery, he shoved his hands in the pockets of his buffalo robe. His .44 was still where he'd left it when he brought Bowdry in. He unbuttoned one button to open his coat and put his handgun in its holster, then thought better of that idea. He'd wait until he reached Tate's where it was warm. He rebuttoned his coat and again ran his hands into his coat pockets.

He stepped up to the boardwalk—and knew he was in trouble. Bowdry and another man came toward him. Gentry knew Bowdry's sidekick better than he did Bowdry. He was Red Duvall, one of a band of outlaws Gentry had sent to prison.

He stopped, waited for them to get closer. Duvall was the more dangerous of the two, he'd take him first. Deep in his pocket, he slipped his finger through the trigger guard of his Colt. The smooth, warm walnut grips snuggled into his palm.

"Howdy, Red. See they let you out earlier'n I figured. Shoulda hung you."

"Nope, Gentry, they didn't hang me. Didn't hang my brother neither. Him an' Bob Benton'll be here in a couple of days. Three more of the bunch is follerin' them. Gonna be good to tell 'em they done made that long ride for nothin'—tell 'em I done killed you."

Gentry felt like he had when wearing a badge. His stomach tightened, his head cleared, and every small thing around him came into sharp focus. "You always was one to drag the pot before seein' the hole cards, Red. You ain't draggin' *this* pot." Not taking his eyes off Duvall, Gentry asked, "Bowdry, you in this game? I gotta kill you too?"

Gentry talked to make them think a bit, make them lose a little of their poise, tighten up. "You gonna give me a chance to chuck this coat so I'll have an even chance?" He tightened his grip on his Colt and tilted it slightly. A gleam came into Bowdry's eyes.

"Even chance? Gentry, you're crazy. You got as much chance now as you're gonna get. Don't even try to unbutton that coat. You didn't give me much chance over there on the Powder. You hauled me outta there quicklike, 'fraid I'd take your woman from you." Bowdry's hand twitched, but he wasn't through talking. "Tell you what, Gentry, after we gut-shoot you, I'm goin' back to your place. I'll have your woman anytime I want. Until I git tired of her—then I'm gonna throw her away."

Angry bile formed in Gentry's throat. He swallowed twice real fast. Don't let them do to you what you're trying to do to them. If they make you crazy mad, they got the edge. A cold calculating fury come over him then. This was the way he liked to be in a fight. He grinned.

"Bowdry, if such happened that two of you beat me, then you got to get by my boy to get to my wife. You ain't even man enough to do that." Bowdry's hand hanging by his holster twitched again, then trembled. Bowdry and Duvall stood close enough Gentry could watch every motion they made.

Duvall's hand slapped for his holster first. Gentry tilted the gun in his pocket and pulled the trigger. A black hole appeared beside Duvall's nose and the whole back of his head spewed a gray and red spray. Gentry swiveled his Colt a hair and pulled the trigger twice. Bowdry was fanning his gun. Gentry had heard somewhere he did that. No wonder he was a second-rate gunhand.

Gentry's first shot knocked Bowdry's right leg from under him, his second turned Bowdry around. It must have hit him in the shoulder. The icy flame in Gentry's head burned brighter. He walked in on Bowdry. He wasn't worried about Duvall; somewhere in the back of his mind he knew he'd killed him with his first shot.

Bowdry was down. His pistol lay just beyond his fingers. Gentry pulled the hammer back on his Colt so slowly each ratcheting sound was audible. "Don—don't, Gentry. I—I didn't mean what I said. I wouldn't hurt your wife. Duvall told me to say them things. Said we could get you mad that way. Don't shoot me."

Gentry squatted by Bowdry, flipped him to his back, and put the barrel of his .44 right between his eyes. "You filthy, slimy trash. Just thinkin' 'bout my wife the way you been thinkin's enough to make me blow your damned head off. If you know any prayers—say them." He squeezed the trigger real easy.

"Gentry! Don't do it. Don't blame you for wanting to, but you'd blame yourself the rest of your life. Ease off on that trigger before you're sorry." Marshal Bruns's words cut through the icy haze in Gentry's brain. He sucked in a deep breath, let it out, and did it again. His thumb tightened down on the hammer. He let it down slowly, then reached past Bowdry's outstretched fingers and picked up the gun lying there. Holding it by the barrel, he handed it to Bruns.

"Thanks, Marshal. Yeah, I'd a been sorry, probably wouldn't of been able to face Anne again. If I'd killed him, with him havin' no chance, reckon I woulda put myself down on his level."

"Yeah, Case, you're too good a man for that." While Gentry stood, Bruns pocketed Bowdry's pistol. His eyes swept Gentry from foot to head. "You hit anywhere?"

Gentry shook his head. "You want me for anything, Marshal? In case you didn't see it, they brought it to me, an' you didn't hear what Red Duvall told me. His brother, Jim, and Bob Benton are on their way up here lookin' for me.

"Reckon puttin' them in prison brought a whole bunch of trouble down on me. Gotta stay here, cain't take a chance on leadin' 'em out to my place and gettin' my family hurt." He punched three spent shells from the cylinder of his Colt, put the casings in his pocket, and reloaded his pistol.

He slanted Bruns a troubled look. "Know what, Marshal? They's three more of them besides the two what are comin' for me. I ain't goin' home 'til my back trail's clear. Might mean not getting home for Christmas. Tomorrow or the next day, Jim Duvall an' Bob Benton'll be ridin' in.

Then—well, I don't know when the other three will get here."

"You got a place to stay while you're here?"

Gentry shook his head.

"Tell you what. Why don't you sleep in the jail, keep the fire goin' through the night, watch whatever prisoners I got in there. Won't be nothing but drunks sleeping it off, and I'll give you four-bits a night for your trouble. You'll be doin' us both a favor. I'll get to spend time with my wife, an' you won't have to spend any of your hard-earned money. How 'bout it?"

Gentry stared at Bruns a moment, wondering if he knew he was stone-cold broke, hoping he didn't. Maybe the marshal had made the offer because he really wanted to spend a night at home. And *he* needed a place to stay. If he stayed in the livery, he'd probably be right back in bed with pneumonia again.

He nodded. "You got a deal!"

All he had to worry about now was the Duvall Gang, and the hell Anne was going to give him for shooting a bunch of holes in a buffalo robe.

CHAPTER FOUR

★ ★ ★

Gentry went from the jail to the livery to get his supplies. He'd keep them in an empty cell until after he met Duvall and Benton.

The liveryman, an old-timer by the name of Tom Rawlings, called Gentry back to his living quarters and office. "Might's well have a cup of coffee while you're here. Ain't much a man can do out yonder in that weather."

Gentry figured Rawlings wanted company. He nodded. "Yeah, reckon coffee would taste good right now. Help thaw the frost outta my bones."

They sipped the hot liquid while Rawlings did most of the talking. Finally, the old man worked his way in the conversation to where Gentry had seen him heading several minutes before. "How's that ranch of yours coming along? Figure it should be shaping up pretty well by now."

Gentry shook his head. "Takin' longer'n I ever thought, Rawlings. I need cows, an' the only place they's any for free is them mavericks down yonder in the big Bend of Texas. I cain't be away from my family long enough to go down there, find a crew, round up a herd, and drive 'em back up here. Reckon I'm gonna have to tighten my belt a few more years an' wait for my herd to grow." He shook his head and took another swallow of coffee. "Just flat didn't figure on it takin' so long."

Rawlings squinted at him over the rim of his cup. Gentry could tell he thought deeply on something. Finally, he nodded. "Might be just the thing for you, young'un. There's a man over west of here, name of Trace Gundy, married to a mighty pretty woman, a widow, Joyce Waldrop."

"I knew Jim Waldrop, a fine man. Didn't know his widow had remarried." Gentry didn't say he also knew Trace Gundy, knew him from his days in Texas, and had known him by another name also, the Apache Blanco.

Rawlings nodded. "Yep, she married this young Texan. Reckon between 'em they have enough land and cows, here and in Texas, to make up one of them eastern states." He stood and again filled their cups. "Anyway, what I wanted to tell you is, Gundy might be able to tell you where you could find some critters for free."

Marshal Ben Darcy down in Marfa, Texas, had told Gentry about Gundy four or five years before, and Gentry had met Gundy once. He'd never heard that Blanco would put a brand on any cow not his. This sounded too good to be true, and despite the surge of hope that streaked through his chest, he took it as just that, too good to be true. He cocked an eyebrow at Rawlings. "Where can Gundy get cows for nothin'? It's mighty close to Christmas, but I don't figure Santa Claus is gonna be drivin' a herd down this way."

Rawlings chuckled. "No, don't reckon he will, but Gundy should be in town in the next couple of days. If you're still here, ask him about them. May not be many, maybe a couple hundred head, and with a lot of hard work you could find 'em."

Two hundred more head on his place would make the difference between waiting several years for his cows to throw that many calves and skimping all the way, or being able to start giving his family the things they needed right away.

It would be at least two or three days before Duvall and Benton showed up. Gentry shrugged mentally. He had nothing to lose. He'd see Gundy. As for it taking a lot of hard work? He had known toil all of his life.

Gentry swallowed the last of his coffee, stood, shouldered his supplies, and told Rawlings he'd wait for Gundy. He stepped toward the stable door, hesitated, and turned back. "Rawlings, would you stable my horse 'til I leave if I feed and water the animals you're keepin' here?"

Rawlings wiped his hand down his cheek, stared at the ground, then looked at Gentry from under the brim of his hat. "You do need them cows, don't you, son?" He nodded. "Yeah, I'll keep your horse in out of the cold, but you don't need to help me. Heck, after you get your ranch goin' you'll bring me plenty enough business to make up for it."

"No, I'll come down here an' help me every day I'm here, Rawlings. 'Preciate the offer, but I sort of like to feel I carry my part o' the load when I can."

Rawlings nodded. "Know how you feel. Come on down." He grinned. "I need the company anyway."

The cold took Gentry's breath when he stepped out the door. He hurried to the jail, dumped his supplies in the front cell, and took his rifle with him into the marshal's office. Bruns picked up an empty cup and looked questioningly at Gentry.

"Don't b'lieve so right now, Marshal. Just had a cup with Rawlings." Gentry sat across the desk from Bruns and stood his rifle on the floor, leaning it against his chair. "Been a long time since my weapons needed to be kept clean inside and out." He opened the loading gate of his .44, emptied the shells into his hand, and started cleaning his pistol. "Reckon the day'll come we don't need guns?"

Bruns shook his head. "Nope. Maybe no shoot-outs every other day, but as long as dishonest men have guns, honest men are gonna need them."

Gentry sighted down the barrel, shoved shells into the cylinder, and shook his head. "Shame, ain't it?"

Bruns walked to the door, threw the cold coffee in his cup out into the street, closed the door behind him, and again sat at his desk. He pulled a badge from the top drawer, held up a ring of keys, rattled them, and said, "These're the cell keys in case you need 'em." He held the badge toward Gentry. "Been a long time since you wore one of these, but reckon you better pin it on if you're gonna take my place in here at night."

Gentry held the badge in the palm of his hand, studied it a moment, and pinned it on. With the badge came responsibility, even though only temporary. He looked into Bruns's eyes and saw he realized the job he'd given him, but more importantly he saw trust there. "Thank you, Marshal."

Bruns's eyes crinkled at the corners. "Thank you, Gentry. It's not every man I'd trust with that badge. I've needed a night off for quite a spell. Now, I'll go see what the missus has for supper."

"I'll make a couple of rounds for you," Gentry offered.

Bruns nodded. "Make one about ten o'clock, that'll be enough. Not many folks out in this weather—even for a drink." He stepped through the doorway, shutting the door behind him.

Gentry sat at Bruns's desk, thinking. There were many men in this town Bruns trusted, but the trust in putting a badge on a man included capability, and Gentry knew of only two men in this area, other than himself, that had that kind of talent. Of course, one was Bruns, and the other had never worn a badge although the Rangers had urged him to join them. Tracy Gundy had turned them down.

His thoughts went from Gundy to Anne. He had to let her know he was all right. He didn't dare go home. After shooting Red Duvall, his brother Jim would crash the gates of hell to get even. Gentry would not take that kind of trouble to his family.

About ten o'clock, Gentry stood, tied the thongs at the bottom of his holster to his thigh, and slanted across the street to the Range Rider Saloon.

When he pushed through the heavy wooden panels, he took the room in with a glance, something he wouldn't have done before pinning the badge on. He saw that most of the men here were either townspeople or off surrounding ranches, and a few soldiers from Fort Keogh, west of town a couple of miles. One man, Red Dawson, owned the Cattleman's Saloon and Cafe over in Ismay, about fifty miles away. Gentry walked about the room, took some ribbing about the badge from those who knew him, and went over to shake Dawson's hand.

"Howdy, Dawson. What you doin' this far from home?"

"Hi, Gentry. Riverboat brought me a shipment of whiskey." He grinned. "That boat might not leave here 'til spring thaw. River's frozen solid since it got here. I come over with a buckboard to pick up what they brought me. That damned wagon's seat's got my rear so sore it takes my mind off the cold. Reckon there's something good about everything."

They talked awhile and Gentry moved on to visit others in the room. One of the ranchers asked about Gentry's family, and it came to him how he might get word to Anne that he was all right. He walked back to Dawson. "Red, when you headed back to Ismay?"

"Figure tomorrow, 'less it blows up a blizzard again. Why?"

"Would it throw you too late gettin' home if you took my missus a message?"

Dawson shook his head. "Don't see that it would. Figured to make camp one night 'tween home and here anyway."

"Tell Anne I'm doin' fine, and I got some business with a rancher west of here. Tell 'er I'll be home for Christmas." He grinned. "An' yeah, She'll feed you and put you up for the night." He didn't say anything about Duvall and his sidekick for fear Dawson might say something to disturb Anne.

Dawson nodded, the corners of his mouth crinkling. "Gentry, I'd ride that far outta my way just to get one of your missus's biscuits." He held up his beer. "Want a drink?"

"No, thanks. Don't reckon I better." Gentry hesitated.

"You got room in your buckboard for a couple of tow sacks—stuff Anne probably needs for the house?"

Dawson nodded. "Yeah. Buckboard's at the livery. Throw your stuff in there tonight though. I'm cutting out of here 'bout daylight."

" 'Preciate it, Dawson. See you next time I'm in Ismay." He left to go put his supplies in the buckboard.

Before he took the gunny sacks to the livery, Gentry took the presents for Anne and the children from the sacks and left them in the jail. He didn't dig deep enough to find the tobacco Leighton hid there.

After the trip to the livery, Gentry again sat at Bruns's desk. He thought of Anne and the children and the closeness of his family. He missed them, but not enough that he'd guide a pack of gunfighters to them. That brought him to Bowdry. He wouldn't worry about him until the skinny gunfighter's leg and shoulder got well. Gentry didn't know where Bowdry might have holed up to lick his wounds, but he'd make it a point to find out in the next day or so.

His thoughts shifted to Gundy, the Apache Blanco. How could Blanco know where there were cattle for free—and what was Gundy doin' this far north?

Blanco had cleaned up a ring of Comancheros raiding along the border and had gotten himself a nice-sized ranch out of the deal, along with a large herd of longhorns. Yeah, that must be the reason he was up here, probably delivered a herd to some ranch in the area. His thoughts shifted to Jim Duvall.

He needed some kind of edge. He'd be fighting more than one man, and if he remembered right, any one of the Duvall bunch were slick gunhands. Luck, a lot of it, had better be riding his shoulders or Anne was going to be a widow. Anger along with the brassy taste of fear gripped his chest and forced his throat muscles to tighten.

He stood, blew out the lantern, went in the front cell, and went to bed.

The next morning when Bruns came in, Gentry had already made coffee and been to the livery to see if Dawson had left town. He had, so Gentry promised Rawlings he'd be back that afternoon and give him a hand feeding.

Gentry studied Bruns a moment. "You look rested, Marshal. Maybe by the time Duvall gets here you'll be back at the peak."

Bruns poured himself a cup of coffee and sat behind his desk. "Have any trouble last night?"

Gentry shook his head. "Everything was quiet. Most of them over at the Range Rider were ranchers or townsfolk just sittin' around jawin'."

Bruns leaned back in his chair. "Way I figured it'd be. Used to have a lot of trouble at the Soldier's Haven, a saloon over yonder across the Tongue. It burned down, and the man running it got himself shot dead, Barton was his name, he owned a ranch east of here, up north of Ismay a ways. Since then this been a right quiet town, until now. That saloon across the river was out of my jurisdiction anyway."

Gentry walked to the front window and looked each way along the frozen street. Hoping not to see Duvall, yet wishing he would so he could get that fight behind him. The icy stretch was empty. He glanced over his shoulder at Bruns. "Don't reckon it's gonna be quiet much longer. Duvall an' his bunch, even without tryin' to kill me, will raise some amount of hell. When they get here, I'll turn this badge back to you. Don't want nothin' I do to reflect bad on the law."

Bruns looked at him a moment. "Gentry, keep the badge. It might make them think a little before attacking you."

"Marshal, they done rode almost two thousand miles to get even with me. They ain't gonna let a badge stand 'tween them 'an puttin' a couple of holes in me." He came back to the desk and sat across from Bruns. "There's gonna be at least five of them. Wish I knew how to make it so I'd not have to fight more than two at a time."

The marshal took a swallow of his coffee and leaned forward. "I'll tell you right now, Gentry, badge or no badge, I'll not let you face more than two at a time, might not let even that many face you."

Gentry locked eyes with Bruns. "Stay out if it, Marshal. I brought this on myself. Don't want nobody hurt on my account."

Gentry paced the office a couple of times, picked up the coffeepot to fill his cup, shook his head, and set it back on the stove without pouring. He again sat across from Bruns. "Tell you what I'm thinkin'. If two of them showed up ahead of the others, I'm thinkin' of takin' it to them—force a fight before they're ready. You got any druthers 'bout that?"

"Hell no, son. If there's any way you can do it to gain an edge, go to it. You and your stubborn pride won't let me help, but maybe this'll tilt the bucket a little."

Gentry felt his eyes go flat and cold. "Ain't nothin' throws a man off more'n a gunfight when he least expects one."

He felt Bruns's eyes rake him from head to toe. "Son, tell you what. Unless I was one of the best gunfighters around, I'd play hell facing you, whether I expected it or not."

Gentry stood. "Reckon I better hightail it down to the livery. Promised Rawlings I'd help 'im feed the stock he's got down there."

When he got to the door, he turned back, picked up his rifle, then tied his holster thongs to his leg. He smiled, his face feeling leathery. He'd better get used to keeping his weapons close to hand.

CHAPTER FIVE

★ ★ ★

About three o'clock, Gentry left the jail and headed for the cafe. He figured if he held his eating to about that time of day, and drank Rawlings's and Bruns's coffee the rest of the time, he wouldn't mind one meal a day. He could eat twice a day on fifty cents if push came to shove, but thought he'd hold off and see how he felt, he might save two-bits a day.

The waitress put his steak, still simmering, in front of him, along with a heaping plate of biscuits covered with a towel. Gentry sat in the warmest place in the room, at the long table next to the counter separating the kitchen from the dining area.

He cut the first bite from his steak. The door swung open, and preceded by an icy blast, a man and a very pretty woman, followed by five ranch hands, judging by their dress, pushed into the warmth. They stood shivering a moment before picking the table next to Gentry's.

"Why don't you an' your missus sit here with me, Blanco? Plenty of room." Gentry, smiling, looked Gundy right in the eyes when he issued the invitation.

Gundy frowned, obviously puzzled, but on his guard to meet trouble head-on. Abruptly recognition spread across his face. "Well, I'll be damned, it's been a long time. What're you doin' up here?" He stepped aside and taking his wife's elbow introducing her to Gentry, then he called out the names of his hands. When he got to Brad Crockett, Gentry broke in.

"You ain't got no prettier these past years, Crockett." Gentry swept them with a glance. "Lordy, this's like old home week."

After the hand shaking and back pounding by those who knew each other, they ordered supper, ate, and settled in to talking about all that had transpired in the intervening years.

Gundy told about his first wife getting killed by Comancheros led by Rance Barton. That he'd tracked Barton all the way from the Big Bend to Milestown and killed him. That he'd hired on with Joy, his wife, to keep from starving during the winter, and that Barton's brother, Lem, had owned a ranch and was rustling cows. That he and Joy's crew, along with several local ranchers, had raided Lem Barton's ranch and gotten the rustled cattle back along with several hundred more, and they had killed Lem while doing it. Gundy slanted Joy a devilish look and said, "Wuz 'bout to head for Texas after takin' care of Joy's troubles when she up an' asked me to marry her."

Instead of rising to the bait, Joy looked at her husband with a smile that told Gentry how much she loved Blanco. "Mr. Gentry, I didn't propose to Trace, but if he'd started for Texas without me, I would have. Truth is, I thought I was going to have to."

This was the longest suppertime Gentry ever spent—but it took that long to catch up on Texas news. And he had to tell Gundy how he came to be in Montana, that he was married, and trying to get a ranch started. Narrow-lidded, he pinned Blanco with a look. "You say you rounded up Barton's cows an' took 'em back to home range? Reckon you left a few?"

Gundy nodded. "Yeah, I'd say we left several hunnerd. It was cold, colder'n what we got now. We made a fast sweep of his range, an' when we figured we had more'n enough to make up for what he'd rustled, we headed for home."

"Reckon if I went over there an' found some of them cows there'd be any trouble with the law?"

Blanco shook his head. "Nope, we took care of all that with the Cattleman's Association. I figure if you work at it you might find six, maybe seven hunnerd head." He studied Gentry a moment. "How many hands you got on your place?"

Gentry felt his face heat up. "Only me an' my ten-year-old son, Gundy."

"I can let you have a few hands to help out. You an' a ten-year-old boy ain't gonna get the job done."

The heat stayed in Gentry's face. He hated to admit his almost destitute state, but he didn't have much choice. "Gundy, I got no money to pay your hands. Mark, my son, an' me'll make do."

Crockett spoke up. "If the boss'll let me, I'll help you for nothing. You gotta have help, son, ain't no time to stand on your stubborn pride. Stockin' a ranch—'cept in South Texas with its mavericks—is a slow process. Let me help you."

Gundy cut in, "Don't give a damn if he'll let you help or not. We'll take four or five hands over there an' drive them cows onto his range, then he can do what he wants with them—even drive 'em back where they come from." Blanco looked at Gentry over the rim of his cup. "Ain't no man too big to need help once in a while. My first wife's pa, her brother, an' a couple of his vaqueros helped me get started. An' by damn, you need help an' you're gonna get it."

Gentry stared at Gundy a moment. "Why you doing this for me, Blanco? You hardly even know me."

Gundy nodded. "Yeah, I know you. Know what you stood for down yonder in Texas; know you left me to show what kind of man I could be when you could have stuck that Ranger's badge you wore slam down my throat. I know you for a decent man—you gonna get help. Come spring, Crockett here, an' four or five men gonna see you get the help you need. Don't wanta hear no more about it."

Gentry, still staring into Blanco's eyes, swallowed fast a couple of times to try to rid himself of the lump in his throat, then blinked rapidly, hoping the moisture that threatened to flood his eyes would not become apparent. "Thanks, Blanco. That's right neighborly of you. Maybe someday I'll find a way to repay you."

"*Da nada*, 'tis nothing. Besides, ain't been but 'bout a month since we made a gather on that land. Crockett knows every hill, stream, an' arroyo over there." Gundy glanced at his watch. "We better get goin', get Joy settled in her room at the hotel." Gundy and the Flying JW crew stood. "See you in early spring."

Gentry watched them go out the door, had the waitress fill his cup again, and sat staring into the black liquid. He came to town without enough money to buy supplies and Christmas for his wife and children. Now, he still had no money in his Levi's, but he had a promise of some—and more than anything else he realized how nice most people were. All you had to do was give them a chance.

Anne had almost the same thought when Red Dawson pulled his buckboard into the yard and explained that he'd made a "little" jog to bring her a message and supplies from her husband. She knew he had ridden several miles out of his way in sub-zero weather to do Case this favor.

"Get down and come in by the fire. You must be about frozen." She looked over her shoulder. "Mark, put Mr. Dawson's team and buckboard in the stable. He'll be staying the night."

Red stepped down from the wagon, locked his hands in the tops of the gunny sacks, and swung them over the side.

When Anne had him seated comfortably by the fire, she unpacked the bags of supplies. Having coffee, sugar, flour, and a few other staples in the house was all the Christmas she wanted—but she *had* hoped Case would manage to get the kids some little thing, maybe some hard candies. Maybe he'd put them in his sheepskin pocket and would bring them with him when he came home.

The first thing she opened was the bag of coffee. She would have been shamed to serve Dawson coffee made from used grounds, but she would have done it.

After grinding the beans and putting them in the old chipped and dented granite percolator, it took only a few moments for it to perk water to the top, into the grounds, and release the most delicious aroma Anne had smelled in a long time. She stood there a moment, her face over the pot inhaling the scent.

Finally, she smiled, and feeling almost like a princess poured Dawson and herself a cup. "How was Case when you left him? Did he look all right?"

Dawson nodded. "Reason he didn't come home before, he almost froze while taking Bent Bowdry into town, caught pneumonia. It took a while to get over it, but he's fine now. Said him seeing that rancher over west of Milestown was very important—might even put your ranch years ahead. Said to tell you how much he's missing you and the kids."

Anne frowned, wondering if Case really was all right. Pneumonia was a serious thing out here on the frontier. "You're not just telling me he's doing okay to make me feel good, are you, Red?"

"No. Fact is he was helping Marshal Bruns run the marshal's office at night until he could see this Gundy fellow. Said, don't worry, he'll be home soon's he sees 'im."

Anne felt better. If Case was helping Marshal Bruns, he must be well. She knew too, Bruns must be paying Case for the help so she could rest easy about him eating, and he'd be most likely to sleep warm. Red broke into her thoughts.

"Notice young Mark there hasn't been two feet from that double-barrel Greener since I got here. You figuring on trouble?"

Anne glanced at Mark and again looked at Dawson.

Pride swelled her heart. "Red, Case told Mark to take care of Brandy and me while he was gone. Mark has even slept with that shotgun since his father left. You can well believe he's taking care of us." She then told Dawson about the way Bowdry had looked at her, and how angry those looks made Case.

Dawson shook his head. "Ain't many in the West would harm a woman, but reckon there's a few. I suppose the more people come out here, the more of that kind we're gonna get. Shame, ain't it?"

"Yes it is. But as long as we raise sons like Mark this'll always be a country to be proud of." She glanced at the big grandfather clock her father had given them when she and Case got married, it was three o'clock. She stood. "Gracious, where has the time gone? Excuse me, Red, while I fix supper. Seems like when I get company, adult company, time just flies."

After supper, Anne shooed the children off to bed, and she and Dawson sat by the fire, talked, and drank coffee until she showed him hers and Case's bed. "I'll sleep in the attic with the children, it's warm and comfortable up there, you sleep here."

Long after they went to bed, Anne thought on what Dawson had told her. She couldn't imagine what business Case could have with another rancher. He had no money to buy cattle, no cattle to sell, not really much of anything to offer an already prospering rancher. She gnawed on the problem awhile, then thought if Case figured on hiring out to bring a few dollars into the family till, she'd balk at that. Poor or not, she wanted her man by her side—especially at night. She smiled into the dark at the thought. Even though she and Case were married, her mother would be shocked to think her little girl had thoughts like that. Her smile widened and she hugged her pillow to her breast.

The next morning when she went out to milk, there was another large buck, ten point, lying on her unfinished porch. Scar was determined to pay any debt he might owe.

She had taken to thinking of the young warrior as Scar for lack of a better name.

After milking, and while she fixed breakfast, she told Dawson about the Sioux warrior and his bringing a plentiful supply of venison and laying it on her doorstep.

Dawson smiled. "Anne, you and these children have made yourselves a friend like few whites ever have. Wouldn't surprise me if young Mark here wasn't getting some unsuspected help in making sure you're safe."

They ate and talked about the growth the railroad had brought to Ismay, then after stacking the dishes, Mark helped Dawson harness the team. Before leaving, he gave both children a quarter. "It'll be too late for Santa Claus to bring you any peppermint sticks to put in your stocking, but it'll taste just as good after Christmas," Dawson said, and tousled Mark's hair before climbing to the hard wooden seat he had only two days before griped to their father about. He shook the reins over the horse's backs and drove off. "Merry Christmas," he shouted over his shoulder.

Anne watched a moment and hustled the children back inside out of the cold. They helped each other unpack the gunny sacks. When Anne came to the tin of tobacco, all the way on the bottom of the sack, she read the note stuck to it. "Case, you wouldn't buy yourself this, but I saw how much you studied on it, or a lesser amount, and finally you didn't buy any. You take it and enjoy every puff. Don't tell me again how much you like kinnikinnick, I'm doing this in self-defense so I won't have to smell that god-awful concoction. Merry Christmas." It was signed, "Your friend, Bob Leighton."

She smiled. Bless you, Bob, she thought, and pushed it to the back of the top shelf in the pantry. That gift of Leighton's would make a great Christmas for her man. She wished the gift had been from her, but like all special days, she and Case would give each other their love, a gift nothing could replace.

*   *   *

Gentry drank the last of his coffee, thinking how lucky Blanco was to be sleeping next to his woman. He sighed. Unless he was the luckiest man alive, Jim Duvall's gang would prevent him from ever having another night with Anne. With the thought, anger swelled into his throat, and his chest tightened with a tinge of fear.

They used to say in Texas, "One riot, one Ranger," well, dammit, he hadn't forgotten all he knew as a Ranger. He'd whip that bunch—somehow.

He stood. It was time he went to the livery and gave Rawlings a hand.

Standing ready to pull the cafe door open, he glanced out the window. Two riders came into view, heavily bundled against the weather, but the hawkish nose and eyes of the rider closest to the cafe were features he'd never forget. Jim Duvall and at least one of his gang were in Milestown. Gentry's hand went to his Colt, massaged the walnut grips, and slowly eased the .44 in its holster. He'd promised himself to take it to them, but along with that he'd best not forget the caution that saved his life more times than one.

He waited inside the cafe, watched Duvall and this man, and glanced back down the street to make sure the other three men weren't trailing behind. The street stood empty. He again touched his Colt and waited.

CHAPTER SIX

★ ★ ★

Gentry tied his holster thong to his leg. He'd figured all along this was the day Duvall would arrive. He'd push them into a fight before the other three got here, but not before he, himself, was ready.

Duvall and his partner reined in at the hitch rack in front of the Range Rider, dismounted, and went in. Gentry studied the door of the saloon as it swung closed. They would have a drink, or maybe a couple of them, before putting their horses away.

He hurried from the cafe to the jail. "Bruns, want to borrow one of them scatter-guns you got there on the wall. My visitors done arrived."

Bruns nodded. "Shells're in the top drawer of my desk." He squinted at Gentry. "Sure you don't want me to side you?"

Gentry shook his head. "This's my bronc to ride, Marshal. Thanks anyway." He took a Greener off the wall, broke the mechanism, and sighted down the barrels. At the desk, he shoved two shells in the chamber, dropped four more in the pocket of his buffalo robe, and headed toward the livery. He wondered that he anticipated this fight, wanted it now that it was here. All of his senses came alive—like in the old days.

Jim Duvall and Bob Benton shoved up to the bar. "Two whiskeys, make them full glasses—thaw the chill out," Duvall grunted.

The bartender set glasses in front of them and tilted the bottle. "Say when." He poured until each glass filled to the rim. He raised his eyebrows, then said, "Four-bits each."

Duvall tossed a cartwheel to the counter. "You know a man hereabouts name of Gentry?"

The big man behind the car, the townspeople called him Pudge, made a swipe at the counter to remove a drop of spilled whiskey. "I might. Why?"

Duvall pinned him with a gaze. "Mister, the why of it is my damned business. You know 'im?"

Pudge nodded. "Yeah, I know him. Don't know where you might find 'im though."

Duvall leaned on the counter. "Don't make any difference, we'll find 'im." He took the men at the bar in with a glance. "Belly up, men. I'm buyin' the drinks. Rode all the way up here to kill one of your citizens—if my little brother ain't already done it."

Pudge stared at him a moment. "What name your little brother go by, stranger? I might know 'im."

Duvall lowered his eyelids to slits. "Goes by his own name, Red Duvall. He rode in here ahead of us. You hear of 'im."

Pudge, a slight smile creasing the corners of his mouth, said, "Yeah, we all heard of him. He's down yonder behind the jail, frozen solid as the Yellowstone. Can't dig a grave until the ground thaws a bit."

Duvall tightened inside. Hate piled onto what he already had inside of him, hate toward Gentry; he was sure it was the ex-Ranger who killed Red, but he asked anyway. "Who done it?"

"Why, the very man you were inquiring about, Case Gentry. He's not a man to go up against."

Duvall, still staring at Pudge, said, "Benton, take the horses down to the livery. We're gonna stay in this town 'til we find Gentry. I'll be here when you get back." He downed his drink, took a full bottle to a table, and sat.

He poured another glassful and sat looking into the

amber liquid, thinking. Six of them had left the state prison in Huntsville, Texas, all bent on killing Gentry; now there were five. The other three were about four days behind him, said they were gonna hole up until the weather got better. But he wanted to put some of *his* lead into Gentry. And now, he had more reason for wanting him. He thought to take Gentry on by himself, then changed his mind. He and Benton would do the job together—make sure of getting him. He took his handgun from its holster and proceeded to clean it.

Gentry wondered for a moment if he would get to face Duvall and Benton one at a time, wondered how he could make it happen. In another hour dark would set in, maybe he could put off the fight until tomorrow. Standing in the livery's hayloft he shoved the pitchfork into the pile of hay and tossed a forkful to the runway between the stalls below. He shook his head. It was no to both thoughts. Knowing the stripe of those he had to face, he'd be facing them both, and putting the fight off until later wouldn't accomplish anything. He'd play the cards the way they fell.

The double doors at the end of the stable opened. Bob Benton, leading two horses, came through and closed the doors. A surge of energy coursed through Gentry. Maybe he'd lucked out. He glanced at the shotgun he'd stood against the ladder railing. It was too far away, and he'd be sure to make noise getting to it. He'd have to count on his Colt, but it was buttoned under his buffalo robe. He grasped the pitchfork tighter and pointed the tines toward the space below.

Rawlings came from his office. "What you need, stranger?"

Benton, his face a frozen mask, said, "What the hell does a man usually want in a livery? Want these here horses grained an' watered. We'll pick 'em up in a couple of days. How much you charge?"

"Dollar and a half a day—each." Gentry almost swallowed his cud when Rawlings said that. He'd doubled the price.

Benton stepped toward the door, turned back, and asked, "You know where Gentry hangs out?"

"Can't say that I do."

Benton shrugged, muttered, "Shoulda known better'n to ask a broke-down old range tramp." he headed for the door.

"You lookin' for me, Benton?"

The little outlaw twisted. His hand flashed toward his gun. The way he acted he didn't know from where Gentry's voice came. He swept the front of the stalls with a glance. Frowning, he looked upward, to the loft.

Too late to try for his handgun under his buffalo robe, and knowing the chance he took, Gentry dived off the loft shelf, holding the tines of the fork out ahead of him. Everything slowed, it took almost forever to fall from the haymow.

Recognition flashed across the gunslinger's face at the same time he tried to bring his gun into line with Gentry. His timing was slow by a split second. Gentry shoved the pitchfork into him. The tines, angled down, went in just below Benton's neck and sank their full length into his chest. A raw, ragged gurgle issued from Benton's throat, bubbled in his throat, and shut off when a glob of blood pushed from his mouth. Benton struggled against Gentry's full weight to stay on his feet and bring his gun into line, but only managed to trigger a shot into the overhead.

Rawlings walked over, stood looking down at the corpse, clucked his tongue a couple of times, and looked at Gentry. "Son, it looks like he found you, an' you was kind enough to keep him from having to get out in the cold, saved 'im a lot of time too."

Gentry stared at the body a moment feeling tension flow from him at the same time his joints turned to water. Fear, or relief the fight was over, always left him weak and tired. He swallowed twice to rid himself of the knot in his throat. He looked at Rawlings. "Yeah, old-timer, I can be right accommodatin' at times. And you know what? If he'd let it ride, stayed in Texas, and gone straight, he might've lived to have grandkids." He climbed back to the loft and retrieved the Greener. Back on the ground, he asked, "You mind puttin' him up 'til I take care of the other half of this business?"

Rawlings shook his head. "Naw, I'll drag 'im out back with the others. He'll be solid ice in an hour. Go ahead. Do what you gotta."

"Thanks, Rawlings. I'll go out the back way, no tellin' what kind of reception I might get out front." Gentry left and walked along the backs of the buildings until he came to the Range Rider. He figured Duvall would be sitting facing the front door, waiting for the return of his henchman. Gentry planned to use the rear entrance, walk down the hall, and come into the bar area close to the back.

He turned the doorknob and pulled the door toward him. The hinges squalled like a Comanche meeting a Texas Ranger. Every nerve in Gentry's body tightened to the point of breaking, his neck muscles tensed. Hating to chance the noise a second time, he stepped through and cast a sour glance at the hinges. He couldn't leave it open with the temperature being what it was. He lifted on the door, taking the weight off the hinges, and closed the weatherbeaten slab of wood. The hinges squeaked only slightly this time.

At the end of the hallway, a rectangle of light showed from the bar area. Gentry cat-footed toward the light. Short of the doorway, he stopped and peered around the framing. The room was full of people, friends, neighbors—and, as he had thought, Duvall sat facing the front door with a half-full bottle of whiskey on the table in front of him.

Gentry studied the people. No one had seen him. He pulled back from the door and shook his head. He couldn't walk into a room filled with people and start shooting. No telling how many of them might take lead from either his or

Duvall's guns. He retraced his steps, went outside, and walked softly toward the front.

Before stepping out on the street, he searched its frozen length before cutting across it to the jail. When he pushed into the room, warmth reached to engulf him. The old potbellied stove in the middle of the room glowed cherry-red. "Bruns, you keep this room this hot you gonna be baked."

The marshal cast him a smug look. "You gotta handle heat in a sensible way, Gentry. What you have to do is jest sit still, don't get your blood to pumping very fast, and let the stove do its job." He grinned. "That way it don't wear your body out too fast." He took his feet off the desk and held out his cup for Gentry to pour him some coffee. When Gentry had filled his cup and one for himself, Bruns asked, "Have any trouble while you were gone? Didn't hear gunshots."

Gentry sipped his coffee, then blew on it. It was scalding hot and thick as pull-taffy. "Wasn't no shots. Stuck a pitchfork in 'im. Now I only got to face one of them what rode in. Started to go in the back door of the saloon and call his hand, but figured others might get hurt. Now, reckon I can take care of him anytime 'fore the others get here."

Bruns nodded, and they sat there in silence drinking their coffee. Gentry sat so he faced the window. His look covered the door of the Range Rider across the street.

Sooner or later, Duvall was going to get concerned about his partner and go see about him. Gentry wanted to shortstop that trip. He didn't want Rawlings to have to explain about Benton, *he* might get hurt.

And regardless how low the temperature dropped, he wouldn't button his coat over his gun again, or he could shoot through his pocket like he did with Red Duvall. He cast that idea aside. He'd already damaged his buffalo robe almost beyond repair and there were not many buffalo left.

The warmth soaked into him. He nodded, his eyes got heavy, ready to close and stay closed. This wouldn't do. He had to stop Duvall before he got to the livery, and he

wanted to be wide awake when he went out the front door.
A glance at Bruns showed him fast asleep.

Gentry poured another cup of coffee and stood in front of
the window while drinking it. He'd drunk about half of it
when the saloon door swung open and Duvall stepped out
onto the street. Gentry's muscles tightened, fear washed
over his body in a flood of weakness. Pictures of Anne,
Mark, and Brandy tried to push into his mind. He closed
such thoughts out. If he allowed himself to think of his
family now, he'd never see them again. He pulled his coat
on, tugged the right side of it back, and hooked it behind
the handle of his Colt, then picked up the Greener. Holding
it in his left hand close to his side he stepped out to face the
man he'd put in prison.

"You goin' to find your partner, Duvall? Or maybe
you're huntin' me. You remember me, don't you? I put you
in prison, but some crooked lawyer got you out early. Yore
brother told me about it. Reckon the only way to see justice
done is put you where they ain't no parole." He talked,
hoping to make Duvall mad enough that his anger would
slow his draw.

Duvall stared at him, his face showed no emotion, not
anger, not fear. He stood there, a big heavy-faced man. He
blinked a couple of times. Gentry thought Duvall's eyes
might have watered from the sharp, frigid wind.

The sheepskin Duvall wore was buttoned over *his* gun.
With an even break, Gentry was not sure he could beat him,
but he couldn't shoot any man without starting even. He
sighed, "Don't put your hands in your pockets. Unbutton
your coat so that you can get your gun. Ain't gonna do you
no good to wait for your partner, I already put three holes
in 'im with a hayfork. He's done joined your brother. Ain't
gonna spoil though, not 'til spring thaw, then maybe they
can bury the three of you in the same hole. Now unbutton
your coat—slowlike."

Duvall's expression didn't change; he continued staring
with that flat snakelike look in his eyes. The fingers of his

right hand worried the bottom button until he pushed it through the button hole. Then, taking forever, it seemed to Gentry, his hand moved to the next button.

Finally, with all buttons free, Duvall's hand went to the opening of his sheepskin and pulled it back.

By now, Gentry's right hand was stiff and numb with cold. His left hand was gloved, and one of those gloved fingers curled through the Greener's trigger guard. Duvall's gunhand had to also be about half frozen. He'd had to take off his glove to free the buttons. He continued that deadly look at Gentry. "We don't have to do this, Gentry. We could shake and let bygones be bygones." He was trying to throw Gentry off guard. He turned his left side toward Gentry as though to go back to the saloon. When he turned, Gentry saw his elbow crook and show behind his back.

Gentry's right hand flashed for his .44, but not trusting the fingers on that hand to work, he rotated the scatter-gun, both barrels horizontal and pointed at Duvall.

Duvall's gun cleared the lip of the holster. Gentry pulled both triggers of the Greener. At the same time he pointed his Colt and thumbed off two rounds. He never knew where his pistol shots hit. Both loads of buckshot hit Duvall dead center in the chest and knocked him backward. The double-aught buckshot almost cut him in two. A single hole Gentry could have shoved both of his fists into showed through Duvall's tattered sheepskin. He lay on his back. First a look of surprise showed in his eyes, then hatred, then only a vacant stare.

Gentry walked to him and turned him over with his boot toe. Where the buckshot left Duvall, they took most of his back with them. Gentry had seen a lot of gore in his life, but never had he been able to look into a man's body and see what was left of that person's lungs, splintered ribs, and half a stomach still holding food only recently eaten.

Gentry always used a handgun or rifle. They left a man pretty clean after being shot. He looked away from the carnage he'd created and swallowed hard to get rid of the lump and the bitter taste of bile. It didn't work.

Despite the cold, the Ranger Rider emptied by the time Gentry turned away from Duvall. There must have been thirty men gathered to slap him on the back. He looked at them and shook his head. "Men, it ain't ever a good thing to kill a man." He shrugged. "Sometimes you ain't got a choice. In this case I took it to him. If I hadn't, I would have had four of them to fight in a few days." Bruns walked up. He had a Winchester in his hands.

"Heard you leave the office, Gentry. Figured I wasn't gonna let such as him kill you, but turned out you didn't need help." He took the Greener from Gentry's hands. "I'll take this back to the office and clean it. You go on in the Range Rider. Get in outta the cold. I'll be there in a few minutes—buy you a drink. Figure you could use one."

"That makes two drinks you gotta put down, Gentry. I'm buyin' you one too," someone said, and others added their offer to that one. Damn, Gentry figured if he were a drinking man he could stay drunk a month.

He again glanced at what was left of Duvall. His taut muscles relaxed. The taste of fear in the back of his throat washed away.

He was tired, and every joint in his body felt like a wet rag. He had long known this feeling; he'd had it after every gunfight. Yeah, he needed a drink. Leighton took his elbow and led him toward the saloon.

CHAPTER SEVEN

★ ★ ★

Anne had been nervous all day. She snapped at the kids, and was sorry for it. It wasn't her moon time so she couldn't think why she was so irritable. Maybe Case was sick again or in trouble. She worried for fear he wasn't eating right. If he was making money helping the marshal he might skip meals in order to have a little left over. Every task she set for herself during the day seemed to go wrong. Her stomach knotted with worry.

She stood at her worktable kneading bread dough. Mark came in from feeding the stock, the shotgun tucked under his arm. "Mark, put that gun down. You're a little boy. Act like one." Her voice was sharp, and she was sorry as soon as she said the words.

Mark stared at her a moment. "Ma, I know something's eatin' at you, but I gotta tell you right now, Pa told me to protect you an' Brandy and that's what I'm gonna do. Ain't puttin' this gun down 'til Pa walks back through that door. Don't mean to be sassin' you, Ma, but that's how it is."

Anne looked at her son a moment, and felt pride and anger surge through her at the same time, then her face crumpled, tears flooded her eyes, and she pulled Mark to her breast. "Oh, son, I'm sorry. I've been terrible to you children today. Do as your father said. I'm so proud of you." She kissed his cheek and pushed him toward the washbasin. "Go ahead, get cleaned up. Supper will be ready in a while."

Another hour passed, and all the while Anne held a tight rein on her nerves. Then about an hour before dark, about the time they sat down for supper, she seemed to relax inside. Her stomach settled down, the tightness in her chest loosened—and her world seemed to right itself. She frowned. Something had happened, something that set to rights whatever had been troubling her.

A glance at the oven and she stood. She pulled the heavy cast-iron oven door open and removed the golden baked loaves of bread. Their aroma filled the cabin.

It's the smell of that bread that made everything right, she thought, trying to find some reason why everything seemed good again. But she knew better. It had been Case she worried about, and now whatever danger he had been in was over and he was all right.

After supper, Anne and Brandy did the dishes while Mark split firewood. He made it a practice to stop and rest every time a V-shaped length split off, and during each rest period he pondered what he and Brandy could give their mother for Christmas. Bought goods were out of the question. Neither of them had any money, and even if they had, the closest store was twenty-five miles away.

Each night after putting Brandy and him to bed, his mother sat by the fire and stitched on a Raggedy Ann doll for Brandy. He had peeked. But she never seemed to work on anything for him. He shrugged. The men of the family didn't really need anything. Pa had told him many times it was a man's place to provide. But he still hoped he might get some little surprise Christmas morning.

An idea as to what he and his sister could give their mother began to form.

After stacking the wood by the stove, they washed up and Brandy climbed to the loft. Their mother tucked them in and kissed them good night despite Brandy begging for a bedtime story. As soon as Mark heard his mother pull her chair close to the fire, he pushed the mountain of quilts to the side and crawled over to Brandy. "Shhh, don't say anything, but come mornin', after we do our chores, me an' you're gonna make Ma a present for Christmas. I got an idea, an' after we get out to the barn I'll tell you about it. Okay?"

In the dim light she stared, wide-eyed, up at him and nodded. He crawled back between the quilts and pulled the shotgun to his side. It was not long until Brandy breathed deeply in sleep. He soon followed.

The next morning Mark said he and Brandy were going to the stable to straighten up some things that needed doing. Anne smiled and patted them each on the head.

In the barn Mark looked around, hoping for bits and pieces of anything that might give him a better idea. Nothing that would make into a better present came under his eye.

"What we gonna make Mama, Mark? You said you had it all figured out."

He set the Greener on its stock and leaned it against the wall. "We gonna make a new breadboard. Gonna cut the top offa your mounting stump with the cross-cut saw an' I'll smooth it with my Green River knife Pa give me."

"How will I climb on my horse if we cut it off. It'll be too short."

Mark shook his head. "Naw now, don't you worry. You've growed a good bit since you started using it. You ain't gonna miss four inches of it. Besides, if it's too short I'll help Pa cut another tree and we'll make you a new one."

Mark stood on the stump to reach the cross-cut saw hung from pegs on the wall, then, one on each end of the saw, they pulled it through the dried wood. Mark had to do most of the work. Brandy was just plain too small to be of much help, but he wanted her to be a part of this present for their mother.

Back and forth they pulled the saw until the slab fell to the ground; Mark picked it up and inspected it from each side. He searched for stress cracks that would have set in during the drying period. "Looks like we got lucky, Brandy. Ain't no cracks. Ma's gonna have a nice breadboard; fact is, it's all of four inches thick so she can use it for a chopping block too. Now I'll smooth it, an' when it's done you can wrap it, don't know in what, but we'll find something."

His mother's voice sounded from the house. "Mark, Brandy, are you all right?"

"Yes, Ma. We're just playin' like we're makin' stuff. Brandy's enjoyin' herself. You need us up there?"

"No, go ahead with what you're doing."

Mark went back to laboriously drawing his knife across the block's surface. In midstroke, he stopped and moved the wooden slab closer to the shotgun. If that man, Bowdry, showed up, he wanted to be able to carry out his father's orders without a hitch.

Thinking of Bowdry, Mark wondered if he could pull the trigger on the man. He had shot deer, sage hens, and a lot of varmints, but shooting a man was going to be different. Then he sharply focused on the man he might have to shoot. *That* man, he decided, he could shoot. Ain't nothing gonna mess with my ma or my sister.

Miles to the west, sitting in a chair by the fire in a shack just outside of Milestown, Bowdry's thoughts were exactly opposite of Mark's. He couldn't get Anne out of his thoughts. He wanted her. He was going to have her. He'd kill Gentry from ambush, if he had to, but kill him he would. He'd kill those two brats anyway. If caught, he'd hang. There wasn't a Westerner anywhere who wouldn't put a rope around his neck.

Using both hands under his thigh for support, he straightened his leg, then tried bending it without using his hands to help. There was only a twinge of pain. He rotated his shoulder. No pain there either. He smiled. He'd leave Milestown behind in the morning. The weather was still well below freezing—but it had stopped snowing. He could make it to the Gentry cabin by midafternoon.

He didn't know whether Gentry had left town or not, but he'd take care of him in his own good time. He'd never forget the way he'd been tied hand and foot and herded into town. The only way to wipe that from his mind, he figured, was to kill Gentry. He took his Colt from his holster. The holster on his left side hung empty. He wanted to get that gun back from the marshal, but it would have to wait until he took care of Gentry and his brood. He admired the silver stars inlaid in the gun's grips and proceeded to clean his one handgun.

He'd hired an Indian woman to clean and cook for him while he nursed his wounds. He thought to leave without paying her, then shook his head. She'd raise hell, let everyone in town know he was gone. He ran a swab through the barrel of his pistol, frowning. He could kill her. He again shook his head. She'd be missed in a day or two and someone would come looking for her—and then they, along with a posse, would come looking for him.

He decided his best bet was to pay her and quietly leave town. That way he should have free rein to take care of Gentry, his kids, and then savor the delectable delights of Anne.

Thinking of her, desire and warmth flooded his lower stomach, his chest tightened, and his breath shortened. His eyes must have glazed over because he had a problem seeing. He had put this off long enough. Wounds healed or not, he'd head out in the morning.

He went to bed that night, still full of the thoughts of Anne, and those thoughts still consumed him when he woke the next morning. He ate breakfast, paid the woman who'd cared for him, saddled, and rode out.

Bowdry stayed about half a mile off the trail that would take him to the Powder and ultimately to Gentry's cabin. He wanted no one to be able to place him close to the scene when they found what he left of the Gentrys.

At noon, he had trouble making himself stop for his nooning. Don't rush it, he thought. She ain't gonna be but a few hours older if you take time to eat. He reined his horse into the lee of a cut-bank and built his fire.

Strong coffee, laced with whiskey, helped wash down the jerky and hard biscuit that made up his meal. Even though anticipating a head-on meeting with Gentry, and then walking into the cabin where Anne would be, Bowdry took time for two cups of coffee, the last almost straight whiskey.

By the time he climbed back on his horse, he was warm and about half drunk. He thought to ride right up to Gentry's cabin door and yell for him to come out and fight like a man. He wallowed around in that thought a couple of miles, thinking how daring and brave he'd be, but by the time he reached the Powder and turned north, the alcohol began to wear off and he had second thoughts. Another two miles and he decided to watch the cabin awhile and maybe wait for Gentry to leave.

Nearing the cabin, he reined in and climbed from his horse, stiff from the cold. His wounds throbbed with each heartbeat, and every painful throb caused him to curse Gentry, vowing to make him pay.

From where he stood, the dark gray outline of the cabin showed through bare, winter-stripped cottonwoods. A skeletonlike limb of an old deadfall served for a hitch rack. One smooth pull and he had his Winchester out of its saddle boot, thought better, shoved it back in its scabbard, then he circled to come up behind the stable.

It took a moment to open the barn door a crack and slip into the stable's dark interior. He stood frozen for a few seconds, listening, trying to sense another presence. Satisfied he had the place to himself, he searched each stall to see if Gentry's big bay gelding was there. When he couldn't find the horse, he had mixed emotions, disappointment he'd not have the opportunity to kill the man he hated, and elation he'd not have to face him. Too, this made his pain easier. He would simply walk to the door, push through it, and take over. First he'd get rid of Gentry's brats, then he'd have Anne to himself.

At the front door of the barn, he studied the cabin. Each window was shuttered tight against the dense, still cold. Bowdry nodded, he'd only have to walk boldly to the door and push it open. He already savored the feel of Anne in his arms, his lips on her lips, on her body. He wiped spittle from the corners of his mouth and eased out the door.

Inside the cabin, Mark heard horse's hooves ring against frozen ground. He searched the trees along the riverbank until he saw a dark shadow. Another, much smaller shadow separated from what Mark supposed was a horse. He followed the smaller vague form's progress until it disappeared behind the stable. The shadowy outline of a man didn't emerge from the other side so Mark kept his eyes on the barn door nearest the house.

"Ma, get Brandy on the floor behind your bed. If we had another gun, you could help me, but we ain't, so just stay down an' let me do my job." He broke the breech and checked the loads in the shotgun, realizing his mother stood there staring at him, hesitant to leave him the trouble. "Do like I told you, Ma. Pile your quilts and pillows 'tween y'all an' the door in case he comes shootin'."

Anne still stood frozen. "Get Brandy down, Ma. Ain't got time to worry 'bout y'all. Do it."

Mark turned his attention back to the space between him and the stable. A tall, slim man opened the barn door a crack and slipped through into the yard. Mark studied him a few moments, and it wasn't until he spotted the stars inlaid in the handle of the man's handgun that he recognized him as the one his pa had called Bowdry. He waited until Bowdry closed to within about twenty yards of the cabin. Mark's muscles pulled tight. He trembled. His breath came in short gasps.

"Bowdry, you done come far enough. Git your horse and

leave here right now. You do that an' I won't shoot you."
Mark's stomach had now begun to hurt he was so scared.

The slim gunfighter stopped, frowned toward the shuttered window, seemed to study on whether Mark was anything to fear, remembering Gentry's words that he would have trouble getting by his kid. Then he smiled.

"Aw, come on, kid. You wouldn't shoot old Bowdry, would you? I don't mean you no harm. Jest figured your ma would give me a feed tonight, an' in the mornin' I could ride on. Yeah, I'll sleep in the barn tonight just like last time."

"You ain't gettin' fed, an' you ain't sleepin' in our barn, Bowdry. Now git while you're still able."

"Kid, I'm cold an' hungry. Now stop messin' around, put your gun down—if you got a gun—an' let me in."

Tension had hold on Mark now such that he trembled so hard the Greener shook. Bowdry had better make his move soon, or Mark didn't know whether he could pull the triggers. Then he made up his mind. He wasn't going to let the gunman call the shots.

Bowdry said, "Aw, hell, kid, if you're gonna be that way, I'll leave." He made as though to turn. Instead, he pushed off on his left foot and sprinted toward the cabin. Mark pulled both triggers at once. Bowdry took two steps, and his legs folded under him.

Mark broke the breech and reloaded both barrels, never taking his eyes off the downed gunman. In what daylight was left, a widening red stain covered Bowdry's thigh. Mark swallowed twice to keep the bile welling in his throat from embarrassing him. He wanted his mother to think of him as the *other* man in the family, and if he got sick now—well, she might never. He looked over his shoulder.

"Ma, you an' Brandy can come out now. He ain't dead, but he's down. I'm goin' out an' see what damage I done."

Before pulling the door toward him, Mark peered through a crack to see if Bowdry had moved. He hadn't.

Mark, keeping the shotgun pointed at the slim, dirty man, eased out the door. Bowdry lay stretched out, lying on his side, his hand, empty, slung out ahead of him. The snow under his leg was reddening now. Mark remembered seeing the gunman wear two guns the last he was here. He looked for them, and saw that Bowdry was lying on one, still holstered, and the holster on the side he could see plainly was empty. "Where's your other handgun, Bowdry? You had two the last time you were here."

Bowdry groaned. "Sheriff's got it. Don't do no talkin', boy, help me."

Still keeping the Greener pointed at the man, Mark circled from Bowdry's back to reach the gun, stooped, and changed his mind. He decided not to chance getting close enough for the gunman to grab him.

Bowdry's face was tight with pain. "What you gonna do, boy? You cain't leave me out here like this, I'll freeze or bleed to death."

Mark stared at him a moment. "Mister, you shoulda thought of that before you tried to bring trouble down on us. I'm gonna give you exactly one minute to start draggin' yourself toward your horse. If you make it, I won't have to bury you. Git!"

"Kid, you cain't do this. You gotta take care of me."

Mark wanted to answer, "The hell I cain't," like his pa would have done, but was afraid his ma would hear him and tan his hide. Instead, he said, "Bowdry, my pa would say you made your bed, sleep in it. Now I'm tellin' you. If you don't start toward your horse right now, I'm emptyin' this Greener into you. An' you make a swipe for that handgun, I'm gonna empty it in you anyway. Now, don't mess around. Go on. Git."

Bowdry twisted, making a half circle in the snow, and dragged himself a foot at a time toward his horse; he apparently forgot the gun in his holster—or maybe he was in so much pain he couldn't use it. He stopped now and then to rest, or maybe find more strength. Mark watched until the bloody trail disappeared into the trees.

When he went in to hang the shotgun on the peg, he

stopped before turning it loose and studied his hands. They were steady. Pa would be proud of him.

From behind, his mother said, "Is he hurt bad, son?"

"If he don't bleed to death, he might get somewhere for somebody to doctor on 'im, but I don't figure he's gonna make it that far."

"Oh, Mark, we can't let him suffer like that. We'll go get him and see what we can do."

"Ma, you ain't goin' out that door. It's gettin' dark an' he might be waitin' out yonder ready to use that gun. Besides that, we don't owe him nothin' but misery, an' I done give 'im that." He carefully placed the shotgun on the pegs and looked at his mother. "Ain't it 'bout time for supper?"

Anne stared at him a moment, knowing she had lost her little boy. He was now a man, and she couldn't be more proud if he'd just been appointed governor of the territory. "Yes, Mark, supper's about ready. After dinner, how do you propose to keep us safe through the night? He might come back, you know."

Mark swelled with pride. His mother had asked *him* what he thought to do. "Well, Ma, I don't figure he'll be back. He's hurt pretty bad, but just in case I'm wrong I figure to stand watch tonight. If I get tired, I'll call you and we can swap off. After supper, reckon I better clean that old Greener. Pa would be pretty upset if he found it dirty." He looked at his mother and smiled. "Besides, Ma, I found I ain't afraid to pull the trigger on a man. Know I can keep you an' Brandy safe now."

Anne wondered if being able to "pull the trigger on a man" was an accomplishment to be proud of. At any rate, she and Brandy were safe with her *other* man watching after them. When she went to the stove, she hummed a tune she had heard at the last barn raising she and her family attended.

CHAPTER EIGHT

★ ★ ★

Gentry wanted nothing more than to take a bottle to the jail, sit quietly, and sip a couple of drinks with Bruns, but he couldn't do that. These men were his friends. They were happy he'd come through the gunfight without a scratch. *They were also curious.*

He had to recount the happenings between him and Duvall and Benton several times, until finally Leighton held up his hands for silence. "Men, Gentry's tired, and he's not a man to take pleasure in killing a man. Now, let's just leave him drink his whiskey in peace."

"Aw, now, looks to me like he thinks he's a right big hero. Anybody could've killed that man with a shotgun."

Gentry searched the crowd around the bar to see who had said those words. He didn't have to look hard. Men pulled back on both sides to form an aisle between Gentry and the one who had spoken. It was obvious the bear of a man had spent most of the day hanging on the bar. Unsteady on his feet, he needed a shave, and the smell of stale alcohol wafted all the way to Gentry.

The man's statement didn't deserve an answer. Gentry turned back to the bar, picked up his drink, and tossed it down.

"You hear what I said, Bad Man?" The man took a couple of weaving steps toward Gentry. "You ain't got your shotgun now. All you got is a lil' ole pistol, and I bet I can shove it down your throat faster'n you can reach for it."

Gentry turned to face the man squarely. The man didn't pack a gun. "Mister, I never done nothin' to you. Fact is, I don't even know who the hell you are. Why don't you go somewhere an' sober up. We'll talk about whatever's botherin' you in the mornin'."

The man stopped, shoulders hunched. He clinched his fists a couple of times. "That's what's botherin' me, mister. You don't know me. Nobody in this town knows me, and nobody seems to want to know me. People where I come from call me Big, so reckon that's my name, Big Battles. I figure if I beat your head in, then people will know me. They'll say 'There's the guy who beat the gunfighter, that's Big Battles.'" He took another unsteady step toward Gentry. "Don't need to go nowhere and sober up. Gonna fix your plow right now."

Gentry didn't want to fight the big man; first place the guy was so big he'd probably whip hell out of him; in the second place, even if he could whip the bear, what was the point?

Gentry opened his mouth to try to mollify Battles, but he was too late. The bear set his feet and swung. Gentry blocked the blow with his left forearm and swung a right to the man's gut. His fist found only a hard, ridged stomach. Big Battles was no barfly. He was in good shape.

Another right came at Gentry's head. He ducked and tried to slip the punch over his shoulder. It didn't work. The ham of a fist sledged its way to the side of Gentry's jaw. He went down, trying to clear his head of the bright lights that exploded in his skull. The big man shuffled toward Gentry.

Gentry rolled to the side, thinking a kick would come his way. The huge man stopped and stood over Gentry. "Git up. I ain't through yet."

Gentry rolled again, farther from his attacker, and climbed slowly to his feet. Another right slammed toward him. He dodged that blow and swung his right to the man's heart. The bear stopped dead in his tracks, his eyes wide. Then Gentry hit him again, another savage right under his heart. Battle's mouth opened. He sucked for air like a fish. But, despite hurting, the huge man swung another right to Gentry's chin. The blow knocked Gentry into one of the tables that ringed the bar. He gathered his feet under him and launched another attack on the bear.

They fought like that for an hour. By this time Gentry was not willing to go down for the count; he'd decided to fight as long as his legs would hold him, and apparently Battles figured it the same way.

Gentry's arms felt like lead weights, and from the way the big man stood, his arms hanging limply, he was in the same shape.

Gentry squinted through a puffy eye. "Don't know what this fight is about, but I'm ready to quit if you are."

There was something pathetic about the big man. He was lonely, and his loneliness ate at his mind. Gentry studied him a moment. "Tell you what, Big. I'll buy you a drink an' you an' me'll sit over yonder and talk awhile. If you got nowhere to sleep tonight, you can sleep in the cell next to mine, then in the mornin' if you're still of a mind to take this up again, we'll tie into it. Okay?"

Battles, a befuddled look replacing his truculent one, straightened. He frowned, "You showed me you ain't afraid of me. An' seems like we got to know each other pretty good. Naw, I don't want to fight you again. You done fought me to a standstill." He stuck his big hand out for a handshake.

"No, I ain't afraid. But I figure it'd be sort of dumb to fight you again when I don't know what it's all about in the first place." Gentry grinned. "An' besides, I think if you started out sober, you'd whip me. I've had all that good stuff I can stand." He fingered the single four-bit piece in his pocket. If he bought Big a drink, he'd have to do without supper, but somehow he thought it would prove to be worth it. He liked the big guy. "Come on. Let's sit down and have that drink. You can tell me about yourself."

Big nodded. "All right, but I'm buyin'. I got money, just

don't have no friends." He went to the bar, bought a bottle of rye whiskey, took it to a table nearest to Gentry, placed two glasses on the table, and tipped the bottle to fill both glasses.

Gentry held his glass up, clinked it against the one held in Battle's ham of a hand, and said, "Luck." They tossed down their drinks and Big picked up the bottle to refill their glasses when Bruns walked to the table.

"Never seen you drink more'n two drinks, Gentry. Who's your friend?"

Gentry winked at Bruns. "Tell you, Marshal, this here man figured to whip me tonight, but the way I figure it, neither one of us won. I talked him into sleepin' in the cell next to mine, an' then when we're both sober in the mornin' maybe we'll find we can be friends." He turned to Battles. "Want to meet my best friend, Big, this here's Marshal Bruns. Figured we'd have about one more drink and then go turn in so we'll be ready for whatever mornin' brings." Gentry looked at Bruns. "You want a drink?"

Bruns raised an eyebrow, grinned, and said, "Yeah, if your new friend here is buying."

Battles threw the marshal a sloppy, drunken grin, nodded, picked up another glass, and poured him a drink.

Big wanted to have another drink after that one, but Gentry figured if they did he might have to carry him to the jail. He didn't relish that thought. He estimated Big to be about six-five and two hundred eighty pounds. He talked him into bringing the bottle and following to Bruns's office.

They sat there and talked well into the night. It turned out that Big hailed from Missouri, had owned a farm back there until his wife died. Then he'd sold the farm, packed what belongings he thought he'd need, and headed west.

Most people, in every town he came to, seemed to think he was a bully, coming to that opinion because of his size, so he'd had to fight his way across most of the plains.

"Hell, Gentry, I don't own much of a gun, just an old Sharps fifty-caliber. I don't like to fight, but seems like people figure I do." He opened his eyes wide and squeezed them closed a couple of times. "I better crawl in that bunk you offered me. Ain't drunk this much whiskey at one sitting before."

Bruns had gone home hours before, so Gentry showed the huge man where to sleep, then he went to his bunk and lay there thinking, missing Anne and the children. He thought to saddle up in the morning and head for home. He cast that thought aside after thinking on it awhile. It might cost him his life, but he couldn't take the chance of leading the three remaining outlaws to his family. Chet Thompson, Gentry knew, was truly a fast gun. He couldn't remember much about the other two men riding with Thompson, but judging by the company they were keeping he had to consider them dangerous.

He thought on a plan as to how he should fight them. He didn't want to take a chance on getting cornered in Milestown, having to fight all three at once. He toyed with several ideas. Finally a plan took form that he thought might save his hide. He went to sleep.

The next morning, sitting in Bruns's office drinking coffee, Gentry looked over the rim of his cup at Battles. "When you want to finish that fight you pushed on me, Battles?"

The big man stared into his cup a moment, then locked gazes with Gentry. "Don't want no fight. Don't like to fight. With my size I might hurt people. Most times I try to walk around trouble, even thought of changing my name to Peace, or Bibles, you know, something that sounds like an easygoing man." He took a swallow of his coffee. "Last night, reckon I was desperate for someone to talk to—even if I had to fight for the right." He looked hopefully at Gentry, shaking his head. "You don't want no fight with me, do you, Gentry?"

Gentry felt a smile break the hard planes on his face. "Never did want to fight you, Battles. I'm a peace-lovin' man. Besides, there's three men comin' in here in the next couple of days gunnin' for my hide. If I beat my hands up on that hard skull of yours any more'n I already have, I might not be able to handle a gun."

Battles frowned. "What you're tellin' me don't sound much like a peace-lovin' man."

"No it don't, but this is what caused it all." Gentry, over another couple cups of coffee, told Big the story. Finally he sat back. "So you see how it is. I got no choice."

"Gentry, I don't know much about gunfightin', but if there's any way I can help, tell me what it is. I'll be there with you."

Gentry studied the bottom of his empty cup. He thought a long time, then locked gazes with Battles. "What you fig-urin' on doing out here in this Montana country, Battles?"

Big shook his head. "Don't know. Gold and silver min-ing seem to be about peterin' out. Most seem to think this is good ranch country, an' I got a few dollars so I might try the cow business. And too, I might find some land I could farm."

A few more questions and Gentry found that Battles knew next to nothing about ranching. "You willin' to work for nothin' for a while to learn Montana ranchin'? I say that, 'cause I got no money to pay you."

"Right now I ain't worrying about money. Yeah, I'd like to learn."

Gentry grinned. "Good. You just got yourself the lowest payin' job you'll ever have." He then wrote Anne a note and drew Battles a map how to get to his place. "Big, 'til I get home, my ten-year-old son will start teaching you, an' don't worry 'bout his age. Kids grow up fast out here, an' Mark al-ready knows more than most 'bout cow critters an' these here winters. Listen to him, am' when I get home I'll pick up business where he leaves off. Oh, yeah, get him to help fix you a room in the stable until we can build you a proper one." Gentry stood, wiped his cup out with a rag, and put it back on the shelf. He looked at Battles. "Don't say nothin' 'bout me gonna have a gunfight. It'll worry Anne. She's got enough to worry her already."

Battles tilted his chair forward and stood. "I start out now I ought to be able to reach my new job by nightfall." He squinted at Gentry. "About twenty-five miles, you say?"

Gentry nodded. "That's about the size of it."

"Good. If I decide to learn ranching, instead of farming, I'll stop by."

He stood outside the door and watched Battles head for the livery to collect his horse and belongings. Soon after Big left, Bruns came in and Gentry told him how he planned to fight Thompson and the two other gunmen.

"I wish you'd let me help, son."

"Nope. We been over that trail before. Now I got to put together a trail outfit. Don't know how long I'm gonna have to be in the weather, just glad it ain't snowin'. I figure I can handle cold. Remember, you got to set 'em onto my trail so they don't go wanderin' 'bout town causin' trouble." He grinned. "Marshal, I'm a pretty good Injun. They gonna have one helluva time once they get on my trail."

Bruns shook his head. "Damned if I don't believe you're looking forward to this fight."

They talked awhile longer, then Gentry went over to Leighton's.

"Hey, Gentry. You already had that second fight with that giant who tried to pick on you last night?"

"Naw, we made friends, fact is I wouldn't be surprised if we didn't get to be right good friends 'fore it's all over." Gentry fidgeted a moment, shuffled from one foot to the other, then said, "Aw, hell, Leighton, I might as well come right out with it. I need you to carry me for some stuff I'm gonna need on the trail while I fight them three what're comin' here to gun me. Don't want to have this fight in town. Someone might get hurt, and I don't want to lead them to my place. I'll sell a couple of beeves in the spring an' pay you."

Leighton looked toward the door, then fastened a look on

Gentry. "Boy, I wish there was some way I could help you fight them, but yeah, take what you need. We're not going to worry about money."

Gentry gave him a jerky sort of nod and went about picking what he thought it would take for him to survive on the trail. He took a couple of Hudson's Bay blankets, extra gloves, three pairs of moccasins, he figured he'd wear them out pretty fast the way he meant to travel, a slab of bacon, coffee, half-dozen tins of beans, and two boxes of .44 shells. And last, he pulled a pair of snowshoes off the wall.

Leighton tossed in several strips of jerky, then eyed Gentry. "Don't look like you're riding a horse on this trip."

Gentry gave him a cold smile. "Leighton, a horse will only get in the way, an' I bet you the time's gonna come 'fore I finish with them gunhawks, they gonna wish they didn't have horses either." He studied the pile of supplies on the counter. "Reckon I better make me a frame to strap to my back for carryin' this stuff."

"You ever figure you might freeze to death out yonder, Gentry?"

"Thought on that awhile, but I'm a pretty good man outdoors, done a lot of it while rangerin'. I'll make it, Leighton, but I'm bettin' they won't." Gentry stacked everything neatly, then told Leighton to tally it up.

"Swore I was never gonna get in debt to you, but reckon comes a time a man's gotta swallow his words, Leighton. I'll write you a note to Anne, tellin' her if I don't get back we owe you for all of this."

"You will like hell. Son, you take care of your troubles and come back this way. You don't owe me anything." He reached behind the counter and pulled a box of lucifers down, then put a one-pound tin of tobacco on top of them. "Better wrap this in oilskin so it won't get damp."

Gentry looked at the added stuff Leighton had put on the counter, and wondered what had prompted him to tell Battles that Bruns was his best friend. Hell, he had two friends like few men on earth ever had. He picked up the pile of supplies and headed for the jail.

He deposited his trail gear in the cell he'd been occupying, went to the livery, and told Rawlings he'd be gone for a while and what he figured to do. Rawlings went to the corner of his room, dug through a pile of junk, and came up with an old A-frame for Gentry to carry his gear on his back. "Wrap your slicker and ground sheet around your pack and you'll be able to sleep dry and warm. Good luck, son."

Gentry spent the rest of the afternoon tying the A-frame securely at each joint with rawhide. The thongs that had held it were dry and brittle. Then he cleaned and oiled his Winchester and Colt .44. He put a razor edge to his Bowie knife and sat back, thinking over his list of trail gear. Finally, he nodded, satisfied he was as ready as planning could make him. Now, he'd wait until he saw Chet Thompson and his two cohorts ride into town. He didn't want to get too far ahead of them, wanting to make it easy for them to follow his trail until they were far out of town—then they were in for more than they ever dreamed of.

CHAPTER NINE

★ ★ ★

Everything packed and ready, Gentry sat by the jail's window, watching for his enemies. Snow had again begun to fall. He sat there for two days, until finally about two o'clock, the afternoon of the third day, three riders ghostly in the light snow, appeared at the end of the icy, rutted road. Gentry's breath shortened, his gut muscles tightened, and his stomach felt like bugs crawled in it. This was it. In a few days it would be over for them—or him. He looked over his shoulder at Bruns.

"Looks like I'm 'bout ready to look at their hole card, Marshal." He again looked down the street. "Figure after that cold ride they gonna stop in the Range Rider to warm up an' have a drink. 'Fore you tell 'em I just rode outta town, gimme enough time to get across the Tongue. Tell 'em I said somethin' 'bout headin' for Billings."

Bruns eyed him a moment. "You certain you want to do it this way, boy? Hell, let us help you. You got a lot of friends in this town."

Gentry nodded. "An' that's the reason I'm not lettin' none of you get involved. You're my friends. Do it the way I asked, Marshal." He stood back from the window so as to not be seen from the outside.

Thompson's bunch did as he'd thought. They drew rein in front of the saloon and went inside. "Marshal, one more thing: act like you don't care who gets killed long as they don't do it in your town."

Gentry waited until the door closed tight behind the three gunmen, shouldered his pack, settled it firmly on his back, cast a regretful glance at the glowing potbellied stove, and went out the door. The warmth he'd left was the last he'd feel for several days. He was thankful the wind hadn't kicked up, but that didn't mean it wouldn't before this was over.

Gentry didn't use his snowshoes. As long as he had the windblown roadway he'd make as good time as possible. And once Bruns told the gunmen where he headed, they'd mostly take time for a couple of drinks, figuring they could catch him anytime they pleased. Too, for easier travel they'd probably stay on the road.

As soon as they entered the door of the Range Rider, Thompson, Worley, and Trent stepped to the side, removed their sheepskins, settled handguns in their holsters, and with a quick sweep of the room determined that Gentry was not there. They bellied up to the bar.

"Whiskey, bartender, a full bottle." Thompson flicked his gaze along the bar, dropped a double eagle to the gleaming surface, and picked up the bottle. "Let's find a table. We got plenty of time." He scooped up his change and turned into the room.

They sat at the table facing the door. Thompson poured each a full water glass of whiskey and sat back, sipping his, feeling its warmth penetrate, warming him from the inside out. "Well, Gentry ain't in here, none of the boys here either. I figured to see the Duvalls and Benton in here. Wonder if they done killed Gentry?"

Lee Trent nervously tapped his fingers on the table in a devil's tattoo. "Hope not. I'd hate to think I rode fifteen-hundred miles for nothing."

Tom Worley pulled at his nose, Thompson wished he would break that habit. Coming in out of the cold it was a wonder it didn't just flat break off.

Worley pulled at his nose again. "We gonna git our

chance. 'Less they all braced him at once, I figure Gentry could take them one or two at a time."

"Soon's we git at least one glass of this firewater down, we'll ask," Thompson said, and took a healthy swallow of his drink. The door swung open. A cold gust of air rushed in. Irritated, Thompson glared at it, then the man who walked into the room. "Shut the damned door."

Bruns walked directly to their table and stared down at them. The first thing Thompson noticed was the marshal's badge. "Howdy, Marshal, if you lookin' to give us a hard time we ain't done nothin'—yet."

Thompson looked into the coldest gray-blue eyes he'd seen since leaving Texas. "You say you haven't done anything yet. Well, hard case, 'yet' better be a long time coming. I don't put up with your type in this town." Bruns words hit Thompson like ice shards. "You three staying or passin' through?"

Thompson felt a shiver run up his spine. This man might be on the shady side of what one would call young, but the gunfighter got the idea the marshal would be a hard man to face. "Depends, Marshal. We come in here to find a man what done us a bad wrong a few years back, and to hook up with three of our friends."

"Your friends wouldn't be named Duvall, two of them by that name, and one by the name of Benton, would they?"

"They're the ones, Marshal. They still here?"

Bruns grinned. "Yep, they're here. Figure they're gonna be permanent residents of this town."

Thompson glanced at his two friends. Worley again pulled at his nose, and Trent sat there staring at the marshal. Thompson leaned back in his chair. "What you figure would make a man want to stay in this town, lawman?"

Bruns grinned. "They ain't got a choice, 'less you want to haul 'em outta here. They're back behind the livery stable froze stiff as an old cowhide. And the man you say did you a bad wrong a few years back is probably the one who caused their early journey down that last, cold trail."

Thompson's confidence deflated. He'd been counting on getting Gentry in a crossfire. He sighed. Three men could set up a whipsaw shootout almost as well as could six. He cocked an eye at Bruns. "Where might we find the man who sent 'em down that trail?"

Bruns planted his feet, his head lowered into what Thompson thought was the most stubborn stance he'd ever seen. "Tell you what, hard case, I don't allow anybody, and I mean *anybody* to have gunfights in my town." Bruns moved a step closer to the table. "But I figure you missed yore man by no more than an hour. Said he was headed for Billings by way of Forsyth, and that makes it fine with me, 'cause now any fighting you and him have won't be in Milestown." He stepped toward the bar, stopped, and faced the table again. "You finish your drink and you might catch 'im by dark." He walked to the bar and ordered a drink.

Thompson stared at Bruns's back a moment, then yelled over the crowd noise, "What name that man go by, you know, the one what headed for Billings?"

Bruns looked over his shoulder. "Generally, around here we call 'im friend, but his name is Case Gentry." He again turned his back to Thompson.

Trent tapped his fingernails on the table. Worley pulled at his nose. Thompson slammed his hand down on Trent's fingers. "Stop that damned racket."

Trent drew his hand to his belt and turned flat, dead, snakelike eyes on Thompson. "What's the matter, Chet, you getting scared now that we're about to find our man?"

Thompson pinned Trent with a look that he hoped would be seen as one of apology. He was a little afraid of Trent who, before going to Huntsville, had a reputation as one of the fastest guns in Texas. He didn't know whether Trent could still handle a gun like he could before going to prison—and he didn't want to find out. "Reckon I wuz ready for Gentry, an' now we find we got some more cold ridin' to do, it's got my fur ruffled."

"Just make damned sure, Thompson, you never, ever touch my hands again." Trent smiled, his eyes still devoid of all expression.

Thompson glanced toward the bar and stood. He wanted to break the tension between Trent and him. Their friendship had never been a strong one, and although he talked of killing Gentry, Thompson had the feeling Trent didn't really care about killing anyone, unless they crossed him. He had the idea Trent wrote off his stint in Huntsville as bad luck. "Think I'll find out what kind of horse Gentry's ridin'. We don't want to ride up on him unawares."

At the bar he asked Pudge for another bottle, and found from Bruns that Gentry usually rode a big bay gelding. Then, satisfied that Trent had time to cool down, he returned to their table. He held the bottle up. "Figured if we wuz gonna have a cold ride a little heat for the stomach wouldn't hurt. Which reminds me; we better stock in some supplies 'fore we head out."

They had another drink, went to Leighton's for supplies, and headed across the Tongue. Thompson didn't think they'd catch Gentry before dark. It was already late afternoon, and he didn't want the ex-Ranger to get too much of a lead or they might not catch him before he lost himself in Billings. It would be better if they had their gunfight on the trail, in order to avoid trouble with the law.

Worley looked at Thompson. "How we gonna track Gentry on this here trail? It's froze hard as some of that rock we come across in Colorado, ain't gonna be no tracks."

"Don't need no tracks. We know where he's headed, an' don't figure him to leave this road or be in much of a hurry. We'll catch him all right, then he's gonna be sorry he ever seen that Ranger badge he wuz so proud of."

About thirty minutes past Fort Keogh, Trent nodded to the front of them. "Rider up yonder. If it's Gentry, we can

get this business settled and be back in Milestown in time
for a good night's sleep."

Thompson squinted into the snow, trying to see the horse
clearly. "Don't know, cain't tell the color of that horse." He
touched spurs to his horse and picked up the pace.

After about fifteen minutes, Worley glanced at his saddle
partners. "Ain't him. That there horse is an Appaloosa.
Slow it down, this here wind is 'bout to freeze my nose
off." Thompson wished it would, then his irritation with
Worley pulling at his beak would be over. They slowed
their pace.

They made camp that night in the bottom of a coulee.
Thompson picked the spot, figuring it would shelter them
from the biting winds. They'd put about fifteen miles behind them since leaving Milestown.

In the bottom of another coulee, less than a mile from
where Thompson and his henchmen camped, Gentry set up
his camp under an overhang of limestone. He cut several
scrubby mountain cedar and piled them in front of his site.
The trees served two purposes; they sheltered him from the
wind, and they cast the reflection of his fire back against
the rock overhang, both warming and hiding his camp.

He fixed supper and sat drinking coffee. Although he had
no fear of anyone seeing his camp, he never looked directly
into the fire for that would take away his night vision, and
he might need to see all around him.

Before leaving Milestown, Pudge had pressed two bottles of rye whiskey on him, "To keep him warm on the
trail," the bartender said. Gentry debated adding that extra
weight to his already heavy pack, but decided it would be
worth it to have a drink before turning in on these cold
nights. He glanced at the two bottles now, and thought to
wait until a better time.

He lay back against his saddle and debated stealing the
outlaws horses, put them afoot on an even basis with him.
He decided to wait and see what the new day brought. Be-

sides, if he took their horses now, they wouldn't have far to walk until they found more. Past Forsyth, out where they would have a hard time coming up with more nags, might be best. He smiled into the dark. Then, with them afoot, he would make their trip a memorable one.

The next morning, before daylight, Gentry packed his belongings, settled his pack comfortably on his back, and walked toward the trail. They were still behind him, by his calculations, and he wanted them ahead, wanted to know where they were and how fast they traveled. The snow had been light but continuous the last few days. He'd not needed his snowshoes.

When he came to the roadway, not entering it, he looked both ways, found a thickly branched cedar, and crouched behind it certain he would not be seen from the trail. The wind, barely strong enough, kept the trail swept clean, except for little swirls that danced their ghostly dance tirelessly across the hard surface.

Gentry squatted in his nest over an hour, getting stiff and almost frozen before he heard the sharp ring of shod hooves. He hunkered closer to the cedar, pushed some of its lower branches aside to edge into it, becoming to prying eyes what he hoped would look part of the tree. He waited.

Finally, the three materialized through the hazy precipitation. They seemed in no hurry. Maybe they figured to catch him in one of the settlements, thinking he'd stop to have a warm night's sleep. What they didn't know was that he knew how to sleep warm no matter the weather.

In only a few minutes the three were abreast of Gentry's hiding place, only twenty-five or so feet out in front of him. He grinned. They looked miserable, half frozen, hunkered down in their sheepskins. Their neckerchiefs were tied over their hats, pulled down tight around their ears, and tied under their chins.

Gentry calculated his chances of getting all three if he cut loose with his Winchester. He shook his head. He had to lessen the odds before taking them on head to head like this. He had no qualms about shooting them without warning. They were hunting *him*, and the only reason they were not wary at this moment was they thought him to be far ahead of them. When the time came, he'd shoot from whatever vantage he could get.

He stayed hidden until they dipped from sight over a slight swell. Then he slipped out close to the trail and followed, but walked at the side of the chewed-up roadway for better footing. Gentry gauged his pace to stay far enough behind that a chance backward look wouldn't catch him skylined. Anytime he thought he might be about to come into the open, he slipped into the stunted growth of cedars. If he could see them, they could see him.

From the time they hit the trail at daylight, Gentry figured Forsyth as only about thirty miles. At the rate they were traveling it should be close to dark when they got there. He wondered if they'd stay overnight, then thought they would. They had to sleep sometime, and would probably think he'd stop in town or camp not far outside of it. Gentry didn't know what he would do either; he'd play those cards like they fell.

Midmorning, Gentry topped a hill just in time to see one of them cast a glance to his rear. He dived into the brush, hoping he'd not been seen. His eyes half shut against the glare, he watched them draw rein and look back. They were apparently arguing.

Thompson shook his head. "Hell, Worley, you done started dodging shadows. I tell you they ain't nothin' back there. Even if there wuz, ain't nobody gonna get a horse off the trail fast 'nuff for us to not see 'im."

Worley cast Thompson a look, with more than a twinge of dislike in his eyes. "Thompson, you done said a few things to Trent, an' now to me, 'bout being scared. Do that one more time, an' I'm gonna find out how much guts you got; fact is, I'm gonna slice 'em right outta you." He stared a moment longer and said, "Now, I'm gonna ride back a ways an' see what I seen." He reined his horse around and headed back.

Gentry held his breath. The rider who turned back came past the brush he squatted in. Gentry hoped when he dived for the tall grass and brambles he'd not left tracks.

The rider reined in a few feet past Gentry's position, rode slowly back toward him, and again stopped. He looked closely at the scuffed tracks in the snow. He raised his gaze, and Gentry thought for a second the peering gaze looked directly at him. Gentry moved his hand under his buffalo robe so slow the movement would not be perceptible and eased his Colt from his holster. He sucked in a slow, deep breath—and held it. The man, Gentry had determined by now the man was Worley, was close enough Gentry could hear his horse breathe. Then Worley said, loud enough for Gentry to here. "Hate to admit it, but reckon Thompson's right, I'm jumpin' at shadows." He again looked closely at the scuffed tracks. "Didn't no horse make them tracks." He nudged his horse back toward the other two vengeance-bound hard cases. Gentry slipped his handgun back in its holster and let his breath out in a long, slow whistle.

About an hour after noon Thompson and his two friends crossed the Rosebud, and stopped in the town by the same name as the river they crossed. They tarried long enough to have their nooning.

Gentry, hunkered in a copse of tangled trees close to the Rosebud's bank, decided to take his nooning also. It would have been nice to go down to the small cafe, eat and have a steaming cup of coffee, but his enemies occupied his space down there. He shrugged and built his fire. His coffee would taste just as good here by the river.

While he drank his coffee, he glanced occasionally at the trail on the other side of the settlement. After about three quarters of an hour, three riders headed out of the town toward Forsyth. Gentry packed his gear, threw several handfuls of snow on the fire, shouldered his pack, walked into the town and out the other side. His blood seemed to flow faster, his senses sharpened. Even if they stayed in Forsyth this night, by noon tomorrow he'd have them where things would start happening.

The murky, snow-laden light of day waned. Gentry closed the distance between him and the outlaws. When they rode down Forsyth's main street, Gentry was less than a hundred yards behind. They rode directly to the livery and stabled their horses. Gentry squatted at the lee side of a building, waited for them to come out and go directly to the hotel. He grunted in appreciation. If they had a hotel room, he could get a place in the livery. He walked to the stable.

The old man who ran the livery raked Gentry with a glance, his look finally settling on the pack. A grin broke up the wrinkles on his face like a dry riverbed in August. "You want to stable that pack? What you want to feed it?"

Gentry grinned in return and pulled his buffalo hat back off his forehead. "Reckoned you might let me sleep in your loft if I paid you."

"Aw, pshaw, ain't gonna charge a man to get in outta the cold. He'p yoreself, youngster." He cocked his head to the side and squinted at Gentry, "Where ye be from, toting that there heavy pack without a horse to he'p yuh?"

Gentry studied the old-timer a moment and, not knowing whether he had a loose jaw or not, decided to play his cards close to his vest. "I got me a small ranch over on the Powder, had to make a trip to Billings, horse went lame in Miles, didn't have enough money to rent another so I headed out afoot."

The old broken-down cowboy stuck out his hand. "Most around here call me Crip. Name's Mabin."

Gentry shook his hand. "Glad to know you, Mabin. Gentry's my name." He shrugged his shoulders out of the straps holding his pack. "You got more than one eatin' place here in Forsyth?"

Mabin told him about three places, then asked if Gentry

felt like he could use a cup of hot coffee to sort of thaw him before going to eat. Gentry accepted.

While talking over a cup of the hottest and thickest coffee Gentry had ever tried to chew, he worked the conversation around to the last riders who'd left their horses with the livery. "They ask any questions, Mabin, like if you seen a man ridin' a big bay geldin'?"

The old man cocked his head a mite, picked a straw out of a bale of hay he had stacked in his living quarters, and chewed on it a moment. "Odd you should ask that, young'un. They not only asked, they checked every stall in here. Made me kinda mad after tellin' 'em no, sorta like they called me a liar right to my face."

He chewed at the end of the straw, threw it aside, pulled a plug of Brown Mule tobacco from his shirt pocket, offered Gentry a chew, and when he declined, Mabin sliced off a hunk and popped it in his mouth. He worked it around his jaw, apparently getting it comfortable, then cocked an eye at Gentry. "Them riders huntin' you, young'un?"

Gentry chuckled. "Don't know right now whether I'm huntin' them, or they're huntin' me. But I figure they think they're huntin' me."

"Tell me the story, Gentry. I got a tight jaw. Ain't nobody gonna shake it outta me 'til you tell me different."

Gentry killed time packing his pipe and putting fire to it. He needed Mabin's help. He decided he could trust the old man to keep quiet about seeing him. Then he told him the story.

"You mean they done rode all the way up here from Texas to get even with you?"

Gentry nodded. "Mabin, when a Texan hates, he does it up right fancy. They was six of them when they started. Didn't have to face them all at once, but looks like that's what I got to do with them you met. He extracted a promise from Mabin to tell Thompson's bunch, when they came to pick up their horses, that a man on a big bay gelding had come in about thirty minutes after them and had left about daylight.

Gentry looked at his watch. "Better saddle up my git-along if I'm gonna get somethin' to eat 'fore them cafes close." He stood. "Thanks for the coffee. "I'll just climb into the loft when I get back. See you in the mornin'."

Gentry walked to each of the cafes Mabin told him about and peered through a window of each to see if Thompson and his cohorts were there, then he chose the one he figured least likely for them to come to. He thought they had probably already eaten, and then gone to a saloon. He ate, went back to the livery, and climbed to the loft. Before closing his eyes to sleep, he planned what he'd do on the morrow. His jaw set in stubborn lines. Thompson's bunch had not seen trouble compared with what he had in store for them.

CHAPTER TEN

★ ★ ★

The next morning Gentry squatted in the loft, shivering with the icy blast along with a heavy flurry of snow that blew in when the big double doors opened to let Thompson and his men in. While they saddled, Mabin talked a continuous stream.

"That man what you wuz askin' about last night, well he come in 'bout half hour after y'all left. Brung that bay he rides with 'im. Left 'im overnight. He cut out of here 'bout an hour ago, said he wuz goin' to Billings."

The three continued saddling their broncs. Thompson pulled his cinch strap tight and looked across his saddle at the others. "Wonder how the hell we got ahead of him? Ain't no way we coulda passed him."

Mabin interrupted. "Reckon I can tell you that. You never pass 'im. He wuz right here in town when you got here. When I said how he wuz ridin' awful late when he brung his horse in, he said he hadn't been ridin' all that while. Said he stopped to see a friend and had supper with 'im. Then after he et, he brung his horse down here." Mabin pushed his hat back and scratched his head. "Why, goldarn it, he might've been sleepin' in the room right next to you in that there hotel. Shame you missed seein' yore friend when he wuz that close."

Gentry slipped closer to the edge to hear all they said—and stepped on a piece of bailing wire. The wire rolled under his boot and scratched against the floor.

Thompson glanced toward the loft. "What the hell was that? Somebody up there."

Mabin looked him right in the eyes. "Naw, I keep grain up there for the animals, danged rats drive me crazy, what with the noise an' eatin' my grain. Costs me a bunch of money."

"Why don't you get rid of them?" Trent asked, "Most of the stores have poisons that'll do it. The cost isn't as much as the grain they eat."

"Well, by jingles, reckon I'll look into it, see if it'll be safe to use it around grain and such for the animals."

Gentry let out his pent-up breath. His tightened muscles relaxed. That old man down there was as good a liar as he'd ever seen. Should have gone to play acting on the stage. He could come up with an answer to anything.

Thompson swung into the saddle. "Let's ride. We gotta catch Gentry 'fore he gits to Billings."

Gentry had a clean view of them. Trent stared at Thompson a moment and turned his look on Mabin. "It's not like we don't thank you for the information, old-timer. _I_ thank you." He dug in his pocket and pulled out a coin of some kind, Gentry couldn't tell from where he stood how much. Trent passed the money to Mabin, mounted, and rode out with the others.

That man Trent came from a good family, Gentry thought, and he's had more than a little schooling. He just took the wrong fork in the trail sometime back. He gave the three time to get well clear of the stable, then climbed from the loft.

"Mabin, anybody ever tell you what a flat-out good liar you are? I sat up there almost believin' them words you told 'em myself. When you help a friend, you go all the way. Thanks."

Mabin brought him a steaming cup of coffee. He sipped on it, or rather chewed it, while he put his pack in order. Gentry had never tasted stronger coffee in his life, unless that he had the night before had it beat.

Finished with the coffee, he threw the dregs out, groped in his pocket for a coin, and pulled out a four-bit piece. It was part of the two dollars and a half he'd saved from what Bruns paid him. "Sorry it ain't more, Mabin, but figure I gotta eat for a while on what I got left."

"Aw, pshaw, young'un, you ain't gonna pay me nothin'. I wuz glad to be of he'p, fact is, I wuz gittin' a kick outta it."

Gentry tried to press the coin on him, but Mabin would have none of it. He eyed the old man a moment. "Thanks, Mabin, see you on the way home." He shouldered his pack and went into the man-killing weather.

Icy wind tore breath from his mouth, and when he breathed, his lungs caught fire. Sometime during the night, winter had taken a serious hold on the land. Falling snow pulled a curtain in front of him about a quarter of a mile out. Caution took hold. The soft, white, beautiful blanket around him muted all sounds. That, in addition to not being able to see far, he could walk in the midst of his predators.

At town's edge, Gentry stopped and strapped on his snowshoes. Thompson and his men would have hard going, and deeper drifts would soon make travel impossible for horses—or men afoot.

Gentry smiled into the shroud surrounding him. The hunt was even better than he remembered. He was surprised how much he missed it, but shouldn't have been. Manhunting had been a great part of his life until the last ten years.

When time for his nooning came, the furry flap Gentry pulled across his face when he left Forsyth was encrusted with ice from his breath. He would bet his reputation as a Ranger that none in Thompson's bunch were prepared for anything like this. He stopped, made coffee, chewed a strip of jerky, and again took the trail.

The white screen in front of him occasionally let up, and he could see farther. Each time it did, Gentry slipped to the side of the trail and studied every snow-laden bush, ridge line, and ravine to make certain his quarry hadn't stopped.

They would camp soon because daylight, in this weather, was even now a murky gray, though midafternoon was not long past.

Another thirty minutes and Gentry looked for a place to camp. He found what he wanted, a cut-bank along a small frozen stream. A huge drift sat in front of the hollowed-out place under the bank. Gentry circled the frozen mass and carried load after load of driftwood into his shelter. Before building a fire he shed his pack and studied landmarks to again find the spot he left, knowing the men he wanted would also make camp. He wanted to know where they were.

If there was even one woodsman in the bunch ahead of him, the sensible thing for him to do would be to camp in a creek bed or a ravine. First, Gentry scouted the same stream on which he'd made camp. No luck. He stepped from the cedar break at the side of the trail onto the frozen roadway to head west again, hesitated, crossed the trail, and slipped quietly along the bank of the stream. He'd not gone a quarter of a mile when he thought he heard a shout.

He stopped, hunkered behind a small sapling, cocked his head, and listened. He squatted there until his knees cramped, then, faint in the swirling wind, another voice raised above the wind singing through branches and across the frozen blanket.

Close to him, not fifty yards away, a man yelled. "I'm gittin' the damned wood. If you want it faster, git your ass out here an' help."

Gentry sank closer to the earth. Now, the sound of a man thrashing about and cursed, just over the bank. It sounded like he tore at the undergrowth, along with an occasional hatchet stroke.

Gentry's nerves tightened until his neck muscles hurt. He put his hand under his buffalo robe and clutched the handle of his .44. Here, along a creek bank, didn't fit his plans for an all-out gunfight.

The sound of footsteps, hatchet strokes, and something

being dragged, Gentry figured it was firewood, continued a few moments, then faded. Gentry, bent almost double, scooted toward where he'd first heard the voice. He wanted to go flat on his belly and crawl, tried it, but his snowshoes hampered that kind of movement. He got to his feet and stayed as low to the ground as he could from a stooping position.

Close to the lip of the bank, he again went to his stomach, and bending his knees to keep from dragging the snowshoes, he slithered to look into the streambed, inched forward another few inches, and looked down on the top of Thompson's head. He swept the camp with a glance and pushed back. A handful of snow and gravel slipped from under his hand and trickled down the bank. Gentry sucked in a slow breath and held it, fear gripped him so he had trouble making his arms and legs respond.

"What the hell was that?" It was Thompson's voice.

"How you 'spect me to know what you're talkin' 'bout. I didn't hear nothin'," Worley growled.

"They wuz somethin' caused that stuff to tumble down the bank. Go see what it wuz, Trent."

There was a moment's silence. "You're the one who seems scared of his shadow in this bunch, Thompson. If you want to know what caused it, go see for yourself."

"Aw, Thompson ain't a scared of nothin', jest careful, Trent. I don't figure it wuz nothin'. Let's fix supper. We ain't seen hide nor hair of Gentry. I bet he's holed up somewhere jest like we are."

"Reckon you're right," Thompson said. "An' yeah, I'm gitten a little spooky. Let's fix supper, have a couple of drinks, an' hit the hay. Shore hope this snow lets up by mornin'. The horses are havin' a rough go of it. Don't know but what we gonna have to hole up a couple of days to rest 'em."

"Cain't take that much time, Thompson," Worley said. "We do, an' we gonna lose Gentry for sure. I ain't rode all the way up here to have him git away when he's right in front of us."

Trent, in his quiet, cold voice, cut in. "We push these horses much harder, we'll kill them. But before we rest them, I want to know where Gentry is. You men stay in camp in the morning, I'll do a little scouting."

Gentry edged back from the stream's bank. And still on his belly, snaked his way about fifty yards from the stream. He kept his knees bent all that distance to hold the snowshoes in the air. Then he stood, and taking careful steps moved silently from their campsite.

The snow would soon cover his tracks, but playing it safe, Gentry, made a wide circle to come on his camp from the opposite direction.

Before building a fire, he tested the wind for its direction. It blew from the west, and would blow smoke and its smell back the way from which they had come; only then did he build his fire, and again thanked the Everywhere Spirit for giving man lucifers for a ready flame.

For supper, he opened two tins, one of peaches and one of beans. He sliced salt pork into the beans and put another few slices on to fry.

After supper, his stomach satisfied, he poured a healthy belt of rye into his coffee and sat back, relaxed. They were going to play into his hands, do what he wanted them to do—split their forces.

Gentry's emotions fought each other. He was glad Trent would come looking for him alone. Trent along with anyone else would be more, perhaps, than he could handle. But he was sorry it had to be Trent he would kill the next day. There was something about the slim, gentlemanly man Gentry liked.

Gentry checked his weapons and again sharpened his knife. He wanted to take care of Trent as silently as possible. Finally, he hoped it could be settled by using his Bowie knife.

He slept warm that night despite the sub-zero temperatures, and when he awoke he dressed carefully, making sure he could reach any weapon, for any kind of fight Trent forced on him. He'd not had need of it before, but now he cut a slit inside the right-had pocket of his buffalo robe so he could reach his handgun.

The gray dawn still stood an hour away when Gentry again checked his gear and knew he was ready. Before heading for the trail, he poured himself another cup of coffee and gave thought to what direction Trent would take. He thought the slim gunfighter would head directly to the roadway rather than angle toward it, if for no other reason the snow was not as deep there, and the road's hard surface would afford better footing.

Finished with his coffee, Gentry glanced at the sky. The leaden clouds hung close to the ground, but were lighter than a few minutes ago. Day would break soon, although it would be hard to tell when it did. The heavy snowfall of the day before had not abated. He sighed, tossed the dregs from his cup, and stood. He wished this didn't have to happen, wished he'd finished the job in Texas, but the final chapter had been out of his hands once the courts had the case. He wondered whether there would be others hell-bent on hunting him down when they left the state prison.

Gentry stashed his cup next to his bedroll and headed toward the trail.

CHAPTER ELEVEN

★ ★ ★

Gentry worked his way through the brush to within about fifty yards of the trail and took cover behind a scrub cedar. Though the new day hid its light behind heavy clouds, the snow blanket gave off its own light. The trail, the brush on its other side, and the stream's bank showed stark in the murky light. Gentry scanned the roadway as far as light permitted. There were no fresh tracks. If anyone had passed this way in the last half hour or so, the snowfall would not have covered them. He settled into his cold hiding place, prepared for a long wait.

He stiffened. Something moved across the way. A dark form against the pristine white background emerged into a man shape. The man moved in jerky motions, lifted his legs high to clear them of the deep drifts, then went ahead another couple of feet. Again, Gentry thanked the Everywhere Spirit he'd brought snowshoes.

Trent, Gentry now certain of the man's identity, stumbled to the center of the roadway. Even along its frozen surface snow lay over a foot deep. In the center of the road, the slim, dapper man stopped, studied the trail from west to east, took a hesitant step in the direction of Billings, and stopped again.

Gentry could almost imagine the frown, the wonder, the question, that came to Trent's mind. Would anyone in their right mind continue a journey in this weather? Then as though to verify Gentry's thoughts, the gunfighter shook his head and stepped across the trail, left it, and proceeded into the brush at its side.

Gentry, certain now of Trent's direction, slipped from brush clump to tree, and tree to brush clump, far enough from the stream's bank to avoid his tracks being seen by his pursuer. He hoped to get far enough from the others' camp-site to be out of hearing of a gunshot.

Gentry let Trent pass him, then he angled in toward the stream's bank and fell in behind the slim form. The outlaw passed Gentry's camp, apparently without noticing it.

The going hard, Trent stumbled, fell, worked his legs until Gentry could almost feel Trent's fatigue in his own thighs.

Gentry followed at a safe distance for about two miles. Then, thinking Trent's partners would be unable to hear any sound he and Trent might make, he increased his pace, closing the distance between him and the gunfighter. Trent never looked back, but kept plodding ahead.

When about twenty-five yards behind Trent, Gentry stopped, leveled his Winchester, and called, "Lookin' for me, Trent?"

The slim gunfighter stopped in his tracks, not moving a muscle for a moment, then, keeping his hands clear of his sides, turned inch by inch to face Gentry. He looked from the ex-Ranger's head to his feet, nodded, and smiled. "Snowshoes." He locked eyes with Gentry. "You never were riding a horse, were you?"

Gentry moved his head from side to side, slowly. "Never was, Trent. Didn't see no need to kill a good horse, along with gettin' myself killed."

Trent stood there expectantly. "Well, Ranger man, if you're going to shoot me, get the job done. You took ten years of my life already, and the rest of it doesn't seem worth much to anyone, not even to me." His smile became whimsical. "Traveling around the country with white trash wouldn't say I'm worth much."

Gentry studied his man a moment. Trent didn't seem to like himself or what he was doing. He seemed to want to

talk, and Gentry stood with his back to whatever additional
danger there was for him. "Stay where you are. Don't
move. I'm gonna circle you and get your back to where
your friends would come from—if they come."

He walked far enough that he could see back the way
he'd come. "Now, turn slowlike, no sudden moves, and
face me." When Trent again faced him, Gentry eased the
Winchester's hammer down. "I know you think I done you
a great wrong, but, Trent, you're the one what wronged
yourself. I wasn't the one what put you away, the courts
done that. I just done my job an' brung you in."

Trent's smile changed from whimsical to chagrin. Gentry
was surprised that the slight gunfighter was saying more
with his expressions than with his mouth. "Yeah, Gentry. I
had a lot of time to think about that. I have only myself to
blame. As the old saying goes, 'You dance, you pay the fiddler.' Well, I paid the fiddler." He straightened, squared his
shoulders, and said, "Now, get on with the job, Gentry. I
don't think I can stand here looking at death much longer
without doing something crazy—like going for a gun I
haven't a chance in hell of getting into action."

"One more thing 'fore we get on with it. Why you ridin'
with that sorry bunch?"

Trent shrugged. "We were all released from Huntsville at
the same time. I had no job, nowhere to go, so I fell in with
them. I've wondered the same thing during the whole long,
cold ride up here to kill you. What the hell am I doing riding with this scum?"

Gentry closed his eyes to a squint. "Gonna ask you
somethin', you a man what keeps his word?"

Again that chagrined smile. "That's the only claim to
honor I have, Gentry. If I give you my word—on anything,
you can take it to the bank. Why?"

Gentry lowered the rifle's muzzle to point at the ground.
"If I don't put a hole in you right here an' now, could I
count on you to head back the way you come. I mean

Texas, not your friends' camp, an' not give me no more trouble?"

Trent stared into Gentry's eyes a moment. Gentry had never seen fear in the slim gunfighter. He saw none now. Trent looked at the ground, rubbed his hands down each sleeve, and looked up. "Gentry, I never wanted trouble with you in the first place. Yeah, I give you my word, I'll never pull a gun or any weapon on you."

Gentry tucked his Winchester under his arm. "You feel like a cup of coffee? That what I made for breakfast ought to be right thick by now."

They walked side by side back to Gentry's camp, slogging through the drifts. At camp, over a cup of coffee, Gentry found Trent knew next to nothing about ranching, or cowboying, but was willing to learn. He said he wasn't afraid of work.

"Tell you what, they's a couple of Texans you might know what's ranchin' west of Miles. Figure they might be willin' to give you a job, an' learn you how to do it. You willin' to give it a try?"

Trent looked over the rim of his cup, lowered it, and squinted into the fire. "Gentry, if there's a chance in hell they'll take me on, and do what you said, I'll try until I die. Hell yes. Who are they?"

"You ever hear of Trace Gundy, the Apache Blanco, or Brad Crockett?"

Trent nodded. "Heard a lot about Blanco, never met 'im, but Crockett's a different story. We rode for the same brand, him for his cow-smart, me for my guns. Can't say we were friends. Our different talents sort of put us on different sides of the bunkhouse."

Gentry laboriously wrote a note to Gundy on a piece of paper sack and handed it to Trent. "Now all you got to worry 'bout is gettin' your horse an' gear outta that other camp."

For the first time Gentry saw in Trent's eyes what made him a feared gunfighter, they had gone flat and deadly. "I'll get my gear *and* my horse. Nothing and no one is going to stand in my way of changing my life." He stood to leave.

"Stick around awhile. I'm gonna show you how to make a set of snowshoes. If you try *ridin'* your horse, you both may die."

Gentry stood, went down the creek a short distance, and came back with two long saplings. "Keep watch, Trent. Don't want yore friends to come lookin' for you." Then he went about bending, shaping, and securing the ends of the saplings. After that he created a web, side to side and front to back, out of a bundle of pigging strings he'd been carrying tied to his saddle skirts. Finished, he held them toward Trent. "I've seen better, but reckon as how they'll get you back to Miles. Stop in an' say 'howdy' to Marshal Bruns when you get there. He'll want to know how I'm doin'."

Trent stood there, gazing at Gentry. His Adam's apple bobbed a couple of times when he swallowed hard. He held out his hand. "Gentry, you're a real man. Thanks." He bent, strapped on the snowshoes, and left.

When Trent reached the roadway, he hesitated, walked to the edge, removed the snowshoes, and hid them under some brush. No point in giving Worley and Thompson the same advantage Gentry had had until now. After ensuring he could find the shoes when he came back, he headed toward the two men, with the likes of whom he hoped to never again be associated.

Close to camp, Trent slid down the bank and walked along the frozen creek bed, picking his way where the drifts were not as deep. Knowing how skittish Thompson was, he hailed the camp when within fifty or so yards.

"Come on in, Trent, we ain't gonna shoot ya." Worley was the one who answered. Trent glanced about the area when he got within the circle of firelight. With the clouds and snow, dark still settled in the creek bed even though it was long into the morning. Coffee was just beginning to boil at the side of the coals. They hadn't prepared breakfast.

Trent went to his pack and methodically began to prepare himself something to eat, aware that each of them kept glancing at him, waiting for him to say something about his scouting trip. It was not until he sat by the fire and began to eat that Thompson asked, "You see anything out there, any tracks, anything that looked like Gentry wuz close?"

Trent looked up from his plate. "Didn't see any horse tracks, didn't even see footprints." He complimented himself on not lying to them. "I *did* see one helluva lot of snow. There is no way we can continue in this weather."

"What you talkin' 'bout, Trent? You 'bout to give up—quit after all the way we come to kill Gentry?" Thompson asked.

Trent finished chewing the rind from a slice of bacon, then nodded. "You, Benton, and the Duvalls came up here to kill Gentry. I came along for the ride. I didn't have anything else to do, so I rode with you. Now, I'm going back."

When he sat to eat he had opened his coat and shifted his holster to a more comfortable position, now his Colt's walnut grips rested within a couple of inches of his hand. He waited for either of them to say something—or pull a gun.

"What you mean, you're goin' back? We ain't done what we come out here to do. You come with us so you gonna he'p us git it done," Thompson said while unbuttoning his coat.

Trent's breathing shortened, his neck muscles tightened. He straightened his right leg to throw his Colt handle closer to his hand. "Thompson, you better have another thought about reaching for that gun. You too, Worley. Fact is, I'll kill you first. Thompson's so damned slow I can put three rounds in you before I pull trigger on him, and I'll still beat him." He smiled, knowing he showed no humor. "Now, I'm going to finish my breakfast, then I'll pack my gear and leave. If either of you tries to follow, it'll be the biggest mistake you ever made." He raised his eyebrows. "You understand me?"

They both nodded. Thompson again buttoned his sheepskin. "Aw, Trent, I wuzn't thinkin' of pullin' iron on you. We're friends."

"No, we're not friends, never have been. We just happened to ride in the same direction. Now, both of you, keep your hands wide of your guns. I'm going to saddle my horse and ride out."

Trent rolled his bedroll, saddled his horse, tied his gear behind the saddle, and led his mustang from the camp. He walked, keeping a wary watch behind. Back-shooting was something he'd heard somewhere that Thompson was not averse to. He thought any fight he had with Worley would be face-to-face.

He waited until he reached the trail before buttoning his coat over his handgun and lashing the snowshoes to his boots. He was a quarter mile down the road toward Forsyth before the curtain of snow closed behind him, sheltering him from a stealthy shot. Not until then did he sheath his rifle. "Well, Mr. Trent," he said to the white flakes falling around him, "with any luck you can dig yourself out of the slime you've walked in for years. You just took the first big step." He smiled and trudged on.

As soon as Trent disappeared from sight, Thompson turned to Worley. "They's just us now, Worley, but that's enough, we can take Gentry, he ain't so much."

Worley stared into the fire, then glanced at the surrounding trees. "I hope you're ready to die, Thompson. Whatever you think, Gentry *is so much*. He's fast with that gun. Most never taken notice of that before 'cause he always shot where he looked, his draw was sorta lazy, like he wan't in no hurry, but I bet if you could get a good look at his hide, you wouldn't find no bullet scars." He nodded. "Yeah, Thompson, he's good."

A chill slipped up Thompson's spine. He glanced at the surrounding trees, snowdrifts, and the edge of the bank above his head. "You sound scared, Worley. You gonna back out on me?"

Worley smiled. "No. Reckon if I had any sense I wouldn't of been here in the first place, but I took cards in this game an' figure to play out the hand. I'll stick 'til I see my hole card. They wuz a bunch of us when we started out. All we got left is a pair, a damned low pair at that. Maybe my hole card will be the wild card, but in poker I'd be awful dumb to call on that chance. Yeah, I'm dumb. I'm stayin'."

Thompson felt that chill again. His eyes shifted to take in his surroundings again. He looked toward every possible hiding place. "What we gonna do, stay here an' rest our horses another day or two?"

"Yeah, we gotta. Them horses gonna die if we take 'em out in this weather again. Good thing 'bout it though is that Gentry's gotta rest his horse too. He ain't gettin' too far ahead of us, if any at all."

"We ought to go look for him maybe. You know, find out where he is an' figure out a ambush."

Looking into Worley's eyes, Thompson felt the poison of contempt, the cold daggers of a man who would kill him in an instant, the look of a man who was ready to walk away from the whole deal because the man he rode with was a coward.

"Thompson, don't know why I ever rode with you. You got no guts. No matter how good Gentry is, I ain't gonna shoot him from no ambush. If I git 'im, I'll be lookin' right in his eyes, through a blast of gunpowder. If you figure to back-shoot him, or ambush 'im, you gonna do it alone. I'm stayin' right here in camp 'til the snow slackens off a little, then I'm gonna start lookin'."

Thompson had never admitted, even to himself, that he was afraid of Trent, but now, looking into Worley's eyes, and having Worley throw it into his teeth that he had no guts and, in fact, didn't have the guts to take offense at Worley's words, something died inside him. He felt he shriveled for all the world to see.

Gentry watched Trent's slim back fade into the snow curtain, stood, and walked the creek bed picking up driftwood for his fire. He figured to wait until dark to make life miserable for Thompson and Worley.

When time came for his nooning, he glanced at the pile

of wood he'd gathered. He grinned. He could stay here three days and still have enough firewood.

He killed the day around the fire and occasionally scouted the perimeter of his camp. Once, in midafternoon, he poured a belt of rye whiskey in his coffee to warm him.

When the gray of night settled about him, he checked his weapons, slipped a sixth shell into the cylinder of his pistol, filled the magazine of his Winchester with seventeen shells, and moved his Bowie toward the front of his belt for easy reach. He stood. He was ready.

Out on the snow, Gentry tested the surface to see if a crust had formed. He was in luck, his snowshoes made little sound, only a quiet swish when the white blanket packed under them. Satisfied, he circled again to approach Thompson's camp from the opposite direction. Taking more than three times the time he would have taken by heading straight to their den, it was almost nine o'clock when he slipped to his belly and snaked his way to the lip of the creek bank.

This time, he used care to keep his hands away from the edge. When he spooked them now, he figured to do a good job of it. The bank's edge was only a couple of feet away when voices broke the night's silence.

Gentry squirmed forward enough to look down into the streambed. Thompson paced back and forth by the fire, waving his arms, ranting and raving.

"I tell you Trent sold us out. I figure he met up with Gentry an' made a deal. He wuz afraid of Gentry, that's what he was."

Worley pulled at his nose. "Thompson, you're a damned fool. Trent wuzn't afraid of nobody. He just flat didn't care 'bout nothin'. You, me, nothin'. He never wuz sold on this trip, or gettin' even with Gentry. He come along for the ride 'cause he didn't have nothin' else to do."

Gentry drew back from the bank a short way and thought about what he had seen. He closed his eyes and pictured their entire camp, then again up to the overhang.

Thompson had stopped his pacing and sat across the fire

from Worley. A coffeepot and a kettle of beans sat in the coals at the fire's edge.

Gentry brought his rifle stock to his shoulder, drew a bead on the coffeepot, triggered two fast shots, moved his sights, and put two shots into the kettle. Beans, coffee, and pots flew into the air. Scalding coffee drenched the two, followed by the thick pot-likker and beans. The gunmen looked like they'd sprouted a midsummer crop of freckles. They jumped up and down, cursing, dancing from one foot to the other, slapping at the beans as though a hive of bees invaded the camp. A gust of laughter spewed from Gentry's tight lips trying to hold it back. Then he threw a shot at the feet of the scurrying figures. They jumped higher and farther. Still chuckling deep in his throat, Gentry stood and moved back the way he'd come, taking advantage of the fact the two outlaws were probably trying to dig themselves a hole in the ice or anywhere to get away from the hail of lead, beans, and coffee.

He shoed his way a hundred yards or so from where he had hung over the creek bank, then ducked behind a thicket and waited for them to take chase.

He could have killed them while they sat by the fire, but that wasn't his way. He wanted to have a little fun, let them know where the lead came from, and give them some slight chance to return fire.

When he thumbed lead into them, he wanted them looking into his eyes. Every time he thought of them, bitter, angry bile surged into his throat. He should be home with his wife and children.

His eyes focused on the tree line bordering the creek. Slowly he moved his gaze from each ghostly tree to the bank's edge, back to the trees, scanned, and scanned again. The third time his gaze covered the area he saw movement. He leveled his rifle at the spot and squeezed the trigger. Fire blossomed from the side of the tree. He'd missed. He'd aimed to hit, and kill this time. But even though he missed, he lucked out. Only one gun spewed flame at him.

CHAPTER TWELVE

★ ★ ★

Still grinning from the havoc he created, he drew sights on the tree, sucked in a deep breath, let it out slowly, held his breath, and squeezed the trigger. As soon as he fired, he bracketed the tree with two more shots, turned, and ran to another clump of brush.

Squatted in the middle of the cedar brake he wondered that no shots followed him into his new hiding place. Maybe he had lessened the odds—at least hit the man, but he couldn't be sure. Maybe his shots did no more than cause his adversary to take cover. He stayed in the thicket a full half hour, then started his slow circle back to camp. He thought neither Thompson nor Worley would be fool enough to try tracking him in the dark. He was wrong.

He'd gone maybe another two hundred yards when fire lanced at him from the side. Simultaneously, an angry whine stung his ears. He launched himself to the foot of a deep drift and lay still. Gentry's gut muscles tightened until they hurt. A cold sweat coated his face. That bullet was close enough to make a believer of him. Whoever he faced was a shooter. He figured it was Worley.

He made sure the drift was between him and the rifleman, then squirmed toward the bole of a large cottonwood. The dark brown of his buffalo robe would be a prime target against the stark white background of the drift. The thought caused him to sweat even more. Once behind the cottonwood, he stood and eased his head out far enough to search toward where the shot had come. At every likely looking spot, Gentry turned his eyes slightly and looked to the side of it. He'd learned long ago that night vision could sometimes see better by not looking directly at an object.

He hugged the tree for another half hour, hoping for his adversary to fire so he could pinpoint his location. Finally, he thought the shooter gave it up. He continued his circle toward his own camp. Every hundred feet or so, he stopped and scanned the area behind and to each side. After a mile of this kind of care, he checked to see how easy his snowshoe tracks were to follow in the dark. Satisfied the snow didn't give off enough light to allow tracking, he walked at a normal pace, sure now Worley headed for his own camp.

Gentry had the advantage. He knew where he was going. Worley would have to guess, and maybe expose himself trying for position. Gentry figured Worley was too cagey for that.

He'd made the gunmen's night interesting. And they'd have a fine time trying to make coffee in that pot. The way it jumped with his shot, he'd put a hole in the side and out the bottom. It was beyond repair. They wouldn't be cooking beans in that other pot either.

Thompson crouched close to the bank. He'd been cowering there since Gentry's first shot knocked the coffeepot across the fire. Worley, the damned fool, had gone hunting trouble.

Thompson strained to pick up sound. Shots, three of them, sounded far enough away he didn't worry for his hide. He figured those shots were Gentry's because of the sound of twigs clipped from small growth downstream, not far away. After a while another shot sounded farther out. He wondered if he'd ever see Worley again. That shot could have come from either of them. He still didn't move from his crouch against the bank.

After a while, a long while, steps crunched the snow. Thompson gripped his rifle tight enough to leave fingerprints in the wood. He held his breath, the fire of fear burned his stomach. His clenched jaws kept his teeth from chattering. "Hello, the camp," Worley's voice, soft but loud enough, came through the darkness.

Thompson's gut muscles loosened. "Come on in, Worley." He kept his voice low. Seconds later, Worley walked to the fire, his rifle cradled in the crook of his arm.

"You get 'im?" Thompson asked.

Worley stared at him across the fire, his lips turned down at the corners, eyes squinted. Thompson continued, his voice weak, "I stayed here in camp in case Gentry tried to wreck it. Didn't see no point in lettin' 'im have his way 'bout ever'thing."

Worley didn't break his stare for a long moment that seemed forever to Thompson, then he said, "Thompson, you stayed heah, frozen up against that there bank, 'cause you're a sniveling, slimy, gutless piece of cow dung." He picked up his cup from beside his saddle, looked at the worthless coffeepot, and tossed his cup back to the ground. "You an' them Duvall brothers talked me an' the others into comin' up here with you. Well, they're dead, just like you gonna be when Gentry gets ahold of you. In the mornin' I'm draggin' my freight if my horse can handle it, an' with no grain, tired as he was when we stopped, I might end up walkin'. You ain't comin' with me, Thompson. You ain't goin' nowhere. I ought to kill you myself, but I'm gonna leave that to Gentry. He'll get the job done."

Thompson stared, his mouth slack. "Worley, you cain't leave me out here alone. Neither one of us, alone, can take care of Gentry."

Worley looked at the ruined pot of beans and, seeming to think he could salvage a plate of them, picked up his plate, then he looked at Thompson, head on. "First off, I not only *can* leave you, I'm *gonna* leave you. Next, you might be right 'bout it takin' two *men* to down Gentry, but in this camp they's only one *man.*"

He went to the kettle, scraped at its contents, and managed to get a half plate full, then turned what was left up-side down over the fire. When he sat to eat, he continued what he'd been saying. "Yeah, Thompson, I'm leavin', an' if I meet up with Gentry I figure to fight 'im. If I go down, I'll go like a man oughtta. And, Thompson, if he gets me you better run fast as yore sorry legs'll carry you. You brought this fight to him an' he don't forget such."

Worley took a mouthful of beans off his knife, chewed on them a little, swallowed, then said, "You're dead, Thompson. I damned near said 'dead man,' but I'd of been wrong. You'll just be a dead nothin'."

After eating, Worley spread his bedding and, not bothering to undress, pulled off his boots and crawled between his blankets. Before drawing the top blanket over him, he put his handgun by his saddle, next to his head, and grinned at Thompson. "Never know what kind of varmints gonna come rootin' round in camp at night."

Worley's grin ran shivers up and down Thompson's spine. He sat, his back against the frozen creek bank, and for the first time in his life took stock of himself. He'd killed men, so what if they weren't gun-quick, but hell, he'd gone against them. They needed killing. He shot a few in the back. Only a damned fool took chances when he didn't have to. He'd done what he had to do to draw his pay. The only reason he never faced a fast gunfighter was 'cause nobody ever wanted one dead—he could have taken them if he had to. He nodded to himself. He was as much man as any of them, and smarter too. The way he fought, he'd outlive them all. He looked at Worley curled up in his blankets.

Without Worley, if Gentry didn't kill him the weather would. He stood, went to his bedroll, and pulled a bottle from it. It held only a couple of swallows. He, Worley, and Trent had almost emptied it, but there was another one they hadn't yet opened. He drained one and opened the other.

After a few more deep pulls at the new bottle, he began to feel better. Who the hell was Worley to look down on him. He'd always carried his load, busted his own broncs. Hell, he could take on Worley and Gentry at the same time. He again tilted the bottle, and before taking it from his mouth, his gaze again fell on Worley. Yeah, he could take Worley and Gentry together, but why not do it the easy way.

He stared at Worley, tilted the bottle, shivered from the raw alcohol, and studied Worley's' tight-knit, short, powerful form. Even though Worley seemed to be asleep, Thompson's gut tightened. His breathing came hard. Gonna leave me out here to fight Gentry alone, huh? Not by a damn sight. He took two huge swallows of the cheap whiskey, knocked the cork into the bottle, put it on the ground between his feet, drew his .44, and thumbed the hammer back, the racheting sound loud in the quiet camp. He swung the barrel toward Worley. Flame spewed from the blankets.

A sledgehammerlike blow knocked Thompson hard against the creek bank. He tried to pull the trigger, but his handgun was heavier than he remembered, the trigger harder to pull, and he felt numb. Why was he numb? Must be the cold. The cold must have frozen the mechanism on his gun too.

Worley rolled out of his blankets and stood. Thompson had to get his handgun back in its holster or Worley would know what he'd been about to do. He looked down to slide his Colt into its scabbard and saw that his sheepskin had come unbuttoned. A black hole oozed something red down his front. It looked like blood, his blood. The red faded to black, his pistol, truly too heavy now, dropped to his leg. He was tired, so very tired. Most days he worked harder than today, but for some reason, today he was tired. He closed his eyes to an eternal black void.

Worley stared at the body of his saddle partner. "You never was any good, Thompson. I never was neither, but I always been better'n you. In the mornin', if I gotta fight Gentry, I'll do it. If I don't cross his trail, I'm headin' for Texas." He picked up the bottle from between Thompson's feet, pulled the cork, and took a couple of healthy swallows. "Even this whiskey don't wipe out the rotten taste you leave in a man's mouth." He turned his back and again crawled between his blankets.

Gentry trudged toward camp. His legs felt like they carried fifty pounds of lead each. His shoulders cramped, and the leaders down the back of his neck were tight as a bowstring. It had been a long day, and come the morrow, he still had a fight on his hands.

He again glanced behind and saw nothing to indicate he had been followed. Studying on it, he figured that last shot someone had taken at him was a means of saying good night. Only a cat could follow the trail he'd laid down.

Finally, in camp, he cleaned his rifle, checked his pistol, then looked at his bedroll, and turned his eyes toward his coffeepot. He decided to fix a pot of coffee, lace it with a little whiskey, and see if it would relax him. In the past such treatment was all he needed to get a good night's sleep.

Holding his coffee cup in his bare hands for the warmth, he backed up to the stream's bank, sat, and relaxed. He wondered what Anne and the children were doing, then realized they had long since been in bed. It must have been past eleven o'clock. He was too tired to look at his watch.

He thought how lucky he'd been to have taken Bowdry to town and met Gundy. If he gathered even half the cows Blanco thought were on Barton's place, his worries were over. Anne and the children could have some of the things they deserved in life.

He finished his coffee, pulled his boots off, and crawled into his blankets. The whiskey-laced coffee did its job. Warm inside and out, Gentry soon slept.

When he awoke, the snow had stopped. A close stillness gripped the land. It was as though the Everywhere Spirit had thought to freeze the world and leave it as it was. No noise, no movement, even the wind rested from its incessant play across the land.

Gentry pushed his blankets down, put on his hat, pulled on his boots, and stood. If he built up his fire, smoke would be seen miles away for it would rise straight up. He grinned. That wouldn't be true in his camp. He cut several cedar saplings and wove them above the ashes of his fire, then built the flames to cook breakfast. The smoke wended its way through the cedar branches and was dispersed by them so as to be seen only a few yards away.

After eating, he broke camp and hid his gear.

He thought to retrace his steps of the night before. His idea was wearysome at the very least, but if they followed his tracks he wanted to meet them and get this over with.

Finally, as ready as he'd ever be, he climbed the stream's bank and headed out.

Every few yards he picked some vantage point where he could see far enough ahead to make certain he didn't walk into a trap. Of the two left, Gentry figured Worley as the most dangerous, so if he had to fight them both at the same time, he'd take Worley first.

When over halfway to the renegade's camp, he stopped and took stock of the situation. From here on in he needed to use extra care. If they started from their end when he started from his, even with the extra time it would take them to track him, he should meet them soon.

The same ground that took him a couple of hours to cover the night before now took twice the time. He moved from brush to tree trunk to cedar brake, any cover he could use to stop and search the area ahead. For some reason, he felt no sense of danger. He shrugged. Maybe he'd lost his edge since leaving the Rangers. The thought urged him to more caution.

Less than a quarter mile from Thompson's camp now, he frowned. They should have been on his trail hours ago. Gentry squatted behind a clump of winter-browned reeds and searched toward the creek. His tracks of the night before showed plainly, though now they were only indentations in the snow. His gaze followed his tracks to where he had sprawled at the lip of the bank. His first thought was to follow them and look down on their camp again. He cast that idea aside. He'd cross the creek and look at them from the other side.

It took an hour to reach the spot he wanted. About ten feet from the bank, he went to his belly and crawled to its lip. He looked down on a dead camp, no fire, no horses, and only one empty bedroll. But Thompson lay back against the opposite bank as though asleep, and his handgun lay along his thigh. Red stained the snow around him.

Still wary of showing himself, Gentry looked along both directions of the creek bed. There was no sign of life. Worley was gone. Convinced now he and Thompson had the camp to themselves, Gentry stood, slid down the bank, and walked to the gunman.

The renegade had been dead for some time. His sightless eyes stared at the bare tree limbs above. His body lay stiff and frozen, one finger still curled about the trigger of his Colt. The .44 was still cocked. One hole, dead center in Thompson's chest, was all Gentry saw.

He shook his head. "You had your chance, Thompson. Worley was too good an' smart for you. You wuz gonna try a sneak shot at him. He didn't fall for it."

Gentry checked the camp, took Thompson's weapons, looked through his pockets, and found them empty. Worley probably took what money Thompson had. A last look about the abandoned camp, and Gentry headed down creek for his gear. He followed horse tracks to the trail. Worley had taken both horses, but rode neither. The mustangs were being led. Gentry's opinion of the gunman raised a bit for his care of the horses. On the roadway, the tracks turned toward Forsyth.

Gentry studied the tracks, thinking now he could go home. But the fight was not over. There was a chance he'd come up on Worley on the trail. If they met, there would be gunplay. If Worley wanted to let it go, Gentry wouldn't let that happen. He wanted the thing over and done with. Worley had to die.

CHAPTER THIRTEEN

★ ★ ★

In his old campsite, Gentry tied Thompson's rifle to his pack, stuck the outlaw's pistol in his belt, shouldered his gear, and walked toward the trail.

Reaching the roadway, he followed Worley's tracks. Two sets of tracks wended their way toward Forsyth. To one side of the trail, a single horse with indentations in the snow of a man on snowshoes, and on the left-hand side of the roadway, two horses and a man afoot left sharper tracks. The sharp tracks would be Worley's.

While walking, Gentry tried to figure what day and date it was, and couldn't, then wondered if he'd get home for Christmas. He'd promised Anne he'd be with her and the children on that day, but now he was not sure, because whatever day it was, and however close Christmas was upon him, Worley came first, and then Bowdry.

With the end of the snow it took until midday for the clouds to break, and even though a wan sun shed its light on the land, the temperature seemed to drop; the snow crusted over and became slick, making use of his snowshoes harder. He wondered how Worley managed any progress.

The day dragged on, the shadows grew long, and Worley's tracks sharpened. Gentry slowed his pace. He was closing on the outlaw and didn't want to with night coming on.

By Gentry's reckoning, the crusted, icy layer on the snowcover forced the Texas gunfighter to slow his pace.

Now Gentry put caution first. He searched every tree line, every ridge, the edge of every snowdrift.

Gentry wanted his camp to be a far piece from Worley's. He didn't want to worry about wood smoke being seen or smelled. And when dark settled, he wanted the flicker of his fire to be far enough away not to be seen. He twisted his mouth in a grimace; what he wanted was a good night's sleep without having to crawl from his blankets firing a six-gun or rifle.

By late morning the next day, Worley's tracks were even fresher. Gentry squatted by them, frowning. Something had caused his man to slow—and it wasn't the weather. Something was going on in Worley's mind, and Gentry thought he knew what it was.

Worley pulled a foot from the frozen mess and took another step forward. With every step, anger boiled deeper in his gut, and his neck seemed to swell. To hell with it, he thought. If me an' Gentry's gonna have it out, we might as well get on with it.

He figured Gentry was behind him, following as closely as he dared in order to not force the fight until *he* was ready. Well, Mr. Gentry, we not gonna play your game. We gonna play it *my* way.

The more he thought about it the madder he got. He started for Texas willing to let it drop, but Gentry wasn't the kind to let something like this end until it was over. They carried the fight to him, and now, Worley knew, the last of the six men who left Texas would lie dead before the ex-Ranger quit. He slowed his pace, and every few feet cast a searching glance behind. Then he looked to the side and ahead for a place to pull off the trail and set up for the fight.

He wanted the spot close to the roadway. His sign leading off for any distance would warn the Ranger of his plans. When he left the beaten path, Worley wanted his cover right at its side so Gentry would still follow his tracks without any indication he stopped or veered off course.

Worley topped a hill, and at its bottom another small creek crossed the trail. His only clue that water flowed there in warmer weather was the line of trees pushing to the edge of the road on each side. That was the kind of spot for which he'd been looking. Holding the reins of the horses, he pulled them toward the line of cottonwoods.

Before every step, every move, Gentry scanned his surroundings. He came on horse droppings, steam rising from them into the cold air. Gentry's first impulse was to hit the ground rolling, to find cover. His breath coming in quick gasps, he glanced to each side of the roadway. He saw only the smooth blanket of snow, then his gaze locked on the trail ahead. The crest of a low hill lay not far ahead. Worley had to be not far on the other side.

Gentry shrugged out of the harness holding his pack, pulled his Winchester from its scabbard, and walked to the side of the road and into the snowfield. He left his pack where he'd taken it from his shoulders.

When about fifty yards from the trail, he turned to parallel it, dropped to his stomach, and snaked his way to the brow of the hill. A man, almost at the bottom, staggered along, dragging on the reins of two horses. The horses stumbled more than the man who pulled them. Gentry had no doubt he looked upon Worley.

When at the bottom of the hill, directly in line with the trees on either side of the roadway, Worley twisted to look back, then pulled the horses into the trees at his side.

Smart move, Gentry thought. Now, I bet he sets up to wait for me. He'll hide the horses, come back, squat behind one of those big cottonwoods, and wait for me to walk into his trap. He lay there and watched Worley do exactly as he thought.

Gentry wriggled his way from the brow of the hill, and when sure he couldn't be seen, stood and went back to reclaim his pack. He squatted by the pile of his belongings to think on what Worley would do.

From what he knew of the man, the gunfighter would wait for him to get within good rifle range and fire a warning shot. Worley, by Gentry's reckoning, was not the kind of man to dry-gulch another. But after the warning, it would be an all-out gunfight, and his adversary would have the edge by having good cover. He, by the other token, would be hung out to dry on that barren, snow-covered hillside.

Gentry sucked in a draft of the cold air, held it a moment, and forced himself to relax. Fear and anticipation mixed to give a contradictory feeling; one of urgency, and at the same time one that urged caution. Finally, he decided how he would play the hand.

He again shouldered his pack and headed at right angles to the trail. He walked straight south about a quarter of a mile, then turned east. The sharp cracking sound of the frozen crust kept every muscle in his body tense. He thought Worley wouldn't hear the noise he made. They were too far apart. The thought did little to relax him.

Gentry rounded the base of the hill from which he'd seen Worley choose his cover and went flat on his belly again. He snaked his way to where the creek wound its way toward the Yellowstone. His gaze swept thc area ahead. He wanted to take away Worley's edge, get into the same line of trees the gunman used, only he figured to come on Worley from the back and slip close enough for handgun work.

The bare, swaying top branches of the cottonwoods came under his gaze first, then the closer he came to the stream, more of the trees showed, until finally he looked on the dark winding line, across the trail and on past it until the bare, skeletal growth disappeared around the base of another hill.

Gentry lay there, panting. He'd heard somewhere an army traveled on its stomach. Well, Lord help them if whoever said those words meant them literally.

He rested a few moments, and while doing so studied the two hundred or more yards between him and the trees. There was not even a swell of snow to take him out of sight of Worley if he should look his way. "This ain't gonna be no picnic, Gentry," he muttered, more for the sound of a voice than anything else. Nothing in his life ever came easy.

Hoping he had Worley figured right, he thought the man would keep his eyes pasted to the trail, waiting for his prey to show himself.

After a few more moments, Gentry sucked in a deep breath. "Ain't gonna get no easier by lying here." He let his breath out slowlike and inched toward the trees.

Every inch he moved forward, he braced against the slam of a bullet, braced for the sharp crack of Worley's rifle, braced to stop the trembling in his arms and legs.

Inch by inch and foot by foot, he closed on the tree line. It seemed they never drew nearer— but they must have because the line of brush at the edge of the trees was only inches from his fingertips. His first impulse was to stand and dive into cover. He kept a tight rein on that thought and continued to slither into the thick winter-killed reeds.

After what seemed hours, Gentry glanced back and saw his legs were into the cover. He lowered his head until his cheek rested on the ground, and lay there forcing himself to relax. He would welcome the smell of dust, a human voice, the warm engulfing feel of parched earth under him—anything to tie him to the world instead of this sterile, pristine blanket.

By his reckoning, it had taken over two hours of snaking his way down the hill to reach his hiding place in the brush. Now, the edge was his.

He rested a good twenty minutes before standing and looking for a place to leave his pack. Not moving more than he had to, he searched the west side for a cut-bank that would protect him from the wind. He lucked out. Only fifty feet or so, the water had over the years eroded the soil under a giant cottonwood, its roots still clinging to much of the dirt the water had been unable to reach.

Easing each foot onto the crusted snow, making it crack almost without sound, he reached the cut-bank and lowered his pack to the ground. Only a light powdering covered the ground where he intended to sleep that night—but before then, he and Worley would meet.

Gentry sat on his pack and checked his weapons. To check his rifle's magazine, he held it under the tail of his buffalo robe so the sound wouldn't carry; he did the same for his pistol, although he thought it wouldn't make enough noise to be heard. Satisfied his guns were all right, he pulled his Bowie knife around within easy reach, braced his legs to stand, and stopped. *Worley's horses.* Where were they? As soon as the thought flicked through his mind, he knew they were somewhere in the streambed between him and the gunman. He checked the wind's direction and found it blew at right angles to the creek. That was in his favor, but there was no way he could get to Worley without passing through or around the worn-out nags. His shoulders slumped.

He sat there a few moments, thinking. Finally, he stood, he had a plan, although, he admitted, not a very good one. He shrugged. He had no choice. If it didn't work, he'd do what he had to do.

Carrying his Winchester in his left hand, he snowshoed his way downstream as carefully as he'd done to get this far, but he still cringed every time the crust snapped underfoot and squeaked.

Gentry moved silently, slowly. After a while, he checked the sun. It stood low in the sky and would give way to night in about an hour. At the rate he moved he might not have enough time. Tempted to move faster, he got a grip on his senses and again caution ruled.

Another few minutes and Gentry saw the horses, standing three-legged, nose to nose. Horses are a social animal, seeming to always want to be sure they have company. Gentry grinned. He couldn't ask for better, unless it was that they weren't there in his way at all.

When he approached he took care to not make any sudden moves to startle them. He had no doubt they heard the snow crust cracking under his feet. A few feet from them, each swung its head to look at him. "Whoa now, boy. Ain't

gonna bother you." His voice low and crooning, Gentry
walked to them, and one at a time covered their nostrils
with his right hand. Their ears peaked, twitched, and relaxed. Now more careful than before, Gentry again headed
downstream. Worley would not be far ahead.

As soon as Gentry had the thought, he saw his man. The
gunman sat leaning against the bole of a cottonwood, staring straight down the trail in the direction from which Gentry would have to come. His hands snuggled in his pockets,
his rifle stood on the ground at his side, the barrel lying
against his shoulder. Gentry opened his buffalo rode and
hooked it behind the handle of his Colt.

"Ain't comin' from that direction, Worley. You guessed
wrong." Gentry expected the gunman to twist and try to get
his rifle in action. He didn't.

Worley slowly turned his head to look at Gentry. He
smiled. "Should a knowed you wasn't dumb enough to do
what a man would figger you to do." He shook his head.
"Well, now you got me cold turkey. You gonna give it to
me straight on—right now?"

Never breaking his gaze, Gentry moved his head from
side to side, real slowlike. "Never shot a man 'thout givin'
'im a chance, Worley. From what I hear you ain't neither."

"Nope. Way I figger it, Gentry, a man what won't give a
man a chance ain't worth killin'; he needs to be strung up
by his thumbs an' whipped to death."

Gentry studied the man who sat before him, calmly
awaiting death. "You say that, but you were sittin' here in
ambush, waitin' for me. What were you gonna do?"

"I thought to fire, let you know I wuz here, an' from then
on I figgered we'd shoot it out."

Gentry nodded. "All right. You want pistols, rifles, or
maybe even knives?"

Worley gripped his rifle by the barrel, stood it against the
tree, twisted on one knee, and stood. "No rifles an' no
knives, Gentry, let's use handguns. I ain't gonna draw first
so pick your time."

"No, I draw when you start yours. Tell you what, we got nobody to count for us, so what say we build a fire and place a branch on two Y-shaped twigs over the fire. When the branch burns in two and falls in the fire, we draw."

Worley frowned, apparently thinking about Gentry's suggestion, and after a couple of seconds, he jerked his head in a nod. "Let's do it."

Together they built a small fire, then Gentry gathered more firewood while Worley looked for a couple of Y-shaped twigs.

Gentry placed a slim twig across the slingshot-shaped branches directly over the fire. They took their places, one on each side of the fire where they could both see when the slim stick burned through and fell.

Gentry watched the fire until the stick began to smoke, then he shifted his gaze to watch Worley's eyes. On the periphery he could see the stick, but watching Worley gave him what he wanted.

The corners of Worley's eyes flicked into a squint and Gentry went for his gun. Only the two men moved in this still, frozen world. To Gentry it seemed they both moved in agonizingly slow motion.

Worley's .44 cleared leather and swiveled to come in line with Gentry's head. Worley's hand seemed to explode in flame. Gentry's gun smoked twice. Two holes appeared in Worley's chest, and instantly turned red at their edges. Fire burned the tip of Gentry's ear. He thumbed the hammer back for another shot, slipped his thumb from the hammer—and nothing happened. His pistol misfired. He thumbed the hammer back a second time—still nothing. Worley's pistol ratcheted with sound when he drew the hammer back on his pistol.

Gentry looked down the barrel of Worley's .44. He figured he'd made his last ride, fought his last fight, but so had Worley. There was no way those two holes in his chest wouldn't kill him. Gentry looked from the gunman's Colt into his eyes.

"Come here, Gentry. Come closer."

His useless pistol hanging at his side, Gentry walked to Worley. "Go ahead, Worley. Get it done."

Worley smiled, a sort of sad smile to Gentry's thinking. "I already got the only job done I'm gonna get done, Gentry." His voice came out in a whispering sort of wheeze, and blood trickled from the corners of his mouth. "If your gun don't misfire, I ain't never gonna get off another shot." He lowered the hammer with his thumb. "I ain't gonna kill you, Gentry. You're too good a man. 'Sides that"—he again flashed Gentry a whimsical smile—"you done killed me." His hand dropped to his side. He took a slight hesitant step forward and fell. Gentry caught him just as he was about to crash into the fire and gently lowered him to the ground. Then, his knees feeling weak as watered coffee, Gentry sat by the pitiful little fire that had already served its purpose. The fire had triggered a fight to kill a good man, a man who lived and died by the code of the West.

Gentry sat by the little fire until it died to gray ash, not even an ember glowed to show the life it once had. Every so often, he glanced at Worley, and wondered that a man with such a sense of honor had not turned out differently. His mind checked off the men he'd killed, and none of them stacked up with the one who lay by the small pile of ashes. He sat there, knowing if Worley had lived with only hate, they would both be stretched out here on this frozen ground. And now, he had one more man to hunt, the last one, he hoped, he'd ever pull a gun on. Even though cold, Gentry sat there a long time, sat there until full darkness shrouded the leafless trees.

He thought how close his family came to being without a husband, a father. He thought what a waste of good men these days were, as well as all the days past when men fought duels, often over some strange concept of honor.

The next man he killed would not fit any code of honor. He'd not fit into any decent society. He needed killing.

CHAPTER FOURTEEN

★ ★ ★

Stiff and cold, Gentry again glanced at Worley, collected his guns and knife, and set off to find his own gear. Come morning, he'd head for Forsyth.

He now had two rifles, four pistols, and two horses he'd not left Milestown with. He could have saved buying Mark's rifle, but maybe Leighton would buy the extra guns. Men in the line of business followed by Thompson and his bunch had excellent weapons, and even better horses.

Gentry rolled out of his blankets an' was on the trail before first light. Walking came easier now with his pack and Worley's gear on one horse, and the other carrying the body. Gentry would not leave Worley for scavengers to eat. He was too good a man.

The horses were hard to get started and keep going. Gentry vowed they would get their fill of grain when he got to the livery. No telling when they last filled their stomachs.

Dark pushed its way into the bottoms when Gentry topped a hill and saw the lights of Forsyth, and full nightfall had settled on the town by the time he got to the livery.

Before he could open the door, it swung toward him.

Mabin looked first at Gentry, raked him from head to feet, then looked him in the eye. "You all right?" and, not waiting for an answer, said, "When that one man come back through here, Trent was his name, he said you was all right, but you still had some cleanin' up to do." He glanced at Worley's body slung across the horse's back. "See you done part of it."

Gentry tugged the two horses into the stable and nodded. "Yeah, all I need to do hereabouts. But I got one more man to take care of somewhere around Miles, then I can go back to my wife and children." He looked toward Mabin's office. "You got any of that mud brewin' back yonder? I shore could use a cup."

Mabin chuckled. "Come on back, young'un. I always got coffee. Made this pot yestiddy mornin', an' added some grounds to it only a few minutes ago. It ought to be about right to cut the hair off'n your tongue by now."

At this point, cold and tired as he was, Gentry didn't care if Mabin had acid in the pot. He'd drink it. He walked toward the back of the livery. "After I *chew* a cup of it, which'll probably take a good bit of time, I'll get the marshal over here an' give 'im the story about the man slung across that saddle."

"Well, gosh-ding-it, I shore am glad you said that, 'cause I wanted to hear about what happened too."

Gentry grinned. "Mabin, my mama didn't raise no fools. Figured if I told the marshal, out of your hearin', I'd have to tell it again. Now, steer me to that coffeepot."

Over coffee, Gentry negotiated trading some of his supplies, some of which he'd taken when he cleaned out Thompson's camp, to Mabin if he would grain-feed the horses and put them up for the night. Then Mabin offered to get the marshal.

When the marshal arrived, Gentry had to tell why the gunmen were on his trail, and about the one lying in a streambed a few miles out of town, killed by the one he'd brought in. "They come after me, Marshal. Didn't have no choice but to take it to them. That there man I brought in was a good man, just had a mixed-up notion of what he figured he had to do in order to keep his self-respect. 'Preciate it you could put some kind of marker on his grave." Gentry dug in his pocket and pulled out a few bills. "Took this outta Worley's pocket, comes to 'bout seventy dollars. What you figure a decent funeral will cost?"

"Ten dollars ought to cover it." He held out his hand and took the sawbuck Gentry held toward him. Gentry stuffed the rest in his pocket.

The marshal glanced at Worley's stiff body. "Reckon we can bury him come spring." The lawman grinned. "I'll have one of the drunks dig a grave after spring thaw. He can pay his fine that way."

After seeing the man with the star head back to his office, Gentry and Mabin drank another cup of coffee before Gentry climbed to the hayloft to sleep. He figured to get on the trail before daylight.

The roadway between Forsyth and Milestown was no better than the one behind him. Gentry trudged down the pristine length of it, breaking trail. No one had braved the weather before him. Even with snowshoes, each step took extra effort to put one foot in front of the other. One night of grain had done little to help the horses. But Gentry wanted those horses and the gear he'd inherited from the outlaws.

Ahead of him lay a long length of white, broken only by the black, stark outline of a tree now and then or a dark line of growth along a stream. Rabbits stayed in their burrows. Birds had long since found their homes far to the south. Even the predators were not hungry enough to brave looking for food.

Gentry caught himself sniffing the air, hoping for a scent—of any kind; he strained his ears for sound other than the crunching of his snowshoes, he would even be comforted to feel a hard knot between his shoulders, one that foreshadowed danger, anything to break the monotonous silence.

Gentry welcomed camp that night. His fire crackling, pushing warmth into his chilled body, wafting smoke-smell by his nostrils, and the horses' occasional blowing, all combined to make him know he was alive. Then the smell of coffee brewing and bacon frying rounded out his sense of contentment. He poured his cup half full of whiskey, topped it off with strong coffee, then lay back against his saddle. The stream's bank under which he camped broke the sharp wind.

He figured to make Milestown by late afternoon of the next day. He took a sip of his drink and sighed.

Bowdry filled his thoughts. The way the slim gunman looked at Anne, it was only a matter of time before he went back to force his will on her. If his wounds had healed, and he'd left Miles, Gentry figured Bowdry would scout the cabin and wait for the best time to attack, likely when he could kill the children without having to face her husband's gun.

Gentry shook his head. With any luck, Bowdry would be the last man he'd ever again have to fire a gun at.

Before sleeping, he built the fire such that he thought it might last half the night. He'd collected enough firewood to last until daylight, and had piled it by his blankets so he could stoke the fire without getting out into the cold.

He was again on the trail by daylight. About midafternoon, Gentry came abreast of Fort Keogh. He cast a glance toward the high, wood stockade fence, wondering if his legs would get him the short two miles into Miles. He'd never been so tired, and the poor horses; he wondered how they'd made it this far. They plodded along, heads hanging, lifting one heavy shod hoof and putting it down a step ahead of the others. Come hell or high water, he would see them fed and rested before taking the trail again.

Another hour and Gentry dragged his weary horses into the warmth of Rawlings's stable. The old liveryman stood in the runway between stalls after taking care of the horses. He studied Gentry a long few minutes. "You all right, boy?" He took Gentry's elbow and led him to the cluttered room he called his office. "Sit down now. Gonna get you a drink, somethin' stronger'n coffee."

Gentry forced a tired grin. "Rawlings, I didn't know they *wuz* anything stronger'n that coffee you make."

Rawlings ignored Gentry's sarcasm and went about finding two granite cups. He poured Gentry's cup to the rim, poured his about half full, grunted, and finished filling it. "Calls for a celebration, you being safe."

Gentry looked deep into his cup full of straight whiskey. "Rawlings, I figure you're tryin' to kill me. Tired as I am, if I drink all this, I'll go to sleep sittin' right here."

"You do that, boy. You go to sleep an' I'll wake you in a couple hours so's you can git somethin' to eat. Now drink up. After you eat, I want to know all what happened to you."

Gentry drank only about half the whiskey before his eyelids felt like they had weights on them. He gave in to his fatigue and let himself sleep.

When Gentry stirred and opened his eyes, Bruns sat across the room on a bale of hay. Both Bruns and Rawlings stared at him.

Bruns lifted his cup toward him. "Awake, huh? 'Bout time. I was beginning to wonder if I needed to tell the missus I wouldn't be home tonight. You feel like sleeping in the jail tonight?"

Gentry nodded. "Marshal, if it's warm, I'll sleep in it." He stretched and yawned. "How long you let me sleep, Rawlings? I feel mite nigh rested."

Rawlings grinned. "Boy, you been sleepin' there close to seven hours. Didn't have the heart to wake you."

Gentry stood. "Them horses I brung in, Rawlings, how 'bout feedin' 'em a batch of grain? I'm gonna drink the rest of that drink you poured for me an' head for the jail. In the mornin' I gotta find Bowdry." He pinned Bruns with a hard look. "Marshal, I done made up my mind to get rid of all my troubles 'fore I head for home."

Bruns shook his head. "Bowdry ain't here, boy. He must of left about the same time you led Thompson and his bunch outta town. Don't know where he might a gone, but he's nowhere to be found. Didn't even come by the office to pick up that fancy side gun of his."

Gentry picked up the drink he'd been sipping when he went to sleep, took a swallow, and said, his voice soft, "Reckon I know where he went. I gotta head outta here in the mornin', 'fore sunup."

Bruns shook his head, his expression showing he agreed with Gentry's unspoken assumption. "Know you got it to do, boy. Hope the weather holds, without more snow."

Before Gentry and Bruns left the livery, Gentry told Rawlings he'd be down to get his horses and gear the next morning.

When Gentry stepped out of the jail the next morning, snow again fell. He squinted into the heavy curtain and figured about three or four inches an hour accumulated. Damn, even if he made good time, another two and a half feet would be on the ground by the time he got home. He hoped Mark had kept a good watch on things, and wondered at the same time if his little boy would be able to shoot a man. Fear tightened his chest. The hair at the nape of his neck seemed to stand out. He pulled his buffalo robe tight around him and walked toward the stable.

Gentry hadn't gone ten yards before he knew he couldn't take the horses with him. He could take his bay, it had several days rest, but in deep drifts even a rested horse wouldn't make good time. He decided he'd be better off to repair his snowshoes and leave the horses where they were.

He packed his gear again. This time his pack held Anne's and the children's Christmas. *His* Christmas, hopefully, lay on a lone, deserted ranch to the northeast, where if he found no more than two hundred abandoned cows, his own ranch would not only survive but prosper.

Rawlings agreed to keep the horses for however long it took Gentry to return for them. Then, before shouldering his pack, Gentry picked the best of the rifles and pistols he'd brought in, weapons as good as money could buy, and tied them to his pack. He swung the pack to his back, went by the cafe, ate breakfast, went by Deadwood Joan's and gave Sara thirty dollars for the care she'd given him, and headed for home.

The sky never lightened with the coming of day, it just opened the lid and dumped more snow on the land. Then wind in ever-increasing strength blew the flakes across the frozen landscape until they weren't flakes, but a veil of screaming, whistling ice needles. Gentry squinted to see through the white shroud, but couldn't see more than a few feet—but he had to get home. Even now, Bowdry might have beaten him there.

By midday, although midnight darkness held the land, Gentry had trouble walking. He looked for landmarks, things he might recognize; bluffs, trees, streams, anything. But the only familiar thing was the white, whistling veil, now part of him. It howled in his head, sank its icy teeth into his body, deafened him, and tore at his eyes such that they filmed over. He had seen nothing to keep him on track since soon after leaving Milestown.

He pushed one foot ahead of the other, making as much headway as his aching legs could stand. Finally, his breath coming in short gasps, he had to rest.

He stumbled, fell, climbed to his feet, and looked for shelter in which to drop his pack and sit down out of the wind.

His feet and hands searched, seeing anything was out of the question. He again stumbled and fell against a bluff or cliff of some kind. Hope pushed its way into his numbed senses. This might be the cliff along the Powder.

The veil swirled harder, tighter, then lightened for a moment, enough to allow him to see. He leaned against a low sharp shoulder of a hill. A hill he'd never seen while riding the lands around his ranch. Gentry's shoulders slumped. He was lost, hopelessly lost with no chance of finding his way until the storm let up.

From experience, Gentry knew he should stay in one place until the weather cleared enough to get his bearings.

But to do that in this weather meant death. He had no shelter, no fuel for a fire. He had to keep going until he found shelter, even if by accident.

He stumbled, slipped, and slid down an incline. The footing leveled off, and instinct told him he walked a frozen streambed. If that was true, there should be trees along its banks. That thought had no sooner entered his head than he fell over an old deadfall.

Groping down the trunk, his hands told him the tree got smaller. He reversed direction. With luck, when the tree fell, tearing itself from the earth, it had left a hole. Soon he felt a tangle of roots, some as large as his thigh. Gentry worked his way to their ends, rounded them, and for the first time in hours could see farther than the length of his arms. A great hole, almost a cave, opened in the bank of this stream he'd walked along. The earth-laden root system of the trees sheltered the cave on two sides. The roots on one side of the tree still clung to the earth that had nurtured it, while those that had torn loose almost covered the opening.

Gentry staggered to the back of the opening, dropped his pack, and sat leaning against the cold earth. He rested only a few moments before pulling his pack to him and searching for a hatchet. He had to have a fire.

Gentry collected twigs, and using his Bowie shaved the twigs into a small pile of tinder, then put other twigs in a tipi-type structure over the tinder. Next he gathered larger limbs, and using his hatchet chopped them to a length suitable for his fire. He stacked those limbs ready to hand. Luckily, within his shelter, wind was only a gentle swirl, but Gentry took no chances. He curled his body around the branch tipi to better protect the flame, struck a lucifer, and held it gently to the small pile of tinder. In but a few moments the fire licked at the larger limbs. He had a fire.

Gentry spent the next two hours gathering and chopping wood. When he had enough to last the night, he fixed supper, using his supplies sparingly, and even then wondering if he would have enough supplies and wood to last out the storm.

After eating, he sat drinking coffee, studying the howling blizzard. If he left camp, he would wander aimlessly, not knowing where he was. Bowdry could have already been to the cabin and done all the harm he intended. He might even now be using Anne to satisfy his lust. With that thought, Gentry reached for his pack, then settled back, staring at the fire. He would do no one any good by destroying himself. He had to stay here. Then if it took the rest of his life he'd find Bowdry.

He stood, put more wood on the fire, walked around it, looked out into the storm, and though he had wood enough to last the night, he picked up the hatchet and went into the storm. He was edgy, and sitting still didn't help.

Gentry worked his way down the trunk, cutting off limbs as he went, then he saw a snag about as thick as his forearm. He nodded. That limb was about the right size. He pulled on it, hoping for it to break off. It didn't budge. One end stuck into the soil under the trunk, and the end attached to the trunk proved too thick to break.

He put his hip against the tree, his leg slightly under it, and swung at the limb. On the fifth swing, the limb gave off a cracking sound. One more swing should do it. Gentry bunched his muscles and swung. The branch popped like a rifle shot and broke loose from the main trunk. The thick bole jerked, rotated, and slipped toward the ground. Gentry snatched his body sideways. He was too slow. The old cottonwood lay with all its weight on his leg—pinning him to the ground.

CHAPTER FIFTEEN

★ ★ ★

Bowdry, dragging his bleeding and crippled leg, pulled himself into the shelter of the trees lining the Powder. His horse stood patiently over him. He struggled to reach the stirrup, needing something to pull himself up with so he could climb into the saddle.

He cursed steadily, hardly stopping to breathe. He looked back through the trees toward Gentry's cabin. "Didn't think the little bastard had the guts to shoot." A tinge of admiration seeped through the pain in his voice.

He grabbed a handhold on his third try, pulled himself up, pushed the foot of his good leg into the stirrup, and climbed to the top of his horse. He urged the hammer-headed little mustang along. He had to find a place to hole up and doctor his leg. He'd gone not more than a quarter of a mile when he knew he had to stop, but he couldn't stop. His head felt light, and the ground rolled and waved in front of him. He gripped the saddle horn and hung on with all his strength. He rode like that until well after dark, by then he ceased to think, ceased to realize he still sat his horse. Only long years in the saddle and a secondary sense kept him atop the mustang. Then the cloud in his brain cleared a bit. His mustang stopped in front of a tipi. He counted three of the cone-shaped dwellings, then his eyes clouded over, and all went dark. He closed his eyes and slipped to the ground.

Bowdry stirred, trying to come out of the deep sleep. His leg hurt and felt stiff. He tried to bend his knee. It remained straight. He opened his eyes a slit and cocked his eyes downward. A bandage of skins encased his leg from hip to ankle. He looked up. A hole, with smoke drifting through it, showed directly in his sight. He shifted his look slightly to his right. A tall Indian with a scar running from front to back along the side of his head stood looking down at him. Bowdry's chest tightened. Had he come this far to get killed by a disgruntled Indian?

Then hope surged through him. If they intended to kill him, they would have done it. That idea came with the thought they wouldn't have bandaged his leg, and an Indian woman squatted by his side with a bowl of something that smelled like venison stew. He looked at the tall one with the scar.

"Where am I? How did I get here?"

"You ride in, fall off horse, we take care of you. You are in the lodge of Wambli Dopa, Two Eagles, my lodge. Who shoot you?"

Bowdry thought to lie, then changed his mind. Two Eagles would not know the Gentrys, or why the boy shot him. "A boy shot me. He lives in a cabin not far from here with his sister and mother. I rode up to ask for a place to sleep an' he shot me without any warnin'. Mean little bastard."

Two Eagles didn't answer. He only stared at Bowdry, his eyes expressionless, then he glanced at the woman by Bowdry's side. "Feed." With no more than that, he walked to the side of the tipi and sat cross-legged.

The woman held a wooden bowl and spooned food from it to Bowdry's mouth. While eating, he felt Wambli Dopa's stare boring into him. He slipped his hand to his side, groping for his handgun. Pistol, holster, and belt were gone. "What you do with my gun, Two Eagles? I ain't gonna give you no trouble. You can give it to me."

"Give gun when right time."

"Time for what? Hell, I ain't done nothin' to you. Give it back an' soon's this here weather clears I'll ride on."

Two Eagles never broke his gaze, nor did he answer. Bowdry squirmed. The damned Indian acted like he knew something. But he couldn't know why Bowdry had gone to Gentry's cabin, besides why should he care what happened to a white squaw.

He lay like that, next to the fire for another hour with no conversation, and only the dead, snakelike stare pinning him. Finally, the tall Indian stood, motioned his woman to tie Bowdry, then they went to sleep. Long after all slept, Bowdry scanned the tipi for his guns. The fire cast flickering little tongues of flame from its burned-down coals. If his guns had been close, he thought he would have seen them. All he saw was a pile of furs in one part of the lodge, and the bedding on which Wambli Dopa and his wife slept. He spent a long time that night trying to loosen his bonds, but the harder he fought them, the tighter they gripped. Daylight was a long time coming.

When the edges of the entrance flap lightened, the warrior's woman stoked the fire and fixed breakfast. She untied Bowdry and went with him outside while he took care of his physical needs. He thought to try to run, but he had no horse, no weapons, and was crippled. To top that, the woman never took her eyes off him, and she held a knife about the size of a Bowie in her right hand. He had no doubt but what she knew how to handle it. They went back inside, ate, and she again tied him hand and foot.

Although they kept him tied, they took care of his wound as if they cared what happened to him. About midmorning, two warriors, their women, and several children came into the tipi. Two of the small ones must have belonged to Two Eagles from the way they acted. They walked directly to the small pile of furs on the other side of the lodge and crawled under them.

The adults talked, and at times the conversation heated up, by Bowdry's thinking, but he had no idea what they

talked about. It was obvious much of it was about him, because every so often they would stop, stare, and point at
him. Every word they said was in a language foreign to
him. He figured the language was Lakota Sioux in that they
were in the middle of what had been Sioux territory. Soon
after they left, he found out what they talked about.

Two Eagles's wife untied him and took him outside. The
other two women waited for her there. The rest of the day
they followed him through the woods making him gather
wood. When he didn't work as hard as they seemed to think
he should, they beat him with sticks. Bowdry tried to make
them feel sorry for him by exaggerating his limp, grimacing
with pain, sitting and rubbing his leg, but his effort only
caused them to beat him harder. He vowed if he ever got
free, he'd come back and kill them all.

The morning of the third day started like most, only
snow fell in ever-increasing heaviness. By ten o'clock or
so, by Bowdry's best guess, the wind increased until a blizzard blew in on them, screaming like a Comanche war
party. Two Eagles, his wife, and son and daughter huddled
under every fur in the tipi. When they had all the furs they
needed, they tossed Bowdry a couple.

Despite the furs, he shivered beneath them, and his
wounded leg felt hot to his touch.

Gentry tried to pull his leg from under the heavy tree. It
wouldn't budge. He lay there, panting, staring at his leg. It
was numb. If the huge bole had crushed the leg, bone and
all, he would die out here—would anyway if he couldn't
get free. The temperature felt well below zero, along with
the blowing snow. He frantically chopped at the part of the
tree he could reach, then he lay back, took a deep breath,
and tried to relax.

Don't panic, Gentry. You've been in tighter places than
this. Think, boy. How you gonna get outta this? Finally, he
swallowed and found that he could do so without choking
on the brassy taste under his tongue. He studied the ground,

his leg, and the tree. After a while he squirmed around to see how far he could reach with his right hand, then he tried his left. He had better position using his left—but swinging a hatchet that close to his leg with his left hand would be stupid. If he hit his leg with the sharp blade he'd lay here and bleed to death. But if he didn't try he'd freeze to death. He figured he was damned if he did, and damned if he didn't. He shifted the hatchet to his right hand.

He decided chopping at the frozen ground would make more progress. And he wouldn't have to be as accurate with the blade. He studied his target a few moments longer, then took his first swing. The blade bit into the ground a good four inches from his thigh. Gentry shook his head. That wouldn't do. He had to cut into the earth much closer, then try to pull the icy chunks from under him.

He gauged where he wanted the hatchet to hit next and hesitantly swung his arm. He hit where he wanted, but his swing was too tentative, the blade bit less than an inch into the hard turf.

He grunted, tried to stay calm. If he let his nerves take hold, he'd never hit where he wanted. He sat there a moment, took a deep breath, and swung hard. The hatchet bit into the ground about three inches from his thigh. He studied the cut he'd made and decided to chop about that same distance down the length of his leg, then using his Bowie like an ice pick, he'd try to break the hard ground into chunks and pull them out.

At the end of about a half hour, a smooth trench ran the length of his trapped limb. Another few minutes of looking at the problem, he tried slicing at the bottom of the trench and picking chunks out with his hands. It worked well, but when he'd taken out all he could reach from his right side, his leg still was pinned tight to the ground.

Well, he thought, a man does what he's gotta do. He shifted the hatchet to his left hand and went to work on that side. He made three swipes with the hatchet, hitting exactly where he wanted, and began to feel better about his chances—but his wrist and shoulder ached from the strain. On his fourth swing the handle turned in his grip and sliced neatly through his buffalo robe and bit into his leg.

Gentry stared at the slice, feeling stupid he'd not taken a few moments to rest. The tendons at the back of his neck tightened, and fear again took hold of him. He shivered with cold and fear. Another deep breath and he calmed. He'd heard of a man who, pinned by a horse, had cut his own leg off—and survived. If it came to that he could do it too. But he put that option at the bottom of his list.

He hesitated, then reached for his robe to pull it back and see how much damage he'd done. The cut, deep and about the width of the hatchet blade, bled steadily, but not in spurts. Good. He'd not hit an artery, and he didn't think he'd hit the bone. He pulled off his neckerchief and tied it around the wound.

He rested awhile, picked up the hatchet, and went back to work, careful now to rest when he thought he might get careless, and he made sure he stopped before breaking into a sweat. Another hour and he pulled the last piece of icy turf from under his leg. From his thigh to his feet felt dead, but the pressure left his leg when it sank into the undercut.

Gentry placed his hands against the ground and pulled. He moved an inch or two. Hope swelled his chest. No matter how badly he was hurt, his family still had a whole man coming home to them.

Slowly, inch by inch, Gentry pulled himself free, then crawled along the bole of the big cottonwood and into his camp.

Before doing anything he piled wood on the fire, then sat close enough to the flames to chance burning himself and dressed the gash in his thigh. After taking care of himself, he melted snow in his pot and made coffee.

Every so often, he glanced over the rim of his cup at his feet, waiting, hoping for feeling to come back into them. After two cups of coffee, and what seemed forever, his toes tingled, just a bit, but enough to bring a churning to his gut, a tightness to his chest, and a smile to his lips. Another few minutes of pain that stabbed all the way to his stomach and he had feeling to his groin. It was not until then did he suck it up and brave inspecting the entire length of his leg. It was swollen, blue, scraped, but when Gentry ran his fingers along the bones and didn't feel a knot under the skin, he thought he'd lucked out. Nothing appeared broken. Not until then did he feel hunger gnawing at his insides. He fixed supper, ate, and crawled between his blankets.

When he awoke, the storm still raged, and muscles he'd never given much thought felt as though they'd pull themselves apart with his every move. His forearms, shoulders, wrists, and most of all his leg screamed at him for mercy. His stomach muscles, every ropy one of them, knotted and doubled him over. But he milked happiness from every painful spasm. He was here, alive, and going back to his family.

Two more days the wind and ice particles tore at him, then on the third day he awakened to an eerie calm. He pulled his covers down, then eased the parka back off his head. Silence.

The incessant whine and whistling of the past few days, and now no noise. Gentry dug his little finger into his ear. Still quiet. He pulled his Bowie and banged it against his coffeepot. The clanging of metal on metal brought a smile to his lips. He hadn't gone deaf—the wind had stopped.

He rolled over and, trying to stifle the groans, stood, dragging his almost useless leg up with him. After stoking the fire and fixing breakfast, Gentry packed snow into his coffeepot and put it on to heat.

All that day and into the night, Gentry put hot packs on the blackest bruises. He repeated this the next day. By late afternoon of that day he was using his leg even though the pain was excruciating. He deliberately put weight on it, and despite the weakness in it, it held without buckling. Exercise, exercise, and more hot packs.

He had to chance leaving camp. He needed to find where

he was, see if he could find a landmark he remembered. He stayed within two or three hundred yards of the place he'd spent the last few days. Not a tree, hill, stream, nothing looked familiar.

Feeling the bitter taste of defeat, he limped back to camp. Again sitting by his fire, he tried to figure what day it was. He looked at the gifts for his family and tried desperately to swallow the lump in his throat. He was certain Christmas had come and gone. When he crawled into his blankets that night, for the first time in his life he felt he had failed.

When he awoke, he fixed breakfast, and while drinking coffee decided to head straight east thinking he'd find the Powder, and once on the river he would walk upstream. If he didn't come on his cabin in a half day, he'd check the other direction.

Gentry tipped his cup to take the last swallow, thinking to pour another cup, when over the rim he looked straight into the eyes of a tall warrior. And his weapons were on the other side of the fire with no chance of his reaching them. He'd not heard of Indian trouble in the recent past, but felt naked sitting there without a weapon of any kind at hand. He'd try to bluff it out.

He nodded. "Howdy," he said and motioned toward the fire. "Want coffee?"

The man walked around the snowbank, and with him came two others, although not as tall. Gentry motioned toward the fire. "I'll make more, ain't enough there for the three of you." He stood and hobbled to the fire, poured the only cup he had with him full, and handed it to the tall warrior. He again packed the pot with snow and placed it by the fire.

"What you do make camp here in storm? Why you not go your lodge?" the leader of the trio asked.

The Indian speaking English didn't surprise Gentry, but his asking why Gentry hadn't gone home did. "I got lost. Couldn't see anything so I holed up. Why're you out here?"

A slight smile broke the hard planes of the leader's face.

"We do same, hole up." The coffee cup came back to him. He drank the last swallow and handed the cup to Gentry. "You got woman, little warrior, and girl." The words were not a question, he'd said it as if he knew of Gentry's family.

Gentry nodded. "Yeah, them folks you just talked 'bout sound like my family." His chest felt like a vise gripped it. He was afraid to ask the next question. "How you know 'bout them?"

The tall one brushed his buffalo hood back from his head. A long scar trailed along the side of his head. The scar looked new to Gentry, and while he stared at the scar, the warrior made a sweeping gesture with his right hand. "We watch from woods."

"They—they all right?" Gentry's voice broke.

The leader nodded, then pointed to his chest. "Me, Wambli Dopa, Two Eagles." He pointed to the others. They Two Dogs an' Many Horses."

Gentry told them his name and looked toward the coffeepot.

In the next couple of hours, Gentry's visitors drank four pots of coffee from the single cup they passed from one to the other. He wondered where he'd gotten the idea Indians didn't like coffee, although he had to admit they drank more sugar than coffee. They depleted his supply of the sweetening quickly.

They didn't seem intent on harming him, so he decided to push his luck. "You show me the way to my lodge?"

Two Eagles, with a flat black stare, looked into Gentry's eyes. "No. We go my lodge."

CHAPTER SIXTEEN

★ ★ ★

Gentry's heart fell to his knees. They had been toying with him. They sat there with a royal flush to his pair of deuces, and were playing with him like a kid with a crippled butterfly.

He glanced at his gunbelt across the fire. Many Horses sat cross-legged only a couple of feet from his weapons. There was no way he could reach them before they killed him.

Wambli Dopa stood. "We go now." He looked toward Many Horses and motioned to Gentry's guns. "You bring."

Gentry's wish for any chance to get to his weapons died. He had Worley's pistol wrapped in his pack and his rifle strapped to the back of it. Neither gun would do him any good.

Gentry dragged himself to his feet, shouldered his pack, doused the fire with a few handfuls of snow, and followed the three from camp.

They walked not more than a quarter of a mile when Gentry smelled wood smoke and the aroma of cooking meat. Two Eagles looked at Gentry. "We hole up 'bout same place, uh?"

They topped another slight rise, circled a clump of cedar, and came on three tipis. "My lodge." Two Eagles nodded toward the center tipi. "You come." He held out his hand toward Many Horses. "Give guns." He pointed to his chest.

They ducked through the flap, and after the bright white

world outside, Gentry waited a few minutes for his eyes to adjust to the darkness. His first glance around the circular structure saw little, then on second look he saw two piles of furs and a lump that appeared to be a man. He kept his eyes on the lump. It was a man, tied hand and foot, and he looked familiar.

Gentry studied him a moment. His vision cleared, and he looked into Bowdry's triumphant gaze. "Got you too, huh? By damn, they's some good about everything."

Before Gentry could answer, Two Eagles's wife left the tipi in response to a few words of Lakota from her husband. In a few moments she was back, leading another woman.

They went to Bowdry, caught him under each arm, and dragged him, none too gently, from the tipi. Gentry wondered what was in store for Bowdry, as well as himself.

Wambli Dopa motioned to a pile of robes. "Sit."

Gentry went to the robes, shrugged out of his pack harness, and sat. They tied Bowdry; he wondered when they would tie him. Again he thought how close Worley's weapons were, yet impossible to reach. Too, he didn't want trouble if they didn't bring it to him. And so far, he still pondered his status in this Indian camp. He figured he'd not stand much chance against three warriors, and he was sure their wives could be just as savage as any man if need be. He sat there until the light faded around the edges of the flap. Two Eagles went about his business, but was never but a few feet from a weapon. He had tucked Gentry's handgun and rifle under a pile of something or other across the tent.

Wambli Dopa's wife came back without Bowdry, and she brought with her a large chunk of roasted venison. She waited for Gentry and her husband to eat before she took a piece of the meat.

Two Eagles wiped greasy fingers on his trousers and looked at Gentry. "Make coffee. We sit here, drink an' go sleep."

Gentry went still inside. Did this mean he wasn't a prisoner? If he ran when he got outside the tipi, would he stand a chance? Running would be a dumb move. With his leg in the shape it was, he'd not get outside their camp. He picked up his coffeepot, threw grounds in it, and went outside for snow.

They sat at the small fire in the middle of the lodge and drank their coffee before Two Eagles motioned it was time for sleep. His two children came in about that time and crawled into their robes. Gentry still hadn't figured out where he stood in their plans—but he felt a lot better about the possibilities. They made no move to tie him.

Wambli Dopa showed Gentry where to bed down, tossed him a couple of buffalo hides, and he and his wife went to bed. Gentry heard Two Eagles call his wife Little Fawn, and in Gentry's opinion, she was just that pretty.

The place the tall warrior spiked out for Gentry to sleep was across the tipi from where he'd dropped his pack. Gentry gazed at the spot long after crawling into the robes. Those guns might as well be in Milestown for all the good they did him.

When Gentry awoke, he judged it to be about an hour before sunup, he crawled out of his robes. All the Indian family still slept as far as he could tell. He studied the places where they slept a few moments, but couldn't tell whether the adults were asleep or not. He decided to push his luck a little more. He went outside the tent to relieve himself, and when he came back, he brought an armload of firewood, placed it as quietly as he could beside the smoldering embers, and stoked the fire.

"You do good, Gen-tree." A few moments of silence, then Two Eagles continued, "Why you no run?"

Gentry looked over his shoulder at the man. "Didn't figure it was no need to. Didn't have my pack, or weapons, an' 'sides, you didn't tie me 'fore you went to sleep. If you'd figured me as a prisoner you would have." He picked up the coffeepot to go after water. "Reckon when you're ready you'll take me to my woman an' kids."

Two Eagles squatted, then sat cross-legged by the fire now beginning to blaze warmly. "I take you when time right. First you fight Bow-dree. He try hurt your woman. Little warrior shoot him. He run. Two Dogs, Many Horses, an' me watch from trees."

Gentry turned his eyes toward the fire. His chest swelled with pride, and the lump in his throat wouldn't go away despite a couple of fast swallows. His small son had become a man, not because he'd shot a man, but because he'd shouldered responsibility and done what had to be done. He stood and left the tipi to get coffee water. His leg felt better, looser. In a couple of days it should be good as new.

After eating some of the same stew they'd had for supper, Little Fawn motioned Gentry to come with her. She and the other two women took him and Bowdry to hunt for wood. Bowdry's legs were tied with a leather thong such that he could take only short steps. No chance for him to run shackled as he was. Gentry's legs and arms were free.

While gathering wood, the women again beat Bowdry with sticks when he didn't work hard. Gentry didn't get hit once. He smiled, thinking rather than kill Bowdry it would be fitting to leave him for the women to use as a slave.

The wood-gathering chore lasted into the afternoon. Bowdry tried twice to say something to Gentry, but the women cut him off. Gentry didn't care what Bowdry wanted to say. Anger smoldered in his gut. Every minute they were in the woods, he wanted to put his hands around the swaggering gunman's neck and squeeze until the last vestige of life left his stinking body. But Wambli Dopa had promised they would fight. He could wait.

When the Sioux thought of fighting, they thought only of guns, knives, or pogamoggans. Gentry smiled. He'd take either of the three, but knives would satisfy him better, not that he figured knives would be more to his advantage, but his Bowie would give him a chance to put more pain into Bowdry's gut. And he didn't want a gun in Bowdry's hand. He might try to kill the Sioux.

Late that evening, Little Fawn again fed them, and after supper, Two Eagles took Gentry's weapons across the tipi and lay them at the side of his pack. When he stood the rifle up so as to keep it clean, he glanced at Gentry and smiled.

Gentry wondered why the warrior trusted him and showed a distinct dislike for Bowdry. He thought on the question awhile and was still at a loss. He shrugged, satisfied that things were as they were.

That night, lying in his robes, he massaged the bruised muscles of his leg until his fingers grew tired. Gentry wanted his leg well enough to be at his best, well enough to cut and slice at his leisure, well enough to kill Bowdry slowly. Before he finished, the slim gunman was going to wish many times he'd never heard of the Gentry family.

He counted on his fingers the days since leaving home, and tried to tie each to an event to make sure. When finished, he knew he'd missed Christmas.

Anne awoke to a cold but calm day. She lay in her blankets, reluctant to get out of the warmth and start another day of futile watching for Case to appear at the bend in the trail. She sighed, took a deep breath, and pushed the covers down. Today was the day before Christmas. She couldn't deprive the children this way. But—something had happened to her husband. He would be home unless something bad had him in its clutches. A shiver not caused by the cold gripped her. She walked to the stove and shoved wood into the embers.

As soon as the stove door rattled, Mark climbed from the attic. "Ma, this the day 'fore Christmas?"

Anne tousled his hair. "Yes, it is, and we're going to celebrate tomorrow just as though your father were here with us. After breakfast, we'll search for a tree and decorate it with all sorts of things. You and Brandy can pick the tree."

Mark stood by her side at the stove, opened the damper a bit to give the fire better draft, then looked at his mother. "Ma, reckon we better let Brandy pick the tree. She's missin' Pa much as we are, but she's tryin' hard not to show it. Figure if we let her pick it, she'll get her mind off of missin' him so much."

Anne swallowed real hard, and blinked to rid herself of tears she wanted to keep from her little boy. She smiled. "That's a good idea, Mark. Together, you and I will handle whatever comes, but Brandy is, well, she's a little young to have to face the hard things in life."

Mark put his arm around his mother's waist. "Ma, you just stop worryin'. The weather's been 'bout as bad as we've ever seen, an' Pa might've had a hard time makin' it. Too, Ma, you gotta remember Pa sent word he had to see that rancher over west of Miles. He might not make it home by tonight, or even tomorrow night, but, Ma, he's gonna be home again." He smiled up into her eyes. "You just gotta stop an' think of the good side of this. We'll have 'nother Christmas when he gets home."

Anne held the tears as long as her aching heart would let her. Abruptly she pulled Mark to her breasts and let the floodgates open. She sobbed, holding her little man close while he stroked her back and crooned meaningless words trying to calm her. When she'd cried herself dry, she pushed Mark from her, dried her eyes, and said, "Shoo now. You're right. We've just got to believe we'll see him soon, and when we do, I'll fix us a nice dinner like I'm going to fix tomorrow. Now, after breakfast, we'll get Brandy and go to the cedar brakes."

Anne fried grits, bacon, and she baked buttermilk biscuits, the kind both children liked, and when sure her small brood was fortified against the cold, they headed out. She carried the ax, while Mark held the Greener across the crook of his elbow. For the first time in days, Anne thought Brandy looked happy. She flitted from tree to tree, and with each tree she seemed to think it grew especially for this time of year.

Anne showed her how to walk around the cedar and inspect each side for symmetry. Mark stood to the side, now holding the shotgun such that he could get it in action if need be.

Finally, Anne approved one of the trees Brandy liked. Mark stepped toward his mother to take the ax and cut the tree when he froze. He held his finger to his lips for quiet. None of them made a sound. Mark motioned his mother and sister to squat, then he turned and headed down the hill toward the Powder. He'd checked the loads in the Greener before leaving the cabin, each hammer rested on a full load.

His steps across the frozen ground made no more noise than a falling snowflake. Scrub tree to scrub tree to brush clump, at each he stopped and searched ahead before moving to new cover. He advanced down the hill to the top of the steep riverbank, then went to his belly and squirmed to a position where he could look on the trees and the ground under them. He grinned. "Thought so," he muttered, and slowly eased the shotgun into firing position. He wanted to make certain of his first shot, then he'd gamble with his second. He'd have no more time than that.

He picked out the largest gobbler in the flock of eight turkey, pulled the hammer back, sighted at the head of the one he wanted, and squeezed the trigger.

With the shot, the flock took off. Pa told him many times turkey were fast, but he wouldn't have believed it unless he'd seen it. He swung the Greener, sighted on another bird, and pulled the trigger. Less than two seconds passed since his first shot. Now, two large birds lay on the ground, the first one, a gobbler, lay by the river's edge, and the second, a hen, lay in midstream. Mark broke the breech, reloaded, and slipped down the bank to retrieve his kill.

When he picked them up, he guessed the gobbler would weigh in at close to twenty-five pounds, the hen would go close to fifteen. Walking back to his mother and sister, he felt like his chest would pop the buttons off his coat. He had their Christmas dinner, with plenty for other meals.

Before he reached them, Anne ran toward him. "Lord, boy, you scared me to death . . ." She stopped in midstride and stared at the birds. "Why, heavenly day, son, why didn't you tell me why you wanted us quiet? I thought we were in terrible danger."

"Ma, if I'd a taken time to talk, we wouldn't of had these here turkey. Pa told me a long time ago, if a man's gonna get a turkey, he's got to be quiet an' fast. I done both. Now we got us a right nice Christmas dinner."

Anne placed a hand on each hip. "Well, I'll swear, I'll be a week getting over the scare you gave me." Her face softened. "You did good, Mark. Your father would be as proud of you as I am. Now, let's cut our Christmas tree and get back to the house out of this cold."

When they came in sight of the cabin, Anne noticed that both children did as she did. They each had their eyes focused on the trail leading from Miles.

Before crawling from his robes the next morning, Gentry again thought of Anne and the children. They would wear the cabin's thick, rough, puncheon floor down to the outside bark walking to the window to check the trail for a sight of him. It caused him to hurt deep inside, caused his stomach to knot, and gave him sharp pain that he brought this kind of hurt onto them. But think as he would, he could come up with no alternative. He had to get rid of Bowdry, or he'd spend the rest of his life peering at trees, ravines, anywhere the gunman might hide for a shot at him—or his family.

Gentry pushed the blankets down and headed for the tent flap, picking up the coffeepot on the way. If they didn't get the fight over and done with, he would run out of coffee. He'd always heard Indians disliked coffee, thought it a bitter drink, but Two Eagles must not have listened when that opinion was passed around.

When he pushed through the flap, braced to face the bone-cracking cold, warmth engulfed him; water ran from under the snow blanket; the sun beat down like a late spring day. Winter wasn't over, but this break in the frigid, man-killing weather brought a smile to Gentry's lips.

Standing at the edge of the riverbank, Gentry frowned. Snowmelt with nowhere to go poured into the river, covering the thick ice, and the Powder was rising—fast. Gentry had seen this before. The melting heavy snow blanket would fill every stream and river; it would cover pasture, drowning cows and people alike. A cow, too dumb to seek high ground, would stand in one spot and let water rise around it until the flood waters engulfed the critter.

When Gentry got back to the tipi, Little Fawn had breakfast ready. He and Wambli Dopa sat chewing their food. Gentry ate without tasting a single bite. "Gen-tree, you think of something. Tell me," Two Eagles broke into his thoughts.

Gentry swallowed and nodded. "How long you had your lodge here?"

The tall warrior shrugged. "Not know. Maybe seven moons, not more."

Gentry brought his gaze level with the Sioux's. "We got a big snowmelt going on out there. Figger water's soon gonna cover this here ground you got your lodge settin' on. Better have your women move 'em to high ground. We better all help."

Without questions, Wambli Dopa stood and spoke rapidly to Little Fawn in Lakota. His words came out faster than Gentry could follow, but there was no doubt what he said.

The Sioux's wife almost running left the tipi. In a moment she returned and set about making bundles of everything in the lodge. Gentry thought she had gone to warn the others. He and Two Eagles helped, though their tasks were usually considered women's work. Gentry finished tying his extra rifle to his pack, cocked his head, and listened. A shrill cry came from the direction of the river, then it came again.

He bolted from the tipi, headed for the Powder, now a

roaring, frothy stretch of white water. He looked over his shoulder. Two Eagles followed close on his heels. "Get a rope, anything to drag me back to the bank," he yelled, not slowing his pace.

At the top of the bank, he skidded to a stop, his eyes searching the roiling, muddy surface.

Another scream and he looked toward the sound. He scanned the waters again, then looked farther downstream. A bobbing little head, with black hair streaming ahead of it, showed, disappeared from sight, and again surfaced. He sprinted downstream to get ahead of the child.

CHAPTER SEVENTEEN

★ ★ ★

While running, Gentry gauged the speed the river carried the child. He stripped his doeskin shirt off while keeping an eye on the bobbing head. When far enough ahead of the small bundle of humanity, tossed at will by the angry waters, he planted his foot and went down the bank.

The icy waters closed over him, burning his skin as though a river of fire bathed him. He surfaced, tried to draw breath into his lungs, sucked, gasped, coughed. His breath froze in his mouth. Abruptly his throat opened to carry a chestful of air to his lungs. He frantically searched the surface for sight of the little one.

He sighted what he thought was a head of black hair and struck out for the middle of the stream. His brain talked to him. "Too fast, Gentry. Water's carryin' you fast as it's pushin' the kid downstream. Get to the middle. Do somethin' to slow you down."

He took long strokes. Kicked his legs until they felt like they'd fall off, then he tried to turn upstream. He managed to face the direction he wanted, but still the water took him along without slowing down. An old snag of a tree pushed to the surface almost in the path he was being swept along. It wasn't moving as fast as him. Must be dragging the bottom, he thought.

Gentry grabbed a large limb that rolled to the surface. It continued to roll and carried him under. He held his breath until he thought his lungs would burst—then he broke the surface. He sucked air like there was no such thing as getting enough. The child was only a couple of yards upstream of him now.

He grasped the limb with one hand hard enough he thought his forearm muscles would break, and stretching his left arm, he swept it across the surface of the angry waters in front of the little warrior. He could now see the little one was Two Eagles's son, Eagle Feather.

Terror shone from the little boy's eyes, but Gentry could not detect panic. He swept his arm in front of Eagle Feather again. The boy grasped his wrist and clung to it with strength Gentry thought unbelievable in one so young.

The tree still rotated in the frigid water. Gentry released his grip on the limb before it carried him and the little boy under. He looked into the boy's eyes. "Hold neck— hold neck," he yelled above the roaring waters.

Eagle Feather nodded and pulled himself inch by inch up Gentry's arm until he could put both arms around Gentry's neck.

Gentry stroked toward the shore, but fighting the water and the cold took its toll. He weakened—fast, but struggled toward solid ground. He used his strength to keep the boy's head above the frothing, churning surface. Every time his head pushed above the surface he searched the bank for Two Eagles, then he saw him.

The tall warrior stood at the water's edge swinging a lariat of some kind around his head, then the serpentine length uncoiled toward Gentry. He grabbed at it and missed. To Gentry, Two Eagles moved as though he had a week to pull the lariat back to him and throw it again. Finally, he swung the rope around his head again and tossed it. Again, Gentry's hand missed grabbing the rope. This time the slick length of rope brushed his hand. Two more times he missed.

Gentry felt like every muscle was weighted with lead. He had to fight to draw small gulps of air into him, and he ceased to care whether he made it or not. When he thought he'd done his best, given it his all, and was about to quit trying, he looked down his body into the eyes of Eagle Feather, and saw pure raw, naked trust. Gentry could not give up. He again scanned the bank.

Two Eagles ran down the riverbank, keeping abreast of Gentry and his son. He swung the rope again and let it fly toward Gentry. A fast stab of his arm and Gentry felt the rope sliding down the length of his forearm. He moved his arm in a circle and felt the lariat wrap itself around until his open, groping fingers grasped it. He tried to yell that he had ahold, but his lungs had too little air to push the words from his mouth. But Two Eagles must have seen. He ran up the bank, the taut length of rope trailing across his shoulder behind him. When he topped the steep slope he turned and began reeling Gentry and his precious cargo to the river's edge.

Gentry held to the rope, feeling the muddy bank slide under him until he gauged he was far enough from the water's edge to turn loose and look at the little boy.

Two Dogs and Many Horses ran to them. Many Horses took Eagle Feather in his arms and scrambled up the bank. Two Dogs tried to pick Gentry up, grunted a couple of times, then grabbed him under his arms and dragged him to the top. There, Little Fawn and the other two women covered him and the boy with buffalo robes. Gentry, lying on his back, twisted to look at Two Eagles's son who lay only a foot or two from his side. The young'un had not uttered a cry or said a word, but he looked at Gentry with worship in his eyes. Gentry lay back and closed his eyes, satisfied for now to wallow in the warmth beginning to penetrate his blue body.

A couple of hours later the women had moved the lodges to higher ground, and Gentry and Eagle Feather lay beside the fire in Two Eagles's tipi. Little Fawn spooned hot broth into each.

Wambli Dopa sat on the other side of the fire. When his wife finished feeding them, he looked at Gentry. "Gen-tree,

Bow-dree try to get loose while we go to river. We find rawhide almost rubbed in two when we get back. We tie him better now." He packed and lit his everyday pipe. His ceremonial pipe came out of its doeskin bag only for religious occasions. Gentry felt the tall warrior's eyes studying him for several minutes while he puffed on his pipe, then he said, "Gen-tree, no need you fight Bow-dree. I kill him for you."

Gentry smiled. Two Eagles was trying to pay him for saving his son, but he couldn't let him do that. Bowdry was *his* problem, and when he thought of the way the man had looked at Anne, and had come back to the cabin to try to kill his family, the only thing that would let him live with himself was for him to fight Bowdry. He shook his head. "Two Eagles, Bowdry's mine. I'll take care of him."

"How you want to fight him, Gen-tree, guns, knives, pogamoggans?"

Gentry shook his head. "Great Warrior, I'm gonna give 'im his choice. He knows he cain't beat me with handguns, so I figger he'll try me with knives or pogamoggans—maybe both." He talked with Two Eagles another few minutes, but after what he'd been through today he couldn't keep his eyes open even out of courtesy. His lids closed a couple of times, then he couldn't open them again, and felt Little Fawn tuck the robe tight around him.

The next morning he awakened to the sounds of Little Fawn fixing the morning meal. He stretched and found muscles he didn't know he had. Every inch of him cried out in pain. He looked toward the mound of robes where Eagle Feather slept and saw the robes empty. He looked questioningly at Little Fawn. She smiled. "He eat an' go play. Him all right."

Gentry returned her smile, remembering that kids bounce back from almost anything better than grown folks. He crawled from his robes, went outside to the woods, then went back to the lodge and ate. After eating, he packed his pipe and settled in to enjoy his smoke when Two Dogs's wife ran into the tipi, gulping great gasps of air.

She talked so fast Gentry couldn't catch many words, but the one he caught several times was "Bowdry." He knew before anyone said anything to him that Bowdry had escaped. He went to his pack, strapped on his Colt, checked the action on his Winchester, made sure the magazine was full, then looked at Two Eagles. "Ain't gonna kill 'im if I can help it. Gonna bring 'im back here to fight in front of your tipi." Two Eagles reached for his bow, and Gentry shook his head. "Stay here. I want to do this alone." The Sioux stared at Gentry a long moment, nodded, and stepped toward the flap. "See how he get loose."

Gentry followed him to Two Dogs's lodge. There they found the rawhide thongs that bound Bowdry a couple of feet from the flap. They were dripping wet. Gentry studied the leather strips a moment and looked into Two Eagles's eyes. "Sometime during the night he crawled outside an' soaked them lashings with snowmelt, they . . ."

Two Eagles cut in, "They stretch, he pull hands out, untie feet, an' go like the deer."

Still looking at the thongs, Gentry asked, "Two Dogs have any guns?"

The tall Sioux nodded. "He have good gun, rifle—but not many bullets."

"Better see if Bowdry took it."

Two Eagles ducked through the flap and almost immediately returned. "He take gun."

Unconsciously, Gentry touched his handgun, his knife, and grasped his rifle by the stock and barrel. "He's got a hurt leg, Great Warrior. I'll catch 'im an' bring 'im back." He nodded, looked at the deep tracks in the soggy ground, and followed them from the campsite.

The footprints headed upstream, staying close to the Powder. Gentry's stomach churned. He figured his cabin lay in that direction, how far, he had no idea, but he had to catch the gunman before he could mount another attack against his family.

Gentry thought he'd left the small Sioux encampment behind maybe a half mile when he squatted beside one of Bowdry's tracks. He'd been hurrying, forgetting Bowdry had a weapon that could reach out a long way. Without his usual caution, he would play into the slim gunman's hands, and lying dead alongside the Powder would not do Anne or the children any good.

With daylight full upon him, the gunman probably would slow his pace, become more careful, knowing he would be pursued. But too he probably would stay clear of the tree line along the river in order to make better time and to see his back trail. Gentry nodded, knowing how how he'd play his hand.

He worked his way into the trees, looking for the tallest among them. A huge old cottonwood came in his sight. He headed for it, then standing at its base he searched ahead for any sign of Bowdry. Finally, satisfied he had this part of the riverbank to himself, Gentry slung his rifle and, groping for handholds, climbed the tree. He stopped halfway up it to catch his breath and to see if he had a good view ahead. He still had other trees in his line of sight. He climbed higher.

Finally, with stopping every few feet, he had the height to see far ahead. Not over a quarter of a mile in front of him, and only a few feet from the trees, Bowdry slogged through ankle-deep mud. Gentry thought to take a shot at him, knowing he could hit his target from that range, but decided against it. He might kill him, and he had other things in store for Mr. Bowdry.

Every ten or fifteen steps the gunman looked over his shoulder, but he never looked up. Then, as though spooked by something, he went into the trees. Gentry grunted. Even though Bowdry couldn't travel fast now, neither could he.

Bowdry's tracks made no difference. They were both

under the cover of the riverbank, and the tall cottonwoods there would shelter each.

Careful to place each step, avoiding limbs or twigs that could crack with a distance-carrying sound, Gentry worked his way toward the spot he'd last seen the slim Texan. He used every tree trunk for cover and worked his way closer to the gunman. With every step he took, Gentry's muscles tightened against the shock of a bullet from the stolen rifle.

He slipped quietly to the bole of another large tree, peered around it, and jerked his head back. Bowdry, looking to his back trail, squatted behind an old deadfall, a tree that had lain there a long time, judging by the rotted state of the trunk. Gentry thought to kill him then, but shook his head. A shot would be too quick, too merciful. He knew what he did made him a fool, but he had to know the man looked at death before it claimed him.

Now, he knew where Bowdry was, he could wait for him to make a wrong move. From the gunman's actions, he seemed unsure he was being followed, but some inner sense urged him to caution. Gentry stood behind the cottonwood waiting for some sound to indicate Bowdry moved on. Then he almost missed it, but the sucking of a boot pulled from mud told Gentry he had outwaited his prey. He waited another few moments before rounding the tree.

Bowdry, his back to Gentry, worked through the tangled undergrowth, heading upstream. Gentry followed. Every time the Texas gunman twisted to look back, Gentry hugged the base of another tree.

The cat and mouse game continued through the long day. Shadows lengthened. Night would fall soon, and Bowdry had become careless, apparently thinking he was free of pursuit. Gentry, throughout his stalking the man, had seen no indication Bowdry suspected his enemies were close.

Another half hour and shadows among the trees cut sight to only a short distance. Gentry stayed as close as he dared, hoping Bowdry would stop for the night, trailing any animal in the dark was not to his liking.

Then, when Gentry figured the gunman would travel all night, the slim Texan stopped, spread twigs in a circle around where he stood, and made camp. Gentry had used that trick many times to help create the chance if anyone followed, they would make enough noise to alert him. The only problem with Bowdry's thinking was that he'd spread the twigs too close to where he intended to bed down. The ex-Ranger smiled.

Bowdry gathered twigs, broke small fallen limbs, and stacked them with the obvious intent to build a fire. Every time the gunman broke a limb, Gentry edged closer to his camp, until finally he hunkered less than twenty-five feet from where Bowdry knelt over the conical-piled twigs.

The fire surprised Gentry, and was a streak of luck he'd not counted on. Bowdry must think he'd risk a fire because either no one followed or he was far enough ahead and his pursuers had made camp also.

Bowdry had taken time to steal the gun, but no supplies. He would have a hungry camp, one without even a cup of coffee to warm him, but Gentry had nothing either. He had made camp many times with nothing to put close to the fire. He'd eat when he got back to Two Eagle's tipi.

Gentry stayed in his spot until Bowdry lay down, clutching the Sioux's rifle close. Gentry thought to wait until the gunman slept, then discarded the idea. He would not take the chance of having to walk into the camp. He waited until Bowdry settled down, then, keeping his voice low and calm so as to not startle the man, said, "Don't move a muscle, Bowdry. You even twitch an' I'll blow you to hell."

Bowdry did as he was told. "Now, loosen yore fingers from around that there rifle. You ain't got a chance of gettin' me, so do like I say."

Bowdry's fingers straightened, but his thumbs stayed hooked around the barrel and the stock. Without thinking, Gentry shouldered his rifle and fired. The rifle flew from the gunman's hands and landed close to the fire's edge.

Bowdry turned wide, scared eyes toward Gentry, then glanced at his hands and back to Gentry.

"Yeah, yore hands're still there. I always hit what I shoot at—or ain't nobody told you that yet? Shoulda put that slug through yore miserable heart, but I'm savin' you for somethin' better; better as far as I'm concerned, that is. Now, shuck that sheepskin, lie down, turn over, and lay on yore stomach. Cross your hands behind your back and lay still. This time you damned sure better not move nothin', or I'll start out by breakin' your legs at the knees—one leg at a time."

Bowdry took his sheepskin off, flopped to his stomach, and clasped his hands behind his back. Gentry edged closer to him, circled, put his toe under the ruined rifle, and nudged it into the weak flames.

He squatted next to the slim Texan, pulled his Bowie, and ran it up Bowdry's back, slitting his shirt from tail to collar, flipped Bowdry onto his back, and stripped his shirt off, then kicked him to his back again.

He split the shirt into strips, tied the gunman with them, and then stoked the fire. He didn't realize until he sat down how bone-weary tired he was. Afraid to sit for long, he rested only a moment, then stood.

He thought to head out in the darkness for the Sioux encampment and discarded the thought. He didn't want to chance walking the dark muddy distance for fear of stumbling and letting Bowdry maybe kick him senseless. He decided to stay by the fire until first light, then he would head back.

He looked at Bowdry. "I ain't gonna sleep tonight, an' neither are you. You gonna be just as tired as me on the way back. You close your eyes an' I'm gonna fix'em where you cain't close 'em—I'll cut yore lids off so you won't never again be able to shut out the light or nothin' else. Now with that on yore mind, see how much sleep you get."

The thought came to him that he hadn't searched Bowdry for other weapons. He took care of that task as soon as the thought hit him, then certain the gunman had nothing but his hands to fight with, he faded back into the brush a ways and sat. His gaze flicked to the rifle he'd kicked into the fire and saw the breech solidly in the flames. Shame to waste such a fine weapon, but it had to be done.

Bowdry lay there, and every so often stretched his eyelids wide trying to stay awake. Gentry had thrown the fear of God into him, and anything short of passing out, he knew the Texan would not sleep. It was a long night.

When Gentry judged daylight to be not far away, he stood, stretched, and walked to the fire. He again built it such that he stood close and warmed his hands and his backside, then slit the bonds that held Bowdry's feet and kicked him in the side. "Stand. Don't try nothin' funny an' you'll live long enough to get back to Two Dogs's lodge. Walk over there about five paces and stand still, with yore back to me."

Bowdry did as he was told. Gentry put the fire out and prodded the gunman toward the encampment.

CHAPTER EIGHTEEN

★ ★ ★

Anne and the children looked at the bend in the trail less now, but she wouldn't allow herself to stop hoping. Still, a thread of doubt crept into her thoughts every now and then, and at night her sleep was broken by dreams of her husband lying hurt somewhere with no one to help him.

She kept the children busy. There were always chores to keep them occupied from dawn 'til dusk. And on the morning when they awoke to find a thaw had set in, she and Brandy washed clothes while Mark stoked the fire under the big cast-iron pot. This was the first opportunity she'd had to hang clothes outside. But while washing, rinsing, and hanging them to dry, she caught herself turning her eyes to look at the trail, and it twisted her stomach into knots when Mark and Brandy did the same. She shook her shoulders, trying to rid herself of the depressing thoughts.

Mark stood back from the pot. "That's the last garment in that pot, Ma. You want I should tip it over an' rinse it out?"

Anne nodded. "Tip it toward the downhill side so it'll run off without scalding you."

"Aw, Ma, you tell me them same words every time." He again looked toward the bend. "You reckon Pa's ever gonna come home? He's been gone a long time now. He missed Christmas, almost missed gettin' to eat any o' them turkey I killed, would've if you hadn't a saved one. Now that a thaw's done set in, reckon you better cook it, or it's gonna spoil."

Anne looked at her son and put her hand on his head to

tousle his hair. "You—you said almost missed getting any of the turkey."

Mark cocked his head to look up at her. "Yeah, Ma. I got a feelin'' Pa's gonna be home in a couple of days. Don't know what held 'im up, but we can bet it was reason enough, an' whatever it was, Ma, he done it for us."

Anne mussed his hair and smiled through tears. "Yes, son, your father has always done all he knew to do for us. Think highly of him, Mark, there aren't many men who stack up with him."

He shoved a sapling under the pot and tilted it on its side. They watched the steaming stream flow down the hill, and together turned and headed toward the cabin. For some untold reason Mark's faith had given Anne new hope. She admitted to herself that within her heart, hope had shrunk to a thread. She again glanced at the trail, only this time a thin smile broke the worry lines.

Gentry prodded Bowdry into the small Sioux encampment. For some time now the smell of wood smoke and the tantalizing aroma of food cooking reached his nostrils. "Tomorrow, gunny, you an' me's gonna fight. Ain't but one of us gonna walk away from it." He stopped in front of Wambli Dopa's tipi, thinking to keep the slim Texan by his side until the fight, then thought better of it. If he showed he didn't trust Two Dogs to guard Bowdry, it would be worse than a slap in the warrior's face. He prodded him toward Two Dogs who stood outside his lodge with his woman and the others of the settlement. "Tonight you watch. When the sun paints the lodge poles with light, bring him to me. We fight then." For a long moment Gentry stared into Bowdry's eyes, then at a signal from Two Eagles went into his tipi.

Little Fawn motioned him to sit while she ladled stew into a bowl. He was so hungry he thought he could eat the bowl if she didn't hurry. Then, while he ate, Eagle Feather sat close to him, allowing only enough room for him to move his arm to put food into his mouth. The little fellow seemed to know he owed his life to Gentry, but his hero worship made Gentry uncomfortable.

Gentry chewed and swallowed the last bite, shook his head when Little Fawn stood to serve up more stew, and then he pinned Two Eagles with a gaze. "Great Warrior, I want you to do something for me if I die tomorrow."

"Gen-tree, I do anything for you. What is it you want?"

Gentry stood and went to his pack. "I got some things in here I wanted to give to my woman an' kids for Christmas. Want you to make sure they get them." He went on to explain that Christmas was a special day, and on that day of each year many families among the whites celebrated the birth of one of their great spirits by giving gifts to each other. And he told him that friends often gave and received gifts also. He opened the pack and took out the mirror comb and hairbrush set for Anne, the doll for Brandy, and the .22 rifle for Mark. "These here are the gifts. Ain't never been able to give 'em anything before, an' I want they should have them even if the special day is long gone."

The tall Sioux stared at them, then at Gentry. "It will be as you say, Gen-tree. They shall have them, but they have them from your hands. When fight is over, I show you way home. Take maybe two suns to reach."

Gentry stared at the spare rifle a moment, thinking to give it to Two Dogs for the one Bowdry stole, then decided against it. Two Dogs had been careless or he would not have lost the rifle. He repacked the presents and gear, glanced at the smoke hole, and saw dark had set in. "Better sleep now, be strong for fight."

Gentry lay there long into the night, thinking about the cattle, thinking some of Barton's bunch of rustlers might have gone back and taken over the ranch after the Apache Blanco had killed Barton. He finally decided nothing would stop him from getting those cattle. He would not jeopardize Crockett and the men he brought with him—but he would have those cows come hell or high water. From the cows, his thoughts homed in on the cabin on the banks of the

Powder. He went to sleep thinking of the three people in that cabin.

He awoke the next morning knowing it was the day he had to kill Bowdry, knowing it was the day he'd looked forward to for so long, he was going home.

When he'd looked back at his cabin from the bend in the trail, he thought to be gone only a couple of days, now it had been weeks. Anne would think him dead, and Gentry wondered how she had prepared the children for that event. He pushed the robes down, went to the riverbank, washed up, went back, ate, and got ready for the fight.

He tested his leg to see if it would take the strain of his weight, spinning, pushing, kicking. He loosened his shoulder and back muscles, flexing them, and then flexing them again and again. He finally felt loose and strong. He looked at Two Eagles. "Tell Two Dogs to bring Bowdry out. I'm ready."

Gentry stood in front of Two Eagles's tipi. Two Dogs prodded Bowdry out the flap of his tipi and over to stand in front of him. He looked into the slim gunman's eyes. "Today you die, droppings from a buzzard. Gonna let you choose how you want it—guns, knives, or pogamoggans. Or maybe you want knives *and* pogamoggans."

"When I kill you, Gentry, what these Indians gonna do with me?"

"If you kill me, Bowdry, I'm gonna ask Two Eagles to give you 'bout half-hour start with no weapons, then hunt you down like the animal you are."

"Hell, Gentry, I cain't win in no fight like that. Give me a chance."

Gentry stared at the slim Texan, relishing the fear he saw in the pale blue eyes that looked back at him. "That's a problem you ain't gonna have to worry 'bout. But however this comes out, you ain't got no other chance. What weapons you want?"

"Knives an' pogamoggans."

Gentry looked at Two Eagles and nodded.

The tall Lakota went into his tipi and came out with Gentry's Bowie knife and his own war club, while Two Dogs fetched Bowdry's knife and *his* pogamoggan.

Gentry walked off a few paces, checked Two Eagles's war club, and at the same time admired the workmanship that went into it. All the plains Indians used a weapon of this nature; a stone head, shaped to the individual warrior's fancy, secured to a supple, strong length of wood with leather thongs. He wrapped several strips of leather around his hand and handle grip—on his right hand.

He watched from the corners of his eyes to see which hand Bowdry would use for the club, watched Bowdry make the same mistake most white eyes made. He put the club in his left hand and took the knife in his right. A slight smile crinkled the corners of Gentry's mouth, but his gut muscles tightened. He swallowed, hard, and willed himself to relax. If he took the slim Texan lightly, he'd lose.

When ready, they faced each other and began circling for advantage, a strategy as old as time. Animals did the same. Gentry moved in first, feinted with the knife, and swung the club. Bowdry leaned back at the last second. The pogamoggan swished past his face so close it tipped his nose.

Gentry moved back a couple of steps. Bowdry stepped forward and swung his knife. Gentry used the handle of the war club to ward off the slice, then backhanded Bowdry with the stone head catching him on the shoulder. The slim gunman fell to the side, caught his balance, and darted in to thrust again.

Gentry dodged and thrust straight out with his Bowie. Bowdry faded back. The Ranger's arm straightened, the tip of his knife stopping only the thickness of a cigarette paper from Bowdry's chest. Gentry stepped to the side, studying his foe. It was obvious the slim Texan figured to use his knife as his primary weapon. Gentry thought to use his pogamoggan to gain the advantage, then use his blade.

He circled to his right, forcing Bowdry to have to swing across his body in order to use his knife, and at the same time rendering the war club almost useless. The pogamoggan's weight should tire the gunman before it took its toll on Gentry. He was bigger, stronger, and heavier muscled.

Bowdry glided toward Gentry, swung his knife, and missed. Gentry ducked low and stabbed straight out with his club. It caught Bowdry above his belt. He gasped, faded back, and sucked for air. Gentry again swung the stone weapon and caught the gunman on the side of his knee—on his wounded leg. Bowdry fell, grasped his knee joint with his knife hand, but held the blade pointed toward Gentry.

The Ranger waited for the slim man to climb to his feet. He moved to the side, forcing Bowdry to put his weight on his sore leg, darted in, swung his club, stepped closer, and thrust with his Bowie. His blade sliced across Bowdry's ribs.

Gentry grunted. That cut would be painful, but not enough to stop the gunman. They backed off, each catching his breath. Then Gentry closed to within a couple of feet, feinted to his left, and again swung the stone-headed weapon. It caught Bowdry on his knife arm. His blade flew from his hand.

"Pick it up." Gentry's voice came out harsh, cruel.

Not taking his eyes off Gentry, Bowdry stepped to his knife, scooped it up, and waited. Then with his right hand, Gentry brought the head of the war club to his left shoulder and swung backhanded at Bowdry.

Bowdry's eyes followed the clubhead. Gentry swung his body with the pogamoggan's weight, letting his blade follow the same route. His knife bit deeper this time, cutting Bowdry across his club arm. The gunman stood there a moment, his face showing shock. Then he reached across his body, cut the thongs wrapped around his hand, and dropped the war club.

Gentry cut his pogamoggan loose at the same time. He stood back, watching, waiting for blood loss to weaken the gunman. Bowdry's face slowly drained of color until it resembled bread dough. He took a deep breath—and rushed, swinging his knife. It cut deep across Gentry's left shoulder. Gentry made a border shift, caught the Bowie with his right hand, and thrust straight out. The tip of his blade went in above the edge of Bowdry's belt buckle and didn't stop until Gentry's hand came flush with the gunman's gut.

The Texan's eyes opened wide, as though to pop from his head. He tried to slice Gentry again, but his knife made only a feeble swipe, then fell from his hand. Gentry jerked his blade free and stepped back.

Bowdry clutched his stomach with both hands, took a step toward Gentry, his legs buckled, and he fell on his face into the mud.

Gentry picked up the pogamoggan and handed it to Two Eagles. The Sioux warrior looked into Gentry's eyes. "Good fight, Gen-tree. Come. Woman fix shoulder. Got medicine make well soon."

Before bandaging Gentry's shoulder, Little Fawn motioned him to sit by the fire, then placed a bowl of stew on the ground in front of him. "Eat. Help make well."

While she took care of his wound, Gentry ate. He glanced at Two Eagles. "Don't know what kind of gear Bowdry brung in here with him. Get his bedroll, take what you want, and give rest to Two Dogs and Many Horses." He hesitated. "They's one thing he brung in here I'd like to have if it's all right with you."

"Gen-tree, you save Eagle Feather's life. Tell Two Eagles what want, I give."

Gentry stared at the fire a moment, then shifted his gaze back to the Sioux. "Hate to ask it, but I'd shore like that there side gun he wore in here. It's one of a pair, an' I know where the other one is."

"The gun is yours. Indian got no use for short gun. No good for hunt." He shifted his look to Little Fawn. "Bring Bow-dree's belongings."

Gentry finished eating, stood, and inspected his pack, making sure it was secure for his trip home. "When you gonna show me the way to my cabin, Two Eagles?"

"We leave when you wear Bow-dree's gun. Sun not move much in sky before we leave."

Little Fawn brought the slim Texan's gear in, along with the clothes he wore during the fight. Gentry knew Bowdry lay in front of the tipi naked as the day he came into the world. She put the bedroll and wad of clothes on the ground in front of Two Eagles, who shoved the clothes toward Gentry. "See what he got in pockets."

The first things the Ranger pulled from Bowdry's pockets were what he expected. A Green River pocketknife, an oilskin of lucifers, a plug of rough-cut tobacco, a few nickels and dimes, and nothing else. He started to toss the trousers aside, then noticed the waistband was unusually thick. Using his Bowie, he slit the cloth and pulled, by a quick count, over two hundred dollars from the lining. He stared at the money, wanting to pocket it. His hand trembled. He shook his head and held it out to Two Eagles.

"Lakota not use white man's money. I take to reservation commissary, and they throw me in jail. Think I kill white eye and take from him. You keep."

Gentry wanted the money so bad he hurt. It could buy many of the things Anne and the children had done without for so long, clothes and shoes at the top of the list. Two hundred dollars was a fortune—more money than he expected to have at one time, even after he sold his first calf crop—if someone hadn't already claimed those cattle Blanco told him about.

"You sure, Two Eagles? Oughtta be somebody to swap it for script for you."

Two Eagles shook his head. "No. Get me in much trouble. You keep."

As much as Gentry wanted the money, he wanted to share it in some way with the Sioux who had befriended him, then he had an idea. "How long you figure to stay here?"

Two Eagles shrugged. "Three, maybe four moons. Go back to reservation for handout—then leave again."

Gentry nodded. "I have a friend in Milestown who owns a store. Soon as the grass turns green, I'll go buy you supplies."

The Sioux smiled. "Get coffee. You keep rest."

They continued to search Bowdry's pack. They found two boxes of .44 shells. Gentry pointed to the Texan's rifle. "They fit long gun. You keep."

After dividing the spoils, Two Eagles motioned they should start for Gentry's place. While Gentry shouldered his pack and tried to make it comfortable against his wounded shoulder, Two Eagles went to the tipi. A moment later the sound of four or five horses coming in caused Gentry to use caution and stay where he was.

A rough voice, directly in front of Two Dogs's lodge, asked, "What the hell you Indians doing here on my land?"

"Our land first," Many Horses said, his voice proud, but with a tinge of bitterness.

Gentry peeped past a gap in the flap. Four riders, all heavily armed, sat their horses only a few feet from the tipi next to Two Eagles's. Quietly Gentry buckled his .44 on and tied the thongs to his leg, then he picked up his Winchester.

He pushed through the flap, pointing the bore of his rifle in the direction of the four. "What makes this yore land? Ain't seen y'all 'round here afore."

Four heads snapped to look in Gentry's direction. A whiskered, dirty rider on the left made a move for his gun. Gentry squeezed off a shot, tearing through the rider's gunbelt. "Next one's gonna go through you—an' any of the rest of you what makes a dumb move." He was in pistol range now, and he didn't miss at this distance. He shifted the rifle to his left hand and pulled his handgun. "Now, tell me what ranch you from."

The tall, skinny rider sitting his horse a little to the fore, and apparently the leader, looked at Gentry a moment before answering. Gentry stared right back.

"Our brand is the Box LB. B'longed to a friend of mine, Lem Barton. I took it over when he got hisself killed."

Gentry, without taking his eyes off the skinny one, said,

"Two Eagles, you and your men get your rifles." He again directed his words to the leader of the bunch. "Barton got killed 'cause he was a damned rustling crook. Reckon if he was a friend of yours I can peg you as the same." He wished he'd centered his shot on the whiskered rider's chest now that he knew them to be part of Barton's bunch. He meant to have every cow on the Box LB.

"Them's right harsh words, stranger. You ready to back them up?"

"Skinny, I ain't only ready—I'm hopin'." From the corners of his eyes, Gentry saw the three Sioux warriors with their rifles ready. "You men want to tell me your names so I'll know what to put on your marker." The squat, powerful-looking rider next to Skinny grabbed for his handgun. Gentry moved the barrel of his .44 a hair and fired—then the clearing exploded with sound.

Three saddles emptied before Gentry could get off a second shot. The whiskered one who'd first grabbed for his gun, dug spurs into his horse, jumped him between two of the tipis, and raced from the encampment. Gentry threw a shot in his direction, but kept his gaze on the three downed riders. At a glance, two of them were shot to rags.

Skinny writhed in agony, holding his hands tight to his gut. He groaned, cursed, and looked up at Gentry. "What for you go and do that? We meant you no harm."

"You should a told your saddle pard that 'fore he grabbed for his gun." Gentry stooped and pulled Skinny's hands from his stomach, studied the hole there, turned the man over, and saw another hole the size of his fist before again flopping him to his back. He looked into the man's eyes. "You gonna die. Ain't nothin' nobody can do for you 'cept try to make you comfortable. What you want on yore marker?"

"Don't want no name." He groaned and clutched his gut again. "You meet anybody who gives a damn one way or the other, tell 'em I swung a wide loop, an' all it got me was a fast trip to hell."

CHAPTER NINETEEN

★ ★ ★

The rustler gasped, his breath left him in a long drawn-out sigh, and his eyes stared sightlessly at the sky. Gentry looked at Two Eagles. "Reckon anything they got b'longs to you and your warriors now. 'Fore we leave, we better find a cut-bank somewhere and bury 'em under it." He stood, went to his pack to shoulder it, frowned, and again looked at Two Eagles. "Be a good idea you move your camp upstream close to my cabin. That'un what got away might bring back some of his friends to cause trouble."

It took only a few moments to strip the rustlers of any valuables, with Gentry keeping all cash. Then they dragged them to a dry wash a half mile away, buried them, and returned to see the women taking down the tipis.

By midafternoon the small band was seven or eight miles from the old camp. Gentry walked alongside Two Eagles's horse. "Better have one of your warriors scout behind—be sure that'un what got away don't bring back more of them."

The tall Sioux looked at Many Horses, said a few words in Lakota, and again turned his face to the front. Many Horses dropped behind, then disappeared from sight into the trees.

They camped that night about ten miles from where they'd struck camp. "I'll take first watch, Two Eagles, wake you when I get tired." Gentry talked while he spread his blankets over his ground sheet.

Two Eagles looked to the northwest. "Not only enemy we watch for. Weather turn cold, maybe snow soon."

Gentry shrugged. "That time of year." Despite his philosophy, he dug in his pack for his buffalo robe.

The women fixed food, the fire died to gray ash, and all turned in to their robes except Gentry.

He walked downstream about a mile, and hunkered next to a large cottonwood. Trace Gundy, the Apache Blanco, would be a welcome sight. Blanco could tell him about how many rustlers he figured were left on Barton's Box LB.

Gentry squatted next to the old tree until his knees cramped. He stood, worked the stiffness from his legs, thought to light his pipe, and decided against it. The faint glow of a cigarette or pipe had cost many a man his life.

He'd no more than settled his pipe at the bottom of his pocket when he heard the sucking clop of horse's hooves.

"Hell, Avery, let's stop this traipsing through the dark. We'll catch them Indians in the mornin'. They're packing their kids, lodges, an' women with 'em."

Gentry strained to see through the black veil of night. The outlaws were close, closer than he wanted. He should have heard them long before now.

"All right. We'll camp, fix coffee, sleep a couple of hours, then we're back on their trail. We let 'em get away with cuttin' us down like they did, we ain't much men. I want 'em all dead, kids an' all, 'specially that white Injun."

Sounds reached Gentry, of men dismounting, setting tinder for a fire, and then the flare of a match. Gentry waited for the fire to catch hold, and as best he could, counted the riders he and the Sioux would have to face. At best guess, he thought he saw six men. The odds were not to his liking, but could have been worse.

Tension set in. Gentry's neck muscles tightened, and a painful knot grew between his shoulders. He sucked in a deep breath and pushed it out slowly. He did this several

times until he relaxed, then turned his mind to how to deal
with the rustlers.

He could rouse Two Eagles and his small band and try to
slip away into the night, or they could stand and fight—
maybe get some of the women and children killed. Or they
could attack. He thought on the problem several minutes,
nodded, and turned toward his friends.

Gentry pulled a foot from the sucking mud carefully to
prevent sound. Then he did it again and again, moving ever
so slowly from the outlaws. Finally he thought he was beyond his sounds reaching them and picked up his pace.

He entered the campsite, went to Two Eagles, squatted,
and placed his hand over the warrior's mouth. The Sioux
nodded, signaling he was awake.

Gentry told him what he'd seen and heard. "Get your
women up. Tell 'em to find a place under a cut-bank—any-
place to hide. Don't make no noise. Have Two Dogs an'
Many Horses get rifles, maybe an extra one an' plenty of
shells. They ought to have extra guns an' bullets from them
men we killed this mornin'. Then follow me. We ain't
givin' nobody a chance to hurt yore women and children."

To Gentry's eyes, the women and children were ghostly
black shapes silhouetted against the darker night. They
were so quiet, if he had not seen their movement, he would
never have known they were there. They scurried about the
campsite a few moments, then melted into the darkness.
The three Lakotas stood at his shoulder. His voice little
more than a whisper, Gentry laid out his plan.

"I figure them men gonna make a fire an' fix more coffee
'fore they hit the trail lookin' for us. We gonna be on every
side of them when their site lights up." He hesitated, not
wanting to say his next words, but he had to if they were to
have a chance. "Warriors, I want you to hold your fire until
you hear me fire, then cut 'em down. Don't give 'em any
sort of break. We gotta do it this way, or we gonna lose
some men, maybe even yore wives an' children." Those
final words were not needed. In a fight, an Indian fought to

win. They didn't understand "fair." "Stay close so you'll know when I stop, then we'll take our places to fight from."

While they walked, Gentry felt the Lakotas' nearness rather than saw or heard them. When he detected a faint whiff of the outlaws' burned-out fire, he held out his arms to hold the warriors where they were. "They're just ahead. Two Dogs, go to the other side of their camp. Two Eagles, you take the side toward the river, an' Many Horses, take this spot here. I'll take the side away from the trees. All of you, be careful not to fire toward one of us. All right—let's go."

Since Gentry last stood in this spot, the temperature had steadily dropped. Two Eagles had been right. A few flakes of wet snow brushed Gentry's cheek. By morning the slush and mud would freeze again. He walked a few more steps, stopped, and gauged where he thought the rustlers' camp to be. Another ten steps and he felt his way into a cedar brake. There he squatted and waited. The colder temperatures were in his favor, it would cause the outlaws to build a larger fire.

He wished he'd thought to have Two Dogs try to cut the rustlers' horses loose, then he figured it was just as well he hadn't. Moving horses might wake the enemy, and the fight would start in the dark. Gentry wanted firelight to shoot into.

Two hours passed—then three. They sure as hell weren't taking only a short sleep. Gentry shifted to put most of his weight on another leg. Then from the camp the sound of men stirring. A light flickered, and the feeble light of a small fire danced on the faces of men huddled over it. "Dancey, go git a pot of water. I'll build the fire up some. Clete, round up some more wood." The voice giving orders was Avery's.

The fire was not yet as large as Gentry wanted. He waited for Clete, whoever he was, to get back with more wood. Then he waited for Dancey to get back.

"Where the hell did Dancey go for that there water?" another of the bunch growled. Gentry wondered the same thing, then it dawned on him. Dancey might have come close enough to Two Eagles for the Lakota to use his knife.

Clete tossed more fuel on the fire. It blazed higher. Gentry waited for Dancey only a moment longer. The fire blazed high enough for Gentry to see every member of the band. Dancey hadn't returned. The Ranger aimed at the one he took to be Avery and fired. The man slammed backward. Gentry held his breath hoping the outlaw leader didn't fall into the flames and darken the site. The dead rustler fell across the edge of the fire, blotting out only part of the light.

Gunfire slammed at the rustlers from every direction. The outlaws seemed confused with the first shots, then dived for cover—but their only cover was the saddles they used for pillows.

A pair of legs showed. Gentry fired, levered a shell into the chamber, and fired again. The legs, a hole behind each knee, dragged toward a saddle. Gentry moved his sights forward of the knees and fired again. The legs quivered and lay still. Gunfire still exploded from every side.

Gentry picked out a saddle with lances of flame spitting from behind it. He centered his sights on the saddle and fired. It jumped like it was loose cinched, with a twelve-hundred-pound steer on the end of a rope tied to it. One of the rustlers lay there, nothing to hide behind. Gentry jacked another shell in the chamber and fired. The puncher jerked like a puppet. Gentry moved his sights, looked for another target. All firing stopped. Silence thundered in his ears. Gentry waited another few moments, waited for a last stray shot. None sounded.

He stood, glanced at the periphery of the rustlers' camp, and walked to the fire. Without a signal, the Lakota warriors emerged from the darkness. Two Eagles looked at Gentry and grinned. "Good fight, Gen-tree." His words were the same as he'd spoken when Gentry fought Bowdry.

Gentry looked questioningly at each warrior. "Anybody get hit?"

One by one, each shook his head. Gentry looked from them to the havoc they'd created. Saddles shot to scrap leather, blankets lying in the crusty mud, cooking utensils lying where they were dropped when the attack started, and men, twisted, bent, bloody, staring at the sky from sightless eyes or lying facedown in the mud. He looked at Wambli Dopa. "You get the one what went for water?"

The Lakota nodded. "Me get."

A hell of a note, Gentry thought, this didn't have to happen at all except for greed.

Then his thoughts centered on who they killed, all remnants of the Barton gang, men who only a few short weeks from now he would have had to fight anyway when he went after the rest of the rustled Box LB cattle, and there were probably still other men at the ranch.

Gentry's basic philosophy had always been, everything happened for the best, and this was further proof of the truth of that belief. He again centered his gaze on his companions. "Look through their pockets for money—anything of worth to you. If you find paper with writin' on it, give it to me. It might say who they were, an' I'll try to let their families know they won't be comin' home."

There were several weapons, rifles, and six-guns, all in excellent shape. "Each of you look at those guns we took in the fight yesterday, along with these, and pick one for each of you. I'll take the rest to Milestown when the grass turns green and trade for goods. I'll split whatever I get with you. Anything else worth takin', take it. I want two of them horses. Figure it's time my son had a decent horse. You men divide up the rest." When he pocketed the money they carried, Gentry couldn't help but think how profitable these fights were.

It took but a short while to clean the camp of everything they wanted. Gentry was of a mind to head back to Two Eagles's camp, but decided he couldn't leave the rustlers lay like they'd fallen. Everyone, no matter how bad, deserved a decent burial.

He threw a couple pieces of wood on the fire and looked at Two Eagles. "Take Many Horses and find your women. Make a fire they can warm by an' fix food. Two Dogs an' me'll stay here an' bury these men. We'll be in when the sun is high in the east."

Without a word, Two Eagles motioned Many Horses to come with him. They had all the plunder tied to the backs of a couple of horses; they rode two others. Gentry and Two Dogs kept the other two. They left coffee and bacon, along with a tin of beans, for Gentry to fix breakfast.

Gentry kept the fire stoked during what was left of the night. The temperature continued to drop, and the snow got heavier. Before the new day dawned, gray and somber, he knew they would have to find some place to cave dirt over the men left here. Even though the weather had warmed, and snowmelt had filled the rivers and creeks, it had been for too short a time to soften the earth more than a few inches, and now a hard freeze set in again. Even with shovels they couldn't dig graves.

Gentry explained to Two Dogs what he wanted to do with the corpses. Two Dogs wanted to leave them where they fell, but Gentry wouldn't hear of it. Two hours after the murky dawn, they'd covered Barton's men as best they could and headed for camp.

Long before raising the campsite, the smell of cooking food and wood smoke told Gentry they were close. When he and Two Dogs rode to the fire, he looked at the small band gathered around four piles of gear. All looked at him, smiling. At the side of one of the piles stood two horses—the best of those the outlaws rode.

"We fix piles for lodges," Many Horses said. "Three tipi, one cab-bin. We take one good long gun each, rest in your pile." He stood there grinning, waiting, Gentry knew, for words of praise. Gentry's chest tightened. He couldn't figure how these people, in such a few short days, had become such fast friends.

He swept the gathering with a smile, nodded, and said,

"You did good, my friends. As soon as I can, I'll make that trip to Milestown."

"We not worry," Two Eagles cut in. "Gen-tree good man."

Gentry was eager to get on the trail for home, but there was one more thing he wanted to make certain of. He'd seen too many weapons carried by Indians, neglected, hardly fit or safe to fire. "You warriors eat, then get your weapons and come sit by the fire." He followed his own advice, got a plate of food, ate, and sat where he wanted them to gather.

When they gathered around, Gentry told them he wanted them to know how to take care of their weapons. He field-stripped the rifle he held, had them do the same with theirs, cleaned and oiled his, and watched while they followed suit. Then he had them do it again, and again, following his instructions each time. Then he had them go through the routine without instruction. When he was satisfied they could keep their rifles in good condition, he looked at Two Eagles. "Have them do this at least five, six times each moon period. These weapons'll last a long time. When you go back to the reservation, leave 'em at my cabin. I'll have 'em there when you return." He grinned. "They might not take kindly to you walkin' 'round better armed than they are."

Soon after the weapons class was over, they packed and headed upstream. Midafternoon Gentry thought they were getting close to his cabin, then he knew they were. Familiar landmarks, a few, then many, came into view. He looked at Two Eagles and saw him smiling. "Woman, little warrior, an' girl wait for you. You go."

Gentry frowned. "Come with me. I want my woman and children to know my friends."

"You go. I come when sun in east."

Gentry stared at his new friends a moment, nodded, and rode toward home.

CHAPTER TWENTY

★ ★ ★

Gentry drew rein about a hundred yards downstream of his cabin. He sat there drinking in the sight of his family. Mark split firewood, the Greener leaned against a block close to hand, Brandy stacked the stove-length pieces of wood, and Anne worked with the hindquarter of a deer tied to the roof's overhang by the back door. He noticed that every so often each of them found an excuse to walk to the front of the house and look upstream toward the bend in the trail. He had no doubt they looked for him. He choked, swallowed, and blinked hard. What was the matter with him, he'd always had control over his emotions? He urged the horse he rode and the packhorse toward the cabin.

Mark was the first to look up and turn his gaze downstream of the Powder. He dropped the ax and ran. "Ma, Brandy, it's Pa. Pa's done come home." Before he got the last word out of his mouth, all three ran toward Gentry.

He climbed from his horse, keeping a tight hold on the reins of both horses. He never knew how he did it, with them smothering him with kisses, hugging him, and each trying to get closer than the others, but he hugged all three at the same time, and still kept hold of the reins.

Finally, he turned the horses over to Mark. "Stable 'em, son, leave that pack with all them rifles in the barn. We'll take care of that gear later, then come on up to the house. We got a lot to talk about." Before Mark pulled the horses toward the barn, Gentry stripped the pack containing the presents from the horse carrying his gear, slung it over his shoulder, put his arms around Anne and Brandy, and stepped toward his own front stoop.

Inside, the first thing Gentry saw was the tree, still decorated. He looked at Anne, a question in his eyes. She just smiled. He lay his pack gently in the corner, at the head of the bed he would lie in with his wife that night. Looking at the neat spread of covers and the pillow she lay her head on brought a lump to his throat. Before turning to again look at his family, he swallowed a couple of times. When he again looked into the room, Anne was busy setting the table, while Brandy poured water in the coffeepot.

"Case, you sit down and rest. Supper will be on the table in a jiffy."

Gentry drank in her trim figure, not wanting to sit, but to take her in his arms and never let go. "Honey, reckon I messed up Christmas for all of you." He shook his head. "S'pose all I can say is 'I'm sorry.' " He sat in his chair in front of the fire and clasped his hands. "Couldn't be helped, Anne. I'll tell you about it after we get the children to bed. S'pose we could let the kids stay up a little later tonight?" He asked the question trying to keep from his voice the hope she'd say no. He needed to hold her close, get his world back on an even keel, then in the morning he'd spend all the time with the children they needed.

Anne locked eyes with him, stared a moment, then shook her head. "No, Case"—a slight smile crinkled the corners of her lips—"I don't care what the date is, tomorrow is Christmas for us, and we'll all be busy getting ready for it. We waited to celebrate it." Her smile widened. "Besides, I'm selfish, I want you and I to share each other as soon as the cabin darkens." She laughed a throaty laugh, full of humor and promise. "If the sun doesn't hurry and set, I'll just drape the windows with blankets and we'll make believe."

Gentry groaned. "Don't do this to me, woman. If we

don't hurry with dinner, I'll drape the windows myself, and try to make the kids believe they already ate."

Brandy stared at them as though they'd lost their minds. Mark came in from the stable and Brandy told him Mama and Papa were going to put them to bed without dinner. Gentry glanced at Anne, smiled, and pulled his little girl to his lap. "Honey, your ma an' me was just teasin'. We wouldn't do such a thing to you an' Mark, but we do have to get to bed early tonight so we can have a good Christmas tomorrow."

Mollified, Brandy snuggled into her father's arms. Gentry pulled Mark onto his other knee and hugged his children. "Mark, I s'pose since takin' care of your ma all by yourself you're 'bout too big to sit on my knee."

Mark leaned back and looked into his father's eyes. "Pa, reckon I might be gettin' to be such, but I ain't there yet." He put his arms around his father's neck and squeezed. "Sure am happy you're home, Pa. I—we all missed you so much."

"Case, if you'll let those hungry children loose, we can eat dinner. I imagine it's been a while since you sat up to a table yourself."

"Anne, if I told you how long it's been, you wouldn't believe me." He released his hold on the children. "Shoo now, young'uns, get to the table."

After dinner, Gentry put bath water on to heat while he and Anne told the children good night. "Reckon I smell a little gamey, but I'll take care of that soon as the children go to sleep."

"Case, I don't care how you smell—just don't ever leave me again. Just be here for me. I—we all need you so badly."

Gentry wondered when he crawled between the covers how he'd ever bathed with Anne refusing to leave his side like she did. They lay there close to each other, letting the bed warm a bit, and Gentry feeling a little shy after being gone so long. Anne turned her body toward him, molding herself to him. "Hold me, Case, hold me tight enough to hurt."

Her words, her warmth, her scent, were all he needed to know he was again where he belonged. He turned to his side and pulled her tightly to him. His lips, and hands, and body said all the things he'd thought and dreamed of through the long, lonely, dangerous days and nights.

After a long while, they lay quietly, then began to say in words what their bodies had already told each other. They talked long into the night. It was then he found out Big Battles had not stopped, and figured he'd decided to farm instead of ranch.

The next morning, a sliver of sun showing in the east, and breakfast barely over, the sound of horse's hooves approached from downstream, breaking into the normal cabin noises. Without a word, Mark went to the wall and took the Greener from the pegs.

Gentry, feeling pride in his son, shook his head. "Put the shotgun back, Mark. I think that's a friend."

Gentry went to the door. Two Eagles drew rein at the edge of the unfinished veranda. He looked at Mark, then Gentry. "Come tell Gen-tree, where we set up lodges."

"Climb down, Great Warrior. Come in. We have coffee." Gentry looked over his shoulder. "Anne, my friend's comin' in. Ain't nothin' to be afraid of."

The tall Lakota moved silently into the cabin. "Case, I didn't know you knew Scar. Where did you meet him?"

Gentry frowned. "Scar? Who's Scar? You know this warrior?" Without giving her a chance to explain, he said to Two Eagles, "Sit, we'll have coffee in a minute, an' me an' my family gonna have Christmas. They waited 'til I got home to have it."

Anne busied herself taking cups from a shelf and said over her shoulder, "The tall warrior and I met before. Notice he has a scar on the side of his head? Well, I dressed

the wound that made it. I don't know any other name to call
him by."

"His name is Two Eagles. He saved my life. I told you
about it last night."

The Lakota made himself at home. He sat on the floor in
front of the fireplace while Anne served coffee. Gentry was
glad he and Anne agreed to have breakfast before opening
their gifts or they'd have been a very hungry family.

Two Eagles told how Anne saved his life. "Get hurt." He
touched the side of his head. "Woman bring me in cab-bin.
Fix head. Big cold outside. I die she leave me."

Mark and Brandy sat wide-eyed watching the Sioux
warrior while Two Eagles talked. But they weren't so en-
grossed in the conversation they didn't cast glances at the
pack their father brought in the night before, or the one
Anne pulled from under the bed before she fixed breakfast.
Gentry knew it was pure torture for them to sit there, they'd
waited so long to have their Christmas.

He looked at Two Eagles. "Remember I told you how
this time of year we give gifts to those we care about?
Well, we ain't give 'em out yet. You wanta watch?"

"Me watch," the Lakota said. Gentry glanced at Anne.
She nodded, stood, and went to the bundle she pulled from
under the bed before breakfast. Gentry picked his pack up
and they placed the two bundles side by side on the bed.
"You open yours first, Anne."

She looked at him a long moment, and he saw in her
eyes she didn't want to spoil whatever he'd been able to afford. "Go ahead, honey, the kids'll like whatever we give
'em."

It was then Mark said he had to go to the barn for something.

Anne picked at the knot in the string she'd tied around
the quilt and unfolded it to expose the gifts she'd made for
each of them. She handed Brandy her Raggedy Ann doll
first. Brandy stared at the doll, hugging to her tiny breast
the carved stick her father had made for her. Then she care-

fully laid her old doll at her side, stood, and took the doll her mother made for her into her arms. "Oh, Mama, she's so pretty." She hesitated a moment, then grabbed her mother around the neck and kissed her. Before Brandy took her arms from around her mother's neck, Mark came back and held the chopping block out to her. "Here, Brandy, you give it to Ma from the both of us."

Brandy held the block a moment, her eyes full of pride, then handed it to her mother. "Me and Mark made this for you, Mama."

Anne stopped what she was doing and hugged them both. Gentry looked on. His family was one to be proud of.

Next, Anne took Mark's deerskin vest from the pile and handed it to him. While he held it up, admired it, and shrugged his arms into the armholes, she poured Two Eagles another cup of coffee, then she handed Gentry the vest she'd made for him. She had only the chopping block, but she wouldn't have traded it for all the gifts in the world—her children had made it.

Seeing her stand there, proud of what little she'd been able to do for her loved ones, with only the one gift for herself, tore at Gentry's heart, bringing a dull pain to the middle of his chest. When he could stand the pain no longer, he tugged at the pigging strings holding his pack together. He and the children had a gift in their hands; he wanted to see Anne with her gift. He pulled it from the pack first.

When he handed the small wooden box to her, she looked at it a moment, then raised her eyes to his. "For me, Case?" He nodded. Never lowering her eyes from his she opened the box, and only then did she look into it. Her eyes widened, her mouth formed an O, then tears threatened to spill over her cheeks. "Case, oh, my dear, Case, it's beautiful." She closed the lid on the box, put her arms around him, and held him tightly.

She didn't ask him if he'd gone in debt for it, how he'd paid for the stuff he brought home. No questions. And Gentry took that as one of the best compliments she could pay him. She trusted him to provide. After holding her for so long, Brandy got impatient and said she wanted to see what else was in his pack; Gentry released his arms from around Anne.

Next he pulled the doll he bought for Brandy, hating to do so because of the one he knew Anne had spent many tedious hours in making. Brandy's reaction to the doll was much the same as Anne's had been when she saw her comb, brush, and mirror set. Then Gentry handed Mark his rifle. "Son, I'll help you work them scratches outta the stock, then it'll be good as any."

Mark took the gun carefully into his hands, caressed the wood with gentle fingertips, and looked at his father. "Pa, I'd take it kindly if you'd let me dress the stock and oil it myself. Reckon you know I've dreamed of someday ownin' my own rifle. I done made believe that old carvin' over yonder in the corner was real for so long, didn't figure I'd ever get a sure 'nuff shootin' gun." He threw his arms around his father's neck, hugged, and then cast an embarrassed glance at Two Eagles.

A smile creased the corners of the Lakota's lips. "Got little warrior like you. Your papa give me my son's life." He shifted his eyes to look at Brandy. "And I have little girl like you in my lodge. Know how arms of little ones feel around neck. Feel good."

A grin covered Mark's face. "You let your little boy and girl come down here to see me an' Brandy?"

"When sun rises on new day, they come."

Mark stood in the middle of the room, caressing his rifle and shaking his head. "Got a gun, an' a friend to play with all in one day. Cain't believe it, Pa."

Gentry laughed. "Believe it, son. Tell you somethin' else, one of them rifles out yonder in the stable's gonna be yours when you grow into it, an' maybe we'll save one for Eagle Feather, Two Eagles's son, so you an' him can learn to shoot together. Sound good?"

They talked, drank more coffee, and Gentry and the

Lakota packed their pipes for a smoke when Anne stood abruptly. "Almost forgot, Case. You have another present, and a note to go with it. You have some mighty good friends in Milestown." She went to the shelf and reached behind some tins of food she'd put up during the summer. After groping blindly a moment or two, she pulled out the airtight tin of tobacco Bob Leighton had so carefully hidden in the supplies.

Gentry looked at the tobacco tin, already tasting the pungent aroma of its contents. Then he looked at his friend sitting stoically by the fire. Gentry thought Two Eagles's face must reflect the hunger he himself felt for a *good* smoke. "Two Eagles, mind you I said at this time of year we always give our friends gifts?" Two Eagles nodded. "Anne, we got anything we can divide that tobacco into? Need to make three piles of it."

Anne found three leather pouches, and Gentry, after dividing the tobacco into three equal piles, filled the pouches. He saved none for himself, and if he ever wanted anything, it was to keep some of the tobacco for himself. He looked at Two Eagles. "One for you, one for Two Dogs, an' one for Many Horses." The smile Two Eagles gave Gentry made him wonder where white people got the idea Indians never showed emotion.

Abruptly Brandy stood from playing with her new dolls and went to her mother. She whispered something in her ear, and at Anne's nod went back to her dolls and picked up Raggedy Ann. Holding her arms tight about the doll, she walked to stand shyly in front of the Lakota. "Mr. Two Eagles, do you think your little girl would want to play with a doll?"

His eyes twinkling, but with a hint of moisture in them, he smiled. "Little woman, Lakota girls play with dolls, same as white eyes." He looked at the doll. "My little woman would play with."

Brandy held the doll toward him. "Tell her to love her

like I do—an', an' bring her when she comes to play with me."

Gentry swallowed the lump in his throat a couple of times, but it wouldn't stay swallowed. Anne had raised Brandy as a duplicate of herself—not a selfish bone in her body.

After a couple more cups of coffee, Two Eagles left. There wasn't much got done around the Gentry household the rest of that day. They spent the time getting to know each other again. Anne and Gentry stayed so close, he wondered how she prepared meals, and to compound the problem, Gentry would have bet she picked up the mirror set twenty times during the day, ran the comb or brush through her hair, and looked in the mirror. That night after putting the children to bed and telling them a story, Gentry again held Anne close. It was after that he told her about the chance they would have cattle to sell in the future.

The next morning Two Eagles brought his son and daughter to the cabin. And true to the Lakota belief that if you receive a gift, you give one, he brought Gentry a new buffalo robe and softly tanned coats for Anne and the children, then he pulled a leather pouch from his pocket and handed it to Gentry. "We not take all tobacco, Gen-tree. You need good smoke. Bring back some for you." Gentry figured they had put it all in a pile and again divided it equally, this time in four parts.

They huddled around the gifts, admiring them, when the sound of several horses approaching broke into their celebration. Gentry reached for his gunbelt.

CHAPTER TWENTY-ONE

★ ★ ★

Mark took the Greener from its peg, and Gentry tossed Two Eagles a Winchester. "Don't shoot 'less I say so." At Gentry's words Mark and the Lakota took stations by the windows. Anne and Brandy went to the bed and squatted.

"Hello the house!"

That voice sounded familiar. Gentry peered around the doorjamb. "Crockett, didn't figure I'd see that ugly face of yourn again 'til spring." He glanced at Mark and Two Eagles. "It's all right. Them men're friends of mine." He stepped through the door to greet ten men, twice the number Gundy said he'd send, so they must be over here for another reason. Gentry had met most of these men before.

"Lordy day, you must of brought the whole Flying JW crew with you. What you doin' so far from home? Y'all climb down an' rest yore saddles."

Crockett and his men swung from their horses. Crockett talked while leading his gelding to the veranda. "That streak of warm weather caused Gundy to figure we oughtta get on with the job 'fore somebody else figured them cows b'longed to them. We'll brand your gather 'fore we head back to the ranch."

It took no more than a glance for Gentry to see they came for a roundup. They brought a chuck wagon, extra horses, and men aplenty. Gentry wondered if Anne had enough food on hand to feed this many men. Crockett took that worry away from him.

"Yore missus don't need to worry 'bout fixin nothin' for the crew. We got our own cook, plenty of supplies, everything."

Gentry locked eyes with Crockett a moment. "Hope I can make all this up to you. You, Gundy, an' the whole crew someday, amigo."

"Da nada, 'tis nothing, old friend. Knowing we got neighbors like you is enough."

Gentry introduced Two Eagles to Crockett's crew, none of whom seemed to think it strange that a Sioux made himself at home on Gentry's place. The Lakota stayed the day, allowing the children to get acquainted, then before dark, Gentry explained that he had to be gone again. The Lakota nodded. "Me watch woman and cab-bin. No worry."

The men slept in the stable that night, and were up an hour before daybreak ready to hit the trail. Crockett told Gentry he thought they should see Red Dawson before going on to Barton's Box LB, find out if any more rustlers hung around town or at the ranch.

Gentry pulled the cinches tight and looked across his saddle at Crockett. "Me an' Two Eagles's crew sort of thinned out some of them we woulda had to worry about. I done told Mark to stay close to that Greener in case any of them come this way. Figure that Lakota band's gonna keep an eye on things around here too. I done made some pretty good friends there, Crockett."

Crockett's eyes crinkled at the corners. "Yeah, Ranger man, you got a talent for makin' friends, maybe not the same kind as most of us would figure, well, sort of like that Trent feller you sent out to Gundy's place. We kept him just like you figured we would. He's workin' like hell to learn cowboyin'. He'll make it."

"Wuz gonna ask 'bout him," Gentry said. He grinned. "Shore was glad to talk him outta killin' me, figure he coulda done it too."

Crockett raised an eyebrow and turned his lips down at the corners. "He said the same thing 'bout you. Glad y'all didn't try to prove who was the best. Saved two pretty good men for this country."

"Don't know 'bout that. Country's gettin' pretty crowded. Hear tell I got a neighbor set up to ranch 'bout twenty miles from here. Gotta get over to see 'im—make his acquaintance."

When all was ready to hit the trail, Gentry went in the cabin to tell Anne and the children good-bye —again. He pulled them all into his arms at once. "Hope this's the last time for a long time, but a great deal of our future is tied up in them cows we find." He tousled Mark's hair. "Take care of your ma an' sister, son. Remember, use the Greener up-close. That .22 ain't gonna stop a man 'fore he does harm." He kissed them all and left, feeling their teary eyed stare on his back when he rode away.

With the chuck wagon along, they made slow time. "Fig- ure we gonna camp one night 'fore we get to Ismay. We could push it an' get there tonight, but it'd be late. Reckon we better not try it," Crockett said.

Gentry hunkered down in his old buffalo robe. He saved the new one Two Eagles gave him for special times. He looked at Crockett. "You're the boss, what with your expe- rience you'll know more 'bout getting this gather under way than I do."

Midafternoon of the next day they crossed O'Fallon Creek and set up camp on the outskirts of the small settle- ment. Crockett glanced at Stick Turner. "Take half the men an' go git yoreselves a drink—not too many. We got a lot of work ahead of us, an' maybe a good bit of fightin' to spice it up some. Tell Dawson the rest of the crew'll be in soon's y'all get the chill outta your bones."

While the cook started supper, the remaining members of the crew huddled by the fire, even the smoke smell made it seem warmer.

It was cold, and snow fell, but not like Gentry saw when he went after Thompson. Crockett eyed Gentry. "From what Trent told us, he left a couple of men out the other side of Forsyth for you to fight. Must a come out in your favor."

Gentry threw a dry grin at Crockett. "Must have. I'm here. He ain't. Naw, it really wasn't so much, I had to fight only one of 'em. He was the *man* of the two. Yeah, I come out ahead."

Crockett stood and poured them each a cup of coffee. "After we get you set up in ranchin', you gotta bring yore missus over to see Miz Joy. Ain't right for womenfolk to not see their own kind."

"Yeah, been thinkin' of doin' that very thing." Gentry frowned. "You know, it's a pure-dee puzzlement to me how a man like the Apache Blanco can settle down an' be a tame sort of citizen."

Crockett looked into his cup, a slight smile touching his lips. "Gentry, they's a lot of men done it. You was feared 'bout as much as Blanco—you done it, an' others you an' me could name. This land is settling down, gunfights are getting to be fewer, 'less of course, things happen like they did for you. But that was part of your past jumped up in front of you."

"Yeah, an' I'd just as soon no more of them 'jumped up in front of me.' "

Gentry glanced toward the town. "Boys're comin' back. Reckon it's our turn to get a drink."

Even though Dawson's saloon was only a quarter of a mile away, they saddled their horses and rode the short distance. When they climbed from their horses, Crockett said, "Main reason I want to stop here is to find out a few things 'fore we go blunderin' into a mess of trouble." He led the way into the saloon.

Gentry walked into the wall of warmth, and would have been satisfied to sit there and soak up the heat without even having a drink. And Dawson's place smelled clean, not like most watering holes smelled, of stale liquor and tobacco smoke.

"Hey, good to see you folks. Stick told me you'd be

comin'," the big Irishman bellowed as soon as they pushed through the door. "Shut the damned door, you're letting the whole outside in."

The seven of them bellied up to the bar. They and Dawson were the only ones in the saloon. Dawson set a glass in front of each of the riders and pulled out a bottle of rye whiskey. They nodded as one man. Crockett held his glass until it was full, then looked at Dawson. "Remember last time we wuz here we headed out to Lem Barton's Box LB?" At Dawson's nod, Crockett continued, "We're comin' through here for the same reason this time. Any of that bunch still out there?"

Dawson looked at Crockett a moment. "You figuring to run the rest of them off?"

"Run 'em or kill 'em. Don't make me no never mind."

Dawson's head jerked with approval. "Good. At last count, I figure there was about fifteen of them."

Gentry cut in, "Less'n that now. Me an' three Lakotas took care of 'bout half of 'em."

"Good. Soon's we rid this country of their kind, folks what are left can get on with living." Red picked the bottle up again. "This's on the house. You boys do a good job."

The door to the storage room opened, and a huge man walked from it, a grin stretching across his face. Gentry, since getting home and not finding him there, wondered where he ended up. "Big Battles. Where the hell you been? Looked for you to be already made into half a cowboy by the time I got home."

Battles, still grinning, said, "Yeah, I got to thinking about being a rancher. Gentry, I ain't cut out for that life. I'm a farmer. Figure to help Dawson 'til spring sets in, then look for some farming country. Think I'll try growin' wheat."

"Well, ain't neither life what a man could call easy. Good luck." Gentry dug in his pocket for money. "Gonna buy you a drink to make my wish a good one."

"Last I saw you, you didn't have enough money to buy anything. What happened?"

"Well, lets just say some of them Box LB riders what don't have no use for money no more is buyin' you this drink."

Battles raised his eyebrows, shrugged, and reached for his glass.

Gentry bought two bottles of rye whiskey from Dawson so the crew could have a drink after they cleaned up Barton's bunch. Then, bottles in hand, he led the crew back to the chuck wagon.

The next night, Crockett called a halt below the brow of a hill, telling them the Box LB headquarters buildings were the other side of the rise, downslope about two hundred yards.

"Gundy burned the cook shack last time we were here. We left the house and bunkhouse standing. Figure if we'd burned 'em all, that bunch would've left. We'll do it this time," Crockett said, and went to the back of the wagon. "I got a long glass here somewhere. Want to take a good look at them buildings in the mornin'."

Gentry ground-reined his horse. "Let me take a look at the setup down there." He held his hand out for the long glass. "You reckon it'll be all right to build a fire, or you figure its glare can be seen from down there?"

Crockett looked at Tom Purvis. "Build a fire, Purvis, but don't make it too big. I don't think they could see its glare from there, but no sense in taking a chance." He held the glass out to Gentry.

The day still clung to the last shreds of the wan grayish light before night took control. Gentry went flat on his stomach before reaching the top of the rise, snaked his way to the crest, and peered down at the three buildings: house, bunkhouse, and stable. Light showed only in the main house.

Gentry trained the glass on the area around the building showing lights. After a while, a man came out, went to a pile of wood, gathered an armful, and went back inside. Next the round eye of the glass focused on the brightest lighted window. If any of them were moving around, Gentry thought he might see them in that room. While he looked only one man crossed in front of the window. Gentry moved the glass around hoping to see something to give him an idea about how to fight what was left of Barton's men. Nothing came to him for a while, then a plan slowly formed. He'd been thinking of a daytime attack. It didn't have to be that way. He inched down the hill to the chuck wagon.

"Crockett, you got any dynamite in that wagon?"

Crockett, his leathery face devoid of expression, pinned Gentry with a penetrating gaze, "Don't think so. What you got in mind?"

Gentry told him what he thought might work. "It'd save puttin' the men in too much danger, an' maybe get the fight over quicker so we could get on with the gather."

Crockett poured another cup of coffee and, holding the cup toward Gentry, looked questioningly at him. He shook his head. "Nope, done had enough."

Crockett looked at the cook. "We got any dynamite in that wagon?"

"Nope. Took it out when I loaded supplies for this trip."

"Looks like we gonna have to fight 'em with guns, Gentry."

Gentry studied his boot toe a moment, then said, "You figure you can keep the men out of sight of them down yonder while I ride to Ismay? Without the wagon I can make it there an' back in one day."

Crockett agreed to keep the men close, and the next morning Gentry headed for Ismay. Riding in, he kept a watch over his shoulder. Then, when there, he bought the explosives, caps, and fuse. He explained to the storekeeper he had a bunch of stumps he wanted to blow out of the ground.

He rode slowly on the way back, for two reasons: he didn't want to happen on one of the rustlers, and he wasn't famil-

iar enough with his cargo to trust it not to go off and blow
him and his horse to hell and gone.

He huddled in his robe, keeping the collar turned up over
his ears. He could hear better that way rather than wear his
hat. If he'd worn it, with the flaps down around his ears, it
would muffle sounds of anyone approaching. To keep his
teeth from chattering he forced himself to relax. He rode
staring between his horse's ears, numb to all around him.
The gelding held to a steady trot. The cold and his horse's
gait lulled Gentry so he nodded, dozed—then came wide
awake. The gelding's ears peaked. Gentry loosened the ties
on his robe, pulled it behind his gun, and thumbed the thong
off the hammer. Two riders rounded a bend in the trail.

They reined in about ten feet in front of Gentry. "Where
you headin' in this weather, stranger?"

Gentry studied the two a moment. "Hear tell they's a ranch
out this way, Box LB, figured to hole up there 'til the weather
thaws a bit." Gentry thought his answer would pull from them
whether they belonged to the LB brand. He was right.

The skinny puncher studied Gentry awhile before answering. "You on the right trail to that ranch all right, but
we ain't hirin'. We don't want no strangers or range bums
hangin' around out there. You might's well turn yore horse
and ride back the way you come."

"Don't reckon I'm of a mind to do that. You talk like
you're the boss of that spread. Ain't never seen no one as
unfriendly as you."

The shorter of the two sidled his horse to get behind the
skinny rider, his left hand toying with the buttons on his
sheepskin. The skinny rider answered Gentry. "Ain't neither one of us what you'd call the boss—but I'm answering
for 'im, an' if I sound unfriendly, it's 'cause I don't like
range bums, an' 'specially don't like you. Turn yore horse
and ride out."

Gentry's right hand hung close to his .44. "You sort a
spiked out the way I feel 'bout you two. Fact is, I don't like
either of you one whit. So you might say I'm sort of a un-

friendly gent myself, so much so that when you get that coat unbuttoned, Shorty, an' reach for yore side gun, I'm gonna blow you to hell." Shorty's hand stopped fumbling for the buttons.

Gentry didn't want a shoot-out. A stray bullet might hit the dynamite and blow them all into the next world. If having a gunfight wasn't enough, that thought brought a brassy taste under his tongue.

The explosive was in a saddlebag on the left side of his horse. He kneed the gelding around so the gelding's body stood between the rustlers and the saddlebag. The skinny rider now toyed with the buttons on *his* coat.

"Go ahead, Skinny, get 'em unbuttoned. Figured to take you first anyway. Ain't gonna draw 'til you have a chance." Gentry had no thought to give them an even break. Two to one was all the break they would get.

The last button taken care of, Skinny swept his coat out of the way and grabbed for his weapon. Gentry, with only a slight motion, thumbed the hammer back while palming his .44 and fired. He swung his gun a fraction and fired again, this time at Shorty. A black hole smoked its way through Shorty's coat about where he would carry his tobacco sack. Gentry swung the barrel of his gun back to Skinny, fired, and fired again. Then he put another shot into Shorty while he fell from his horse.

Smoke still curling from his gun barrel, Gentry shucked the spent cartridges from the cylinder, put them in his pocket, and reloaded. He kept his eyes on the two, dismounted, and walked to Skinny. Three holes, only now beginning to bleed, marred the front of the thin man's coat, one in the middle and one on each side of his chest. He was already dead.

Gentry looked at Shorty. It didn't take a close look to know he died—fast. Gentry's second shot into him had torn the side of his face away.

He went through their pockets, turned up one hundred forty dollars and fifty-three cents between them. He shook his head. He had more money than anytime since he and

Anne were married. But he found no name of anyone he could write about how the two met their end. He pocketed the money, thinking how well off Barton's bunch had made him. He had known bounty hunters who made less.

He dragged the two bodies into the brush, found a ravine, and pushed them into it, first taking their guns and looping the cartridge belts around the saddle horns of the horses they wouldn't need anymore.

Gentry took the reins of the extra horses in hand and headed toward camp. While riding, he tried to calculate whether they were close enough for the shots to be heard from the ranch. He shook his head. The wind blowing from the ranch in his direction, along with the snow, would dampen any noise before it carried that far. Now, if his calculations were right, they would have no more than five or six of the rustlers left. He liked those odds.

When he rode to the chuck wagon and off-loaded the rustler's guns, Crockett stared at him a moment, his face looking like he wanted to grin. "Dawson give you them guns, the storekeeper givin' 'em away, or you find 'em lyin' 'longside the trail?"

Gentry returned his look. "Naw. Not none of what you said. Run into a couple of the LB riders along the trail what figured them horses yonder wuz gettin' plumb tuckered out carryin' them and the guns too. I went 'em one better. I unloaded *them* an' the guns." He looked at Stick Turner. "Unsaddle 'em, Stick, an' turn 'em in with the remuda."

When he turned back to Crockett, he faced a coffee cup full of rye. He took the cup and held it up in a toast, then took a healthy swallow, and said, "Way I figure it, we ain't got but five or six of them left to fight."

Gentry sat by the fire, drank his whiskey, finished warming, walked to his bedroll, took his boots off, and turned in. Tomorrow promised to be an interesting day.

CHAPTER TWENTY-TWO

★ ★ ★

The next day they sat around the fire, told lies, drank coffee, and made their gear ready for work—or fight. Gentry looked up from cleaning and oiling his guns. "You men listen up, now. We gonna do this my way. Every one of you're stickin' yore neck out for me. Ain't lettin' none of you go down that hill with dynamite. That's my job." He snapped the loading gate open and punched shells into the cylinder. "We're takin' a lesson from the way y'all did it last time when Gundy was along, only 'stead of Gundy goin' down that hill, I'm goin'." He locked eyes with each of them and waited for a nod before looking at the next man. When he had a nod from all, he returned to checking his gear. He'd gone over everything he could think of several times, but having something to do kept him from thinking about that trip down the hill.

Soon after dark, Gentry set the fuses to the explosive sticks. When the men offered to help, even though he didn't feel much like grinning, he grinned and said this was a job he'd rather do himself. His guts churned, tied themselves in knots, then churned some more. When this day was over, he could get on with trying to set himself up as a well-to-do rancher or a dead one. He set the fuse on the last stick, inspected it closely, and, satisfied, again looked at the men.

"While I'm slidin' down that hill on my belly, you men take stations around the clearing. When that first stick goes off, I figure they's gonna be men coming out windows, doors, any way they can get outta there. If you have a chance to take 'em alive—do it, but don't put yourselves in no more danger than you have to. Okay, let's get started."

When he topped the hill, he studied the lighted windows and saw no movement. The snow would silhouette his dark robe whether he ran, slid, or crawled down the hill. If he got shot doing any of the three he'd be just as dead. Bitter bile welled into his throat, his neck muscles tightened, and the hair at the back of his neck bristled. Scared? Damned right. He hesitated only a second, sucked in a deep breath, and pushed off on his right foot.

Fear put wings to his feet. Every five or ten yards he zigzagged, every muscle in his body tensed against the sharp impact of a rifle slug. The house drew nearer, seeming to take forever, then he skidded to the wall. Had he made too much noise when he slid to a stop and bumped the wall? He hunkered close to the ground, waited, listened. Only loud voices and laughter came from inside.

Gentry took a packet of lucifers from his pocket and pulled one of the sticks of dynamite from behind his belt at his back. He held a match to strike it against his belt buckle, stopped. Maybe they had a man outside, at the back or front standing watch.

He cursed under his breath and inched his way toward the back of the house. There, he eased his head around the corner far enough to check along the entire wall—no one. He turned and made his way to the front and repeated his inspection. Still no one. He again placed his hand to strike the match and again stopped. He had to break the window glass in order to make a smooth path for the explosive to follow. He had three sticks he wanted to get inside the house, all three in one room wouldn't do the trick.

Despite the cold, sweat poured down his face, it soaked his shirt inside his robe, and each drop of the salty fluid wrung from his body had fear stamped on it. He had to space the explosive front to back. That ain't gonna be easy, Gentry. But if it had seemed easy, he'd have been suspicious. He groped for rocks and finally found three, each the size of his fist.

He dropped two of them into his robe pocket, crouched under the window where the talking took place, and holding the three sticks in his left hand, the rock in his right, he pulled the fuses close together so as to light them with one match. He prayed he'd cut the fuses long enough. If they went off in his hand, it was all over.

Holding the lucifer between thumb and forefinger, his other fingers curled around the rock, he struck the lucifer, held it to the fuses, and when all three started sparking, dropped the match and heaved the rock through the window. In the same motion, he plucked one of the sparkling sticks from his hand and tossed it into the room.

As soon as the one left his hand, he dipped into his pocket and took hold of another rock while he darted to the next window. The rock broke the window and a sparkling stick followed it.

Yelling, cursing, and sounds of wild scrambling sounded from the house. He had barely gotten rid of his last stick through the third window when the first one detonated.

Gentry didn't have time to get away. He threw himself flat, pulled his robe over his head, and curled into a ball. Almost simultaneously, the other two went off, shaking the earth around him. All hell broke loose. A couple of men ran into and through the window when he threw the first stick. They hit the ground not twenty-five feet from Gentry. Splintered lumber rained around him. He stayed still until a quiet settled on the land, then he pulled his buffalo robe down a fraction and looked toward the two who'd escaped.

One of the men, gun in hand, drew a bead on him. Gentry rolled to the side at the same time the rustler's gun spewed flame. A hot streak burned its way down his side. His hand flashed for his .44 and rolled out two shots, sounding almost as one. The man, still on his side, was knocked to his back. He jerked with the impact of each slug, tried to roll back to his side, struggled, tried to jerk his body into doing what he wanted. He didn't make it. With a long sigh the rustler groaned, sank to his back, shuddered, and lay still.

Gentry trained his six-gun on the second man. In the dim light, he couldn't tell whether the rustler had a gun in his hand. He fired into him, placing a shot in his chest and another in his head. He crawled toward the outlaw. When close enough, he saw he'd wasted those last shots, a board, split down the middle, stuck through from the man's back to come out his chest.

Gentry wanted to lie flat and let the tension and fear flow from him; instead, he crouched against a jumble of timber and searched the area. Only the soft fall of snow moved. He sighed, let his legs from under him, stuffed new loads into his Colt, then leaned against the pile of rubble and closed his eyes.

A few moments later sounds of men coming from the hills caused him to sit up.

"Gentry, hey, Gentry, you all right? Where are you?"

"Over here, Crockett." For the first time he took stock of himself. As far as he could tell, he didn't have a scratch, except for the crease down his side, and figured if it was bad he wouldn't be sitting here. "Yeah, I'm all right."

The next thing he knew, Crockett and the Flying JW men stood over him, staring. "My God." Crockett's voice sounded awed. "I thought the Apache Blanco wuz the only one what could raise so much hell in one night. You feel like walkin' back up that hill for a good, healthy shot of rye whiskey."

Gentry grinned, and it even took an effort to do that. "Yeah, reckon that's about all would get me back on my feet. Let's go."

Three weeks later, riding drag behind seven hundred eighty-three head of mixed breed cattle, Crockett looked tiredly at Gentry. "Looks like you're in the cow business, Gentry."

Gentry stared over the backs of more cattle than he thought he'd ever own. "Crockett, why don't you an' me split this herd, you take over what's left of the Box LB an' turn rancher."

Crockett shook his head. "Naw, Gentry. Gundy's done told me I got a job with him the rest of my life—down yonder in Texas. That's where I b'long, Ranger man, not up here in this cold." He grinned. "Much obliged anyway. Come down Texas way to see me when you get rich." Crockett squinted across the herd, then looked to each side. "How far we from your land?"

Gentry frowned. "Reckon we been ridin' on it since shortly after sunrise. Why?" Then he realized why Crockett asked the question. "Let's cut these cows loose. My cabin's just over that rise yonder. This herd ain't gonna stray far, better grass down here, besides they all got my brand on 'em."

Crockett glanced at the herd once again. "Come spring you gonna have a whole bunch more cows. A good three quarters of these heifers are heavy with calves." He looked at Gentry. "You ride on ahead an' see yore woman an' children. I'll have cookie fix us supper. We gonna head back to the JW in the morning."

Gentry locked eyes with the crusty old-timer. He swallowed twice—hard. "Crockett, ain't nothin' nowhere I wouldn't do for you an' yore men." He swallowed again. "Thanks, old friend. If you or them ever need me, for anything, give a yell, I'll be there."

"*Da nada,* this's what friends are for, Gentry. But, yeah, I'll remember. Now, go see yore woman." He slapped Gentry's horse on the rump.

Gentry's horse jumped and broke into a hard gallop. When he topped the hill, Anne, Mark, and Brandy stood outside staring in his direction. They must have heard the bellowing of the cows and rumble of hooves. He kicked the gelding into a hard run.

Barely waiting for the gelding to stop, Gentry threw himself from the saddle and pulled them all into his arms. He finally turned them loose. "On the other side of that hill yonder is a whole bunch of cows—all ours." He looked Anne in the eye. "Honey, we're through doin' without. You an' the kids'll have the things you need." He dropped his gaze and stared at the ground. "Reckon now I can be the husban' I been wantin' to be. Ain't lettin' nothing stand 'tween you, the kids, and me never again."

He studied Anne's face. "See you been usin' that mirror an' hairbrush. You get prettier ever' time I look at you." He felt all mushy inside. He gave her a tender smile and said, "That there hairbrush an' mirror don't have nothin' to do with it, you wuz born pretty—from the inside out."

Anne stepped back a step and looked at him, a smile trying to form. "Case, you've always been the husband I wanted. Cows, money, nothing could change that." She did smile then. "And if you're not too tired, tonight after the children are in bed, I'll prove it."

"Woman, I ain't never been that tired." He looked at the sun. It stood at about the three o'clock position. "Reckon it's time for the kids to get tucked in?"

A special offer for people who enjoy reading the
best Westerns published today.

If you enjoyed this book, subscribe now and get...

TWO FREE WESTERNS

A $7.00 VALUE—NO OBLIGATION

If you would like to read more of the very best, most exciting, adventurous, action-packed Westerns being published today, you'll want to subscribe to True Value's Western Home Subscription Service.

TWO FREE BOOKS

When you subscribe, we'll send you your first month's shipment of the newest and best 6 Westerns for you to preview. With your first shipment, two of these books will be yours as our introductory gift to you absolutely *FREE* (a $7.00 value), regardless of what you decide to do.

Special Subscriber Savings

When you become a True Value subscriber you'll save money several ways. First, all regular monthly selections will be billed at the low subscriber price of just $2.75 each. That's at least a savings of $4.50 each month below the publishers price. Second, there is never any shipping, handling or other hidden charges— *Free home delivery*. What's more there is no minimum number of books you must buy, you may return any selection for full credit and you can cancel your subscription at any time. A TRUE VALUE!

Mail the coupon below

To start your subscription and receive 2 FREE WESTERNS, fill out the coupon below and mail it today. We'll send your first shipment which includes 2 FREE BOOKS as soon as we receive it.